Hoodwinked

Also by Frank Palmer

Testimony
Unfit to Plead
Bent Grasses
Blood Brother
Nightwatch
China Hand
Double Exposure
Dead Man's Handle
Dark Forest
Red Gutter
Hot Toddy
Murder Live
Black Gold
Final Score

HOODWINKED

Frank Palmer

Constable · London

First published in Great Britain 1999
by Constable & Company Limited
3 The Lanchesters, 162 Fulham Palace Road
London W6 9ER
Copyright © 1999 Frank Palmer
The right of Frank Palmer to be
identified as the author of this work
has been asserted by him in accordance
with the Copyright, Designs and Patents Act 1988
ISBN 0 094 79540 1
Set in Palatino 10 pt by
SetSystems Ltd, Saffron Walden, Essex
Printed and bound in Great Britain
by MPG Books Ltd, Bodmin, Cornwall

A CIP catalogue record for this book
is available from the British Library

The East Midlands and the East Riding police forces are fictional and so are their characters and cases. In real life, the Isle of Axholme is a pleasant and peaceful place, well worth a visit. No point in looking for the Cottage Hospital, Temple Hall and Westport, however. They are fictional, too.

For Brian and Chris,
my fellow travellers

1

WINTER

'PRIVATE AND CONFIDENTIAL,' he tapped out. He stopped and studied what he'd typed.

What's the point of that? he asked himself angrily. The whole job's riddled with more leaks than Whitehall.

Nothing, absolutely nothing, would jump into his head; a total block.

Go public then, he slowly decided; call a news conference.

'<Del' was poked to delete. 'DEA . . .' Blast, forgot to knock off the capitals. '<Del' again and then 'Dear Officer'.

The first murder was nine months ago, he reminded himself, so he wanted this letter to go to recently retired officers too. 'Colleague' was substituted for 'Officer'.

Back arched, he sat on the front edge of his swivel chair and stared at the screen, his mind blank again.

Short and sweet, he recalled his wife advising. No reminiscing about your dear departed grandad and beat officers like him being the eyes and ears of the force. And not too many 'I this' and 'I that', she'd added.

OK, then. His fingers hovered like a concert pianist's, then came down, playing with only two fingers. 'An announcement will be . . .'

Wrong chord. It had already been announced in the papers, unofficially anyway.

He flopped back in his chair.

Oh Christ, he sighed. I had no idea management would be like this – chewing over every word, fretting about how the media will play it, wondering when the budget will go bust, nursing the egos of senior aides, one of whom will have to go, unable to decide who.

He straightened his back. Get on with it then, he ordered himself.

*

Dear Colleague,

An official announcement will be made next week that a co-ordinated ... go back ... combined? ... no, joint inquiry is being launched into the series of armed sexual assaults on women on the Isle of Axholme and two murders on motorways that serve the locality.

Computer analysis indicates that two quite separate and highly dangerous offenders are at large.

Attached are summaries of all crimes under review, along with maps and copies of postcards received after each murder.

The leads that come out of computers are only as good as the information put in, so we need everyone's help. Does any fact remind you of incidents you've previously encountered? Anyone on your patch with a fascination for knives? Anyone who writes in the strange printed style on the postcards? Any names we should be following up?

If so, please submit suggestions to HQ until an incident room is established and the numbers circulated. If not, keep your ears and eyes open.

He sat back again, reasonably pleased with himself. OK, he'd succumbed to 'eyes and ears', but no 'I's. On the whole, not bad. Better, certainly, than the stiff formal stuff that normally comes out of HQ.

He'd ask his secretary to clean up the draft, copy it and get it out in that half-alive half week between Christmas and New Year. But, with such gory detail in the enclosures, signing off with 'Happy New Year' would be inappropriate. He tapped out 'Kind Regards' instead.

Then followed his name: 'Phillip Todd'. He stopped, deleted the 'lip'; more matey. On the next line his new title came into use for the first time: 'Assistant Chief Constable (Special Assignments)'.

He read what he'd written yet again, then moved his cursor to delete 'Kind' and restore 'lip' to 'Phil'. New assistant chiefs can't be too kind or matey, he resolved.

2

Not a line made the papers, even though the letter had gone out five days earlier. 'The media mole's gone to ground,' said the force's public relations chief, a plump, rather bossy ex-newspaperwoman.

Gone shy, more like, Todd mulled.

'The silence is deafening,' she went on, rather gleefully. Like all journalists who became PRs, poachers turned gamekeepers, she was paranoid about leaks.

Over the last couple of days, Todd's phone had been red hot with several divisional commanders calling to cover their backs. 'Writing to officers directly at their homes sets a dangerous precedent,' griped one. 'You're going outside channels,' complained another.

Had he been more confident in his new authority, he'd have replied, 'What really worries you is that some village bobby may already have come up with a name that you've filed away and forgotten and you're terrified you'll be rumbled.'

Diplomatically, he'd said, 'You know as well as I do that not every beat officer reads the bulletin board.'

The PR raised the news conference she was fixing for the start of the first full working week of the New Year. She'd enlarged the maps to display on the wall behind the platform, complete with flags in two colours. She padded out his letter into a written release and thinned out the grisly items from the case summaries for public consumption.

Presentation, Todd thought glumly. Everything these days is glossy presentation.

She waved photocopies of the two postcards among the enclosures. 'Will you want me to hand these out?'

He had no need to reread them. In the fortnight before Christmas, he'd read up everything on file and committed most of it to memory.

One card had arrived after the murder of a prostitute picked up at a motorway service station and dumped, semi-naked, bound, her throat cut, forty miles further north.

The superintendent in charge had told the press at the time, 'We've found no handbag and think robbery may have been the motive.'

The postcard came by second class post a week later, addressed to the superintendent at police HQ. On the front was a photo of a crooked church spire, Chesterfield's landmark.

The message was in handwritten pencil but resembled a print-out from a primitive word processor. Stripped of the +s between letters, ... between words and o's that dotted the i's, it said: 'You have made a mistake. The wages of her sins will be found at the power station.'

The second postcard arrived last month in the second class post three days after the murder of another prostitute who vanished from dockland streets. Her body, stripped to her briefs, bound, her throat slashed, was found just off a motorway that runs through the Isle of Axholme.

The card was again addressed to the superintendent and had a picture of William Wilberforce's column in Hull. The message was in pencil and in the same strange style,

'H+e+r ... w+a+g+e+s ... o+f ... s+i+n ... a+r+e ... a+t ... t+h+e ... g+o+l+f ... c+o+u+r+s+e ... n+o+r+t+h ... o+f ... H+u+m+b+er ... B+r+i+d+g+e.'

Todd nodded at the PR and said, 'Please.'

'Who'll be with you on the top table?' she asked, making it sound like a dinner engagement.

He hesitated, about to reveal a major decision.

She pressed him. 'We'll need to print their names on place markers.'

Such bullshit, Todd groaned inwardly. 'Carole Waites and Ben Nixon.'

Her head came up from the big pad on which she was taking notes. Her eyebrows were arched in surprise – nothing to compare to the shock wave the news will send through the force, Todd realised. 'Not Ray Trench?'

He shook his head.

'He's virtually fixed up a slot on *Crimewatch*,' she said, almost an objection.

'Carole will do it.' Todd shrugged, trying to seem unconcerned.

She wrapped up her briefing with 'And wear your uniform on

Monday.' She rose and walked to the door, both rather ungainly movements because of her weight.

Then she turned back. 'Post Mortem Morton will be there, by the way.' She smiled a rather sickly smile.

Only when the door had shut did he return the grim smile.

In his white shirt-sleeves behind his huge new desk, he sat thinking during his first wholly free few minutes of the day.

The PR and her ever-increasing staff may scour every national and local newspaper and monitor every radio bulletin, but they didn't read between the lines.

Long before Todd had been put in charge, she'd been driven to distraction by the leaks – the reported rows between forces about how many sex crimes committed near motorways should be reviewed, where the inquiry should be based, whether a psychological profiler should be called in.

All the pieces had appeared in various newspapers under various staff bylines, but all, it was suspected, had come from one source – Harry Morton.

Like Pam, the PR, he was an ex-journalist. These days he specialised in paperback crime – non-fiction. Within a week of a headline case finishing, he'd be on the bookstalls, with serialisation to follow in a Sunday paper.

To be that quick off the mark, of course, most of the book had to be prepared and partially printed well before the verdict. He couldn't merely rehash the court reports which had run over page after tabloid page for day after day.

Morton solved the problem of access to advance information with approaches to the detective running the investigation and, after an arrest, the defence solicitor. It wasn't always cash in hand. Sometimes a good write-up would do; recognition, fame.

To fund long-term research, he'd sell major developments on to Fleet Street as the case progressed.

Ray Trench had run one big inquiry on a double child killer which had been given the Post Mortem Morton treatment and an extremely good write-up he'd got.

Some of the facts, however, had never been made public in court. One of the victim's families protested to their MP about unwarranted intrusion and breach of confidentiality.

Todd, in his previous post as chief superintendent in Complaints, had investigated, but got nowhere close to making a disciplinary case.

Practising what he preached, like his dear old grandad had taught him, he'd kept an eye and ear open, however.

In the nine months that Trench had run the first vice murder case, despite several cock-ups, not one word of criticism about him had made the papers. He'd separately arrested two men he'd later had to let go. On no more than a hunch, he'd publicly linked his case with other unsolved sex crimes. And not a hint about that postcard correcting his false assumption on motive had come out.

Not hard evidence, a long way from proof, but, to Todd, reading between the lines, confirmation enough.

Trench walked into the warm, spacious office after a single tap on the door; breezed was a better word, so self-assured did he always appear. Tall, slender and light of step, he seemed to float in on the howling winds that were seeing out the Old Year.

Not yet forty, four years younger than Todd, his short, neat hair was the colour of frost. Eyebrows that were jet black made Todd wonder if he used dye on one or the other.

'Got your letter, thanks,' he said as he walked on, patting his deep blue jacket at the heart.

Closer to, his handsome face wore a look that wasn't so full of his usual confidence, troubled almost. Uninvited, he sat on a high-backed chair only recently vacated by the PR. 'For internal consumption only, I take it.'

'Sorry to drag you in when half the force is still off,' said Todd, evasively and apologetically.

Trench put on an understanding expression. 'You'll want to discuss the news conference.'

'Yes.'

'I mean . . .' Trench touched his jacket again. '. . . you're not releasing all of this to the press, are you?'

'Yes,' said Todd flatly.

Trench's black eyebrows arched into a steeper angle than the PR's. 'Is that wise?'

'Someone may recognise the odd writing.'

'And it will result in postbags full of copycat cards.'
'We'll have to hope the handwriting experts can spot the difference.'
'We'll be inundated with crank messages.'

True, Todd privately agreed. Still, he could withhold the facts that the cards were written in pencil and carried 20p stamps. That might sort out some hoaxes from genuine articles. He saw no point in disclosing the tactic.

Trench crossed one sharply pressed trouser leg over the other, a failed attempt to look comfortable. 'It makes us look silly.'

Us? repeated Todd to himself. Us didn't go on record claiming robbery as the motive.

'I mean, I didn't know she was on the game. We hadn't even put a name to her then.'

Not true, Todd knew. Trench had a name, but had been slow to check on her background. 'No one's blaming anyone.'

'What's it going to look like, being corrected, lectured to, by a psycho we haven't caught yet?'

'It would look a lot worse if he struck again when someone could have recognised his handwriting.'

'It's obviously disguised.'
'It's well practised, then.'

Trench leant forward, a pleading expression on his face. 'You could be making a mistake. I'm asking you to reconsider.'

Todd sighed, more in relief than in frustration. A difficult task was being made easier for him. 'Those are my tactics . . .'

'I think they're wrong.'

Their eyes latched on each other's. 'If you've no faith in them,' said Todd slowly, 'then we've come to the parting of the ways.'

Trench's head went back a fraction.

'I'm combining the two motorway inquiries . . .' Todd took the plunge. '. . . under Chief Inspector Nixon.'

Trench's face registered utter disbelief. He and Nixon were from different police schools. He was smooth, articulate, ambitious, image-conscious.

Nixon was older, rougher, smoked and drank too much, mistrusted the press, PRs, psychologists and new tech. But his work rate was phenomenal. He would travel miles on his own time to pin down the thinnest of leads.

Besides, to Todd, it was a question of trust.

'But it's my patch and my case,' Trench protested with a flustered little wave of a hand.

'The first victim was snatched off your patch and the second dumped on us. Nixon could argue the same in reverse.'

'But I outrank him.'

'And I outrank you both and these are now my cases,' Todd wanted to shout. Instead, he flannelled a reply about needing financial input and staff from Nixon's force, East Riding. He ended with a lame, 'Sorry.'

'I know why this is,' Trench said, in a low, almost threatening tone.

Todd said nothing.

'You think I'm Morton's mole.'

Todd decided not to deny it.

'You think I sold out to him on that double murder. I wasn't his source, and I told you so then, and I'm not now, never have been.'

'It's just a question of fresh minds and legs,' said Todd, appeasingly.

Trench smirked and Todd knew why. He had a gammy leg, the result of a shotgun wound five years ago. These days, on-the-road detectives regarded him as a desk jockey. He felt compelled to expand. 'Nixon's case is fresher and so are his leads.'

'Leads.' A sneer. 'He's got no bloody leads.'

Todd was losing patience and gaining confidence. 'Neither, to be honest, have you and you've been on it for nine months.' A sorrowful expression as he repeated, 'Sorry.'

Trench rose, face almost as grey as his hair. 'You'll regret this.' In long, easy strides, he swept out of the office without looking back, slamming the door behind him.

Regret it? Doubt that, thought Todd, alone again, at peace with himself. Far from it, in fact. He felt good about it. With the mole gone, he could and would manage the news now, as well as the inquiry.

3

The bossy PR looked more than a touch miffed when she saw that Todd had turned up for her news conference in civvies.

'The missus hasn't stitched on my new badges of rank yet,' he apologised; true, but not the real reason.

His wife Em had a down on police chiefs who wore uniform on TV. 'Looks like pigeons have crapped all over their shoulders,' she'd mocked.

Em had been a journalist and had interviewed many high-flyers in a broadcasting career that had just ended with a part-time spell as a breakfast-time newscaster. Now, with the hike in pay that came with his promotion, she'd quit.

She could still make five hundred for a morning's work introducing corporate videos. Her husband regarded the fee as obscene or handy, depending on his mood.

He'd only appeared in one previous TV interview, about a hunt for a jailbreaker in his Special Op days before that shotgun wound in his right leg had taken him off the streets.

In the mainly chairbound years since, in Special Branch and the Complaints Department, he'd operated a policy of never be seen, never be heard in public, and he'd grown to like it that way.

That one brief newsbite he rated a coup in that he'd eventually married the reporter who asked the questions. It was a view that his wife sometimes shared and sometimes didn't, depending on his current behaviour.

'Not too many I's,' she'd repeated in her final coaching session. She had a particular down on police chiefs who said on TV, always with a grim face, 'I want to speak to . . .' or 'I want to hear from . . .'

'Everybody knows they do bugger all, except dress up for and speak to the media,' she'd grumbled; with some ACC's, not much of an exaggeration, Todd agreed.

'They belong to the Carmen Miranda school of policing.' And

she'd rumbaed round their cosy lounge imitating the old Hollywood musical star singing: 'I-I-I-I-I like me very much.'

Egos, she was saying. 'And don't wear that bloody uniform,' she'd concluded.

He was always more inclined to listen to his wife than the force PR.

Todd looked up from his desk with his appeasing expression. 'I am in my Sunday best.' Em had picked midnight blue mohair, a pale blue shirt (because white sometimes glared in camera light) and a striped two-tone grey tie for contrast; all bullshit, of course, he'd thought, but hadn't said.

'Mmm,' mmmed the PR, unimpressed. Her eyes inspected Carole Waites sitting in a high-backed chair.

She was wearing a tailored jacket, broad black and white checks, and a black pleated skirt that ended at the knee. Her shapely legs were pressed together at an angle to the maroon carpet, model-style. Her fair hair was short and neat. A detective chief inspector based on the south bank of the Humber, she didn't look her forty years.

The PR smiled briefly and approvingly and her eyes moved on to Ben Nixon. He was lounging in a low armchair, wearing a crumpled grey suit with brown shoes. His hair was thinning and straggly. His gaunt face had been badly shaved. He didn't look in his forties either, closer to pensionable age.

Todd thought he saw the PR's eyes go heavenward and was thankful she hadn't got too close to him. He'd smelt of last night's booze and cigarettes when he arrived after a longish trip from his station in Hull opposite the Wilberforce monument on the second postcard.

'Right,' she declared, not quite clapping for attention. 'Eight locals, four nationals, two agencies, three freelances . . .' She stopped and looked down at Todd. '. . . including Post Mortem Morton. Four radio. Three TV crews. Four still photographers.'

'A good turn-out,' Carole enthused.

The PR didn't look so certain. 'The lecture hall is pretty big and will look rather empty for the pan shots.' She brightened. 'I've press-ganged a few clerks in civvies to sit at the back and make up the crowd.'

'A load of old bollocks,' Nixon grumbled.

The PR gave him a sour look. Todd smiled to himself, finding it difficult to disagree.

Well, thought Todd. It's going reasonably well. He was sitting, quite relaxed, at a green baize table on the platform with more than half a dozen microphones in front of him. Nixon and Waites were at either side.

He had stuck closely to the prepared release, reading slowly and evenly, looking up now and then at the steeply rising rows of faces in front of him, not really seeing them.

Carole Waites had risen elegantly from her seat and, with pointer to enlarged map, had given the dates and places of the eight knife attacks on the Isle of Axholme, but not the names of the victims.

She added a description of the wanted man: short, stocky, always wore dark overalls and face mask, local accent, agile and, therefore, probably youthful, no known means of transport.

Nixon had stumbled and mumbled now and then with his briefing on the two murders, but had struggled on gamely to the end.

'Any questions?' announced the PR, standing behind them.

From a front row seat, a thickset man, overweight and too old at around fifty for a tight, trendy leather jacket, spoke first in the elongated vowels of South Yorkshire.

He didn't introduce himself, but Todd knew him to be Morton. 'Earlier reports suggested up to twelve other sex crimes, including murder, are being connected with your motorway jobs, if I recall accurately,' he began.

And so you should, thought Todd cynically. You wrote them, dubbing the killer the 'M-way Madman', as I recall.

'Are you now ruling them out?' Morton demanded.

'All unsolved murders and attempted murders associated with motorways had been reviewed,' Todd replied. 'None of the others had the same sort of wounds and – '

'Which are?' Morton interrupted.

'I've already told you that,' Nixon came in gruffly. 'Pre-mortem knife wounds, final, fatal injury to the throat in both cases.'

'So both were tortured?' asked a woman journalist, wide-eyed.

'We're dealing here with a homicidal sadist,' said Todd, sidestepping slightly, 'and – '

Morton butted back in. 'Are these masked attacks and murders connected?'

'We don't think so,' replied Carole cautiously.

'Why not?' Morton wanted to know.

She looked at Todd, passing the buck. He took it up smoothly. 'The murder weapon was a pair of scissors.'

He gestured at Carole. 'The masked attacker my colleague is seeking uses something like a Stanley knife, not capable of such deep penetration, but nonetheless inflicting dangerous and painful injury and terrible trauma. There are other major differences, too.'

A moment's meditation. 'The bindings and knots used, for example, but we don't want to reveal the rest.'

Not least, Todd added privately, that the masked man lets his victims live, something that ought to have occurred to Post Mortem Morton with his obsession with death.

While Morton's head went down over his small red notebook, a TV girl got in a question. 'Why combine the inquiries then?'

'Because both necessitate trawling through records of previous sex offenders and information can be immediately interchanged.'

An evening paper veteran began with a hesitant preamble. 'All these, like, non-fatal, er, masked attacks have happened within – what?'

'Eight months, from May onwards.'

'They started after the first murder, right?'

'That was in March, yes.' Get to the point, Todd wanted to say.

'Well, I mean, do you think the murderer read about these knife attacks and dumped his second victim on the Isle to confuse matters?'

Never crossed my mind that, a brilliant theory, Todd conceded admiringly but secretly. 'It's crossed our minds,' he heard himself saying.

'These postcards . . .' A radio man waved his copies. '. . . did they lead to the recovery of any money?'

'In both cases, handbags containing cash, yes,' said Nixon,

quite pleasantly, for him, 'which obviously indicates they were from the killer.'

Morton came back again, nagging. 'But are you saying no other M-way murder is linked?'

He'd oversold his next book as a hunt for a mass killer and feared his advance would have to be returned, Todd suspected. He didn't let his glee show. 'Catching our two offenders may, of course, lead to other crimes being solved.'

Far from being assuaged, Morton pointed rudely at the platform. 'Superintendent Trench isn't present. What do we read into that?'

'Saves duplication, that's all. It's a joint operation between two forces and DCI Nixon is the East Riding team leader.'

Todd was expecting: 'Has Trench been sacked?' and resolved to reply, 'He's on a command officer's course' and to rush back to his office to turn a lie into truth. No follow-up question came.

A man from the *Axholme Herald* wanted to know if the incident room would be based locally.

Waites fielded his query with her local knowledge. 'The only station on the Isle isn't big enough to accommodate us, so we're having to look elsewhere. Certainly, our aim is to bring all three inquiries presently centred on Chesterfield, Hull and Scunthorpe under one roof and work together as a team.'

The *Herald* man did have a follow-up question. 'This computer analysis you mention – are you employing HOLMES?'

'Yes.' Waites looked around the rows of faces and, spotting young ones among them, seemed to feel obliged to expand. The Scunthorpe end of the inquiry, her end, was already using the Home Office Large Major Enquiry System.

Todd had to fight against shaking his head. The Home Office had used both large and major, which amount to the same thing, to shoehorn HOLMES out of it. HOMES, he knew, didn't have the same forensic ring.

A woman from the rival and delightfully named *Epworth Bells* pointed out the Isle could easily be sealed.

Cleverly, well into her stride, Waites didn't reveal that spy cameras were about to go up on every bridge and road to the Isle, and talked instead of the frequency of her road blocks.

'Were any of the victims raped?' the reporter asked.

'None.'

'None?' she double-checked.

'There's no medical evidence of intercourse in any case in either series.'

'Doesn't that indicate a link then?' Morton nagged on.

'Told you that, too,' snapped Nixon. 'There are differences, apart from the weapon used, and we're not revealing them.'

The murderer had stripped his victims to their pants, but hadn't removed them. In some cases, the masked man had cut his victims' briefs off and taken them away; as trophies, Todd suspected. To have disclosed that might encourage the killer to change tactics and confuse his hunters.

'This wages of sin business...' The radio man waved his postcards again to attract Todd's attention. '... does that point to a religious crank?'

'Possibly,' said Todd.

'Are you getting psychological profiles?'

'It's on our agenda,' Todd hedged.

'Yes...' Morton again, rather rattily. '... but are you getting 'em?'

Todd felt his shirt sticking to his back, but managed to smile down at him. 'It's on the top of our agenda.' Immediately he wished he hadn't been so positive.

'Terrific,' cooed Pam, the PR, as if they'd just broken a leg at the Royal Command Performance.

She was leading the way back up a wide, panelled staircase to the polished flight deck and Todd's new office in the headquarters of the East Midlands Combined Constabulary, an old but sadly modernised manor house.

'Wonderful,' she added for good measure. Carole straightened her back, preening a little. Nixon mumbled under his bad breath.

A pale-looking woman in civvies Todd had vaguely noticed at the back of the lecture hall among the press-ganged clerks had tagged on to the end of the procession. He assumed she was an assistant from the Press Bureau which seemed to have as many staff these days as the Vice Squad.

Pam opened the heavy door for everyone and shut it behind them as Todd headed for his desk. Half-way there, Carole called him back, motioning towards the newcomer. 'This is Deborah Thompson, our chief HOLMES operator.'

Todd smiled and offered his hand. 'Never worked with HOLMES before.'

She took his hand and smiled rather timidly.

'She'll look after you,' said Carole breezily. 'She does me.'

'Sit down,' he said, spreading both hands.

Nixon already had, reclaiming the easy chair. Todd went behind his desk. Carole perched herself on the edge of it. Deborah took the high-backed chair. The PR stood with her back to the oak door, as if on guard against gatecrashing reporters.

Todd looked at Deborah. She was in a plain knitted dress, bottle green, loose, rather frumpy for someone in her mid-thirties, and was wearing large flesh-coloured spectacles.

Not surprising if she sat at a terminal all day reading bloody HOLMES, he reasoned.

There was no wedding ring on her third finger, but then neither was there on Carole's and she was married to a business executive and had two teenaged sons.

'Service or civvy?' he asked Deborah.

Civilian, she replied, seconded on a two-year contract from her computer company. She lived on the coast at Cleethorpes and was operating on the masked attacker at Scunthorpe with Carole.

'We worked together on Fish Finger Freddy as well,' Carole chipped in. She paused, then, seriously, 'I've been thinking, sir.'

Nixon stirred uncomfortably and Todd knew an old sore was about to be scratched.

In their meetings before Christmas, Carole had pushed for Dr Mervyn Peck to be brought in as the psychological profiler. She had engaged him last year in a hunt for an extortionist who had threatened to contaminate fish at a big freezing plant.

Peck's report hinted at an inside job – an ex-security guard, perhaps, who knew the set-up, had been sacked, was going bust in a new business venture. He had been spot on.

Nixon had also used him, on his chief's orders and very much against his will, in a search for a serial arsonist.

Peck concluded he'd be an immature youth who got sexual charges out of fire-raising and hearing the bells of the engines. He'd predicted that the offender would live within a mile of the fires and urged that close attention be paid to the callers who'd alerted the brigade and bystanders who'd made heroic efforts to fight the blazes.

The way Nixon amusingly told it was that he'd ended up with an itinerant old lag who set fire to places in which there was nothing to steal to fund his booze.

Superintendent Trench had enthusiastically backed Carole at those pre-Christmas meetings. Todd had remained on the fence.

He had no more experience with profilers than with HOLMES. It wasn't an exact science, like DNA or fingerprints, in his view. On the one hand, it could be useful in narrowing down a field of suspects. On the other, he feared, over-reliance on a profile could lead to tunnel vision.

He had checked out Peck with other forces and found his experience limited and his forecasts patchy. Profiling was not his full-time occupation. He lectured at colleges on both sides of the Humber and was a consultant at several clinics.

Todd had approached two much better known psychologists in the business, but both had caseloads that were too heavy.

'You know Dr Peck occasionally operated from a clinic on the Isle?' said Carole, using subtle tact today.

'I bloody well hope you've checked out all his old clients then,' said Nixon, not so tactfully.

Carole smiled thinly. If she hadn't, she would now, Todd knew. 'It's closed and empty, but it could be useful as a base for us, perhaps.'

'Where is it?' Todd asked.

'Grey Green, a village almost next to the motorway,' she replied, displaying more geographical knowledge. 'A tarted-up stable block in the grounds of the Cottage Hospital.'

'NHS-owned?' Todd queried.

She shook her head. 'It still belongs to Lord Harvard.'

The boss of the frozen fish firm, whose ex-member of security staff was awaiting trial for commercial blackmail, Todd knew.

'He gave his big, old place to the health authority years ago, and lives in the lodge,' she went on, 'but rented out the stable block to Three Counties Clinic.'

'Well,' said Nixon, slowly, stretching his legs, 'if the customers were all nutters, they couldn't call the clinic Axe Home, could they?'

Carole, beginning to lose patience, didn't smile. Todd did.

'Lost its funding,' Carole continued. 'The director has moved on.' She had visited Dr Peck there while he was assisting on the Fish Finger Freddy inquiry. 'It's in good nick.'

'Is it big enough for an incident room?' asked Todd.

'We won't need a lot of space,' said Deborah, coming in for the first time.

The incident rooms Todd had operated from in his CID days often covered a whole floor, so he frowned.

'Just room for half a dozen or so in the computer team,' she went on, 'and offices, of course, for the two separate squads.' Almost as an afterthought, she added, 'And you.'

Todd frowned still and she launched into a little lecture about HOLMES being able to dispatch details of inquiries and actions required to almost any station via phone modems from its data bank. 'You don't need scores of officers on site.'

He told Deborah and Carole he'd have a look at the premises. He told himself to cost it carefully, because he had a budget he couldn't bust without going with a begging bowl to Finance every month.

Nixon shuffled, about to get up and start an even longer drive down south to see a kerb crawler in custody on a charge of robbing a prostitute at knife point.

Carole finally got round to what Todd knew was uppermost in her mind. 'So what about Dr Peck then?'

'He's local and normally available,' Deborah added.

Yes, but is he any good? Todd wondered.

From the door, Pam, the PR, added her considerable weight. 'You virtually committed yourself to a profiler in there, you realise.' She threw her head back in the general direction of the lecture hall.

Todd realised, all too well. He accepted, too, that psychological input was all the rage, had been regarded as *de rigueur* since *The Silence of the Lambs*. No detective novel, TV film or real life major inquiry seemed to be complete without it these days.

'Might as well employ Mystic Meg,' moaned Nixon, hunched forward.

'In your case, he wasn't working from a database,' said Deborah, edgily.

Todd asked what she meant and she delivered another technical talk. In the extortion investigation, she'd downloaded case histories to Dr Peck. On the arson job, the old-fashioned card index system had been used, not HOLMES, and Dr Peck had virtually been working blind.

She was, in effect, accusing Nixon of not co-operating, but, mercifully, he didn't pick up on it.

'I'll have a word with him while I'm up there looking at the stable block,' Todd promised.

Nixon surrendered with a sighing headshake. 'You're the boss.'

That was what Todd liked to hear.

4

Pam, the PR, walked into Todd's office with her clipboard tucked under a chubby arm and a self-satisfied smile on her pleasant face. 'Didn't I always tell you publicity pays?'

In her job, she's bound to say that, Todd thought.

Coverage of the news conference had brought in forty phone tips, and still counting. All had been rerouted to Carole and Deborah, who were feeding them to HOLMES.

Todd's wife Em had been unusually complimentary about his performance on TV; he less happy, hardly recognising his own voice, broader and flatter to his ears than Post Mortem Morton's.

In a tabloid feature, Morton had been doughty in defence of his advance for a book on the M-way Madman. He'd pinched the title of a film, an old trick, to dub the killer Scissorhands, used a slight misquote ('Catching him may lead to many more answers') and unilaterally ruled back in the other eight unsolved murders.

Pam pulled her board from under her arm and sat down. 'We've had Lord Harvard's office on. He's happy for you to inspect the vacant premises.' She paused and turned the smile to full beam. 'And he's prepared to put up a substantial reward.'

Todd paused, not smiling. 'Why should he do that?'

She looked down at her board where she had several cuttings not from today's papers. 'He's an Ionian, born and bred.'

So were a large number of the seventeen thousand or so who populated the Isle, calculated Todd, so there had to be more to it than that.

'And, according to the *Sunday Times*, he's among Britain's fifty richest people,' she added.

No one else on Axholme could claim that, Todd conceded, but the question remained. 'How much did catching Fish Finger Freddy save his company?'

Recalling and scrapping contaminated frozen foodstuffs had cost half a million, she reported, looking down. 'But had Carole Waites not nabbed him so quickly, who knows?'

Inwardly, Todd was acknowledging the undoubted incentive a reward would give to public appeals for information and tried to suppress his doubts. 'What do we know about him?'

She looked down again at her notes and began to clip her phrases. 'Born '35, father owned a fleet of trawlers, educated Eton and Cambridge, three years in the army, commissioned naturally. He was among the pioneers of the switch from canned to frozen foods, veg as well as fish, with products available in every supermarket. Made a life peer in the seventies for services to the food industry. He's still company chairman, but currently concentrates more on good causes. Widower, one married daughter, one son.'

She looked up. 'No convictions.'

Todd laughed uneasily. Doubts about the ethics of accepting hand-outs from a satisfied customer remained.

Pam gave him no time to debate them. 'I've arranged for you to see him in an hour.'

The Isle of Axholme isn't quite an island, Todd had discovered on a solo swan around in weak December sunshine just before Christmas, giving his eyes much-needed rest from the heavy reading of the case files.

The River Ouse runs along the top, the Trent down the eastern side and the Idle across the bottom. The western boundary is peat bog, desolate and impenetrable in places. The moors have eerie names like Wastes and Chase. On the latter, the second murder victim had been found a month earlier.

Midway up runs the M180 linking the Humber Bridge with

South Yorkshire. Most motorists speed through without noticing or even knowing they are on the Isle.

Todd felt a touch sorry for them. He'd found it an enchanting spot, full of history, two hundred and fifty square miles, like a slice of Ireland transplanted and tucked away between the steel town of Scunthorpe and the railway town of Doncaster.

In Epworth, the capital with three thousand inhabitants, was a small but busy square with the stump of a stone column with round steps. It was where the town's most famous son, John Wesley, first preached his Methodism.

It stood in front of an old manor, almost two hundred years old and mercifully unmodernised. Below the grey slate roof was a blue-faced clock with gold Roman numerals.

Up a flight of uncarpeted wooden stairs was a cosy library founded and funded by the New Mechanics Institute. Todd had a soft spot for the organisation, not because it was a forerunner in adult education for artisans, or anything remotely left wing like that. He'd used the institute's branch in the centre of his university city to read the papers or play snooker or just shelter from the rain when he was a penniless student. He was inclined to remember kind hospitality.

On his tour, he'd spent a warm hour inside, studying old maps, learning about the draining of the Isle and the riots it caused, reading about the rectory round the corner where Wesley had been born, trying to get a feel for, a sense of, the place.

Across the square was a long, white pub, where he'd spent another hour over soup and sandwiches by an open fire.

No time to browse or snack today, though.

It had been a slowish journey in his Volvo S40, R-reg, brand new, silver, all mod cons, his Christmas toy, his promotion present to himself.

He'd never topped fifty, not so much because he was running it in (no need, these days), or because he wanted to listen to two Beethoven piano concertos back to back on his dinky CD player. The road from HQ had been partially flooded here and there from heavy rain. Skies that looked like lead threatened more.

Soon after crossing the high, brown River Idle he'd been held up by a line of cars and scruffily dressed walkers heading towards a village up a hill to his left.

They were being observed, rather than watched and certainly not marshalled, by a rather short, portly police sergeant.

For a gut-tightening moment, Todd thought another attack had taken place and a manhunt was being launched and, because of a foul-up, he hadn't been alerted.

He buttoned down his window, poked his head out, didn't introduce himself, urgently called, 'What's up?'

'The Haxey Hood Game,' said the sergeant. Politely, he added, 'Sorry for any hold-up.'

'What's that?'

'Annual rough and tumble,' he replied, rather quaintly, thumbing over his shoulder towards the village. 'Just a day out.'

Nothing to do with me, Todd decided, relieved. 'Have fun then.' He fingertipped the window up and drove on.

He ignored the signs to Epworth centre and rectory, was held up again at traffic lights, and drove on for a few more miles.

Before the motorway, he took a right at a mini roundabout overlooked by a war memorial and followed signs to the Cottage Hospital into a narrow lane.

He entered well-tended grounds the size of a royal park. Some distance away, on a rise to his right, stood the hospital, a rambling three-storey building with a walled terrace and lots of extensions from the elaborate Victorian era and plain modern times.

Closer, to his right, was a smaller, much more beautiful Georgian house, two storeys, with white-framed windows and a shiny black door.

The lane passed right in front of the door, no garden, just a gritty square on which stood a dirty, quite old Land Rover.

Beyond the house, on a curve with a view of the motorway almost a mile distant, was the stable block, same fascia, small bricks, matured with great age; same sloping grey-tiled roof, same shiny black paint on arched, closed gates.

He didn't drive on for a quick recce. He was already ten minutes late.

For Britain's forty-something richest man, Lord Harvard appeared underdressed and understaffed.

Wearing baggy green cords, tartan shirt, no tie, and grey pullover, threads snagged here and there, he opened the black door himself. 'Ah.' A creased face smoothed out in welcome.

'Sorry I'm late,' Todd began, 'but I – '

Harvard flicked his hand, as if brushing away a fly, not an apology. 'Come in. Do.' His accent was more stylish than his dress sense.

He shut the door and led Todd through an echoing hall with chequerboard tiles and a dog-leg staircase. Over his shoulder, he asked, 'Have you lunched?'

'A sandwich at the desk.'

'Join me in another then,' he said, entering a huge kitchen with pine fittings and a large square table scrubbed almost white.

Not for fish fingers, Todd hoped. He hated them.

Lord Harvard scooped up two or three newspapers from the table and placed them on one of half a dozen chairs around it. He bent forward to remove one patterned plate from the top of another.

Todd looked down on daintily cut sandwiches, smoked salmon on brown; a mouth-watering sight.

'Beth always prepares too many,' said Lord Harvard with a helpless little headshake.

He must be talking about the housekeeper, Todd decided. Best not upset her. He'd help out.

'Sit down, please.' Lord Harvard turned his back as Todd sat and went to a fawn worktop where a kettle was boiling. He poured coffee beans – Cuban, Todd noted – from a glossy blue packet into a small round grinder.

Over the noise of both electrical appliances, Harvard explained that his housekeeper had taken the rest of the day off for the Haxey Hood Game.

'Yes.' Todd seized on the chance to get in his excuse for being late. 'I got held up by lots of people on their way there. What happens?'

'A piss-up and a punch-up.'

Both laughed.

Pouring the boiling water over the grindings, Harvard said in an amused tone, 'I'll explain the rules of the game. There are none.'

Still standing, he described how, years ago, some gentle lady out riding lost her hood in the wind. Locals fought to retrieve it and claim a reward.

To commemorate the event, teams from local pubs still spent all afternoon and often into the evening in a massive scrum, trying to get the Hood, a leather-bound cylinder these days, from a field outside the village to their local.

'A bit like the Eton Wall Game without the wall and for a better class of people.' He laughed lightly.

Todd smiled, wondering if he was hinting at unhappy schooldays or being self-deprecatingly upper class. He was tall, slim, retained a military bearing, no spectacles. Only greying hair, what there was of it, betrayed his sixty-plus.

'Some private scores get settled in the scrum,' he went on, rather pleasurably. 'It's quite a sight to see the victors, all muddy, heaving their way down the main street in a steaming cloud.'

'What's the prize?' asked Todd.

'Drinks all round.' He looked down at a heavy gold wristwatch. 'Hope to catch a bit of it myself.'

Explains his casual dress, thought Todd, especially if he plans to join in.

Harvard returned to the table and poured coffee from a silver pot into two brown mugs. He plonked the mugs beside both plates and said, 'Dig in, please.'

Todd removed one sandwich from the pile and put it on the empty plate, nibbled.

Harvard helped himself and finished his in one. Suddenly, as if they had already been discussing the topic, 'Yes, of course, you can have the stable block.'

Not so fast, thought Todd, eating slowly and politely.

'Have you seen it?' asked Harvard.

'In the distance.'

Like an estate agent on a hard sell, Harvard tripped through what was inside the closed gates – own courtyard, two floors in parts, secure, several offices, conference room, kitchen, toilets, overnight accommodation. He smiled. 'Even a padded cell.'

The clinic, he explained, had catered for patients on referral from family doctors or courts. Some had to be kept in for observation. 'Well,' he backtracked, 'not quite padded, but barred certainly.'

Todd asked how long it had been empty.

'A month,' Harvard said, quite sharply. 'Cash flow problems.'

Todd wondered if debts had been left behind. It made him think of money. 'What's the rent?'

'Oh...' A short breezy wave. '... have it on us.'

Todd stopped munching his third sandwich and looked away.

'Only too pleased to have it lived in this weather,' Harvard went on.

Todd eyed him doubtfully. Looking a gift horse in the mouth? he was asking himself. He picked up his mug and took a long sip of coffee that was rich and strong.

Harvard seemed to sense some reservation on his part. 'Of course, you'd have to furnish it, have the heating and phone lines reconnected and foot those bills.'

Still a major saving on the budget, Todd calculated. 'I can't put a time on how long we might need it. I mean, we don't want to get settled in and then...'

Harvard was shaking his head, quite vigorously. 'We've no immediate plans for it.' They'd once had a vague idea of converting it into a motel to encourage tourists on day trips to Wesley's birthplace to stay and spend a bit more money locally, but a lakeside complex on the other side of the motorway had beaten them to it.

Todd wondered who 'we' and 'they' were. 'I'll take a closer look, if I may.'

'Toby will show you.' Harvard didn't explain who Toby was. 'Now...' He rose from the table and Todd thought their meeting was over with three more sandwiches to go, all his, he estimated, as the host had eaten far faster.

Instead Harvard moved to a cabinet on a wall opposite a long black cooking range. Both hands went inside. 'Did my office mention to yours a reward?'

'Yes,' said Todd, hurrying up his nibbling. 'What do you have in mind?'

Smaller plates, not matching the two on the table, were in Harvard's hands. Pudding, too, thought, Todd, delighted.

'Twenty-five thousand? Something like that, my PR advises me.'

Public relations, thought Todd sourly. Publicity pays. 'That's very generous.'

What's in it for him? he wondered. His firm's slogan on the side of police cars: 'This patrol sponsored by Fish Finger Freddy's Favourite?' One day in the hard-up police service, it would come to that, he feared.

'The least I can do.' Harvard returned to the table with a tray of cheese, biscuits and butter on a dish, along with the small knives and plates. There was a clatter when he put the tray on the scrubbed table.

He sat and waited until Todd had cleaned up the plate of sandwiches, talking all the time about the awful atmosphere that had descended on the Isle, the trauma the victims had suffered, anxiety of families, his duty to locals, some of whom worked for him on South Humberside. He had an obvious and deep affection for the place.

Todd realised his main concern was, understandably, catching the hooded knifeman terrifying his neighbourhood, not the double killer whose victims came from some distance away. 'We're looking for two unrelated offenders.'

'So I see.' Harvard nodded at the newspapers he'd put on the chair. 'Mmm.' He mused. 'Difficult, I suppose.' Another pause. 'To split into neat, round figures, I mean.'

He seemed to be acknowledging the problem of giving one inquiry a higher financial priority than the other. Without further thought, he added, 'Make it thirty thousand then and divide it equally.'

Astonishing, thought Todd. Another five thou, just like that. That would take my Em ten half-days to earn. He smiled to himself, a smile that faded with the thought that donating any of her fees to the maintenance of law and order would never have occurred to either of them. Astonishing.

It would, he thought on, look effective on 'Wanted' posters. 'What about publicity?'

'We want none.' Harvard's chin had come up. 'Absolutely none.' He'd become very animated. 'Not a single word. Say a benefactor, if you must, but not local; no clues. Agreed?'

Todd nodded gravely, wondering: Then what, in God's name, is in it for him?

'Frankly, I'd be happy if you gave the impression it was coming from police funds,' Harvard added to underscore the conditions he was placing on his offer.

He's genuinely public-spirited, Todd finally conceded, a touch shamed. 'For information leading to arrest and conviction, we'll say.'

'That's entirely up to you.'

'And if we're successful...'

'When you're successful.' Harvard used a positive tone.

'... who'll decide what info brought in the results?' Todd continued.

Another dismissive little hand gesture. 'How it's allocated I'll also leave to you.'

Todd recognised the sort of chairman who decides policy and leaves his managers to manage.

And, like a chairman moving briskly through an agenda, Harvard changed the subject again as they started on disappointing red cheese and rather hard biscuits. He gestured to the newspapers on the chair. 'I see you're using HOLMES.'

Todd nodded, conscious of the noise the biscuits were making in his mouth.

'Clever name that,' Harvard went on.

Not so clever when you work it out, thought Todd.

'Read Conan Doyle?'

Another nod. As a boy, Todd had. His grandad loathed the contemptuous way Holmes treated professional policemen, regarded him as élitist, a drug addict and probably a woofter. He'd have gladly stuck his violin bow somewhere very off-key.

Harvard smiled playfully. 'Have you got yourself a Dr Watson?'

Todd smiled back. As a matter of fact, he had. Not Post Mortem Morton, either.

He always put his best cases down on tape for an old workmate, 'Jacko' Jackson. They'd been together, Jacko's last job, on the day Todd was shot in the leg. Jacko's intervention had saved him.

In retirement, Jacko was writing crime novels, basing his plots on their old cases, fictionalising them, changing names and locations.

There was nothing in it for Todd – only his life. No one outside of him and Jacko and their wives knew. He aimed to keep it that way, especially when he'd just sacked Morton's non-fiction source. So he smiled and shook his head.

Harvard rose again and returned with the coffee pot. As he poured refills, he said, 'Freud was very impressed by Holmes' powers of deduction, you know.'

Todd didn't and ate on.

Harvard put the pot on the table and sat down. 'I see a psychologist is on your agenda.'

He's well read, Todd realised. 'We're considering it, yes.'

'Have you considered Dr Peck?'

Another nod, guarded.

'He's a good man.'

Another hard sell coming, Todd feared.

Harvard was off again. He had a keen interest in psychology, he said. He'd been an officer in the Royal Army Medical Corps. 'Just a lieutenant on admin,' he added modestly.

He'd collated detailed interviews, masses of them, with ex-PoWs for a study on the long-term effects of captivity. 'It became a standard work,' he said, rather proudly. 'I'd have liked to have stayed on in the army . . .'

Todd believed him. Forty years on, he'd still got an officers' mess lilt and that sense of mucking in.

'. . . but, you know . . .' A sad little shrug. 'Family and business commitments and all that.'

He'd first used Dr Peck when his company introduced aptitude tests in assessments on executives. 'I'm a firm believer that they help sort out the wheat from the chaff.'

Todd sipped his fresh coffee and broke a long silence. 'Did you suggest him to Chief Inspector Waites for the . . .' He just stopped himself saying Fish Finger Freddy. '. . . extortion case?'

Harvard gave the question some thought. 'I seem to recall it as a meeting of minds. He did a first class job.' Hurriedly, he decided to share the credit. 'Both of them.'

Todd probed on. 'He also treated patients at Three Counties here, I gather.'

'Yes.'

'With emotional problems?'

'A good insight, I'd have thought, for the work he does now. He wants to make a speciality of criminal profiling, you know. Would you like to speak to him?'

Without waiting for a reply, Harvard got up again, a jack-in-the-box this mealtime, and left the kitchen.

Am I being railroaded here? Todd asked himself anxiously.

All he'd heard for several minutes was a one-sided conversation, not near or loud enough to catch, before the call came: 'Here. Have a word.'

Todd rose and walked into the hall. Harvard was standing at a polished antique table beneath the dog-leg staircase. He handed over a white phone receiver and immediately walked back into the kitchen.

They introduced themselves. Before Todd could explain his presence here, Peck said, 'I've heard about you from Carole Waites.'

They still keep in touch then, Todd realised. He got round to his explanation. 'I'm having a look at this clinic you used to run . . .'

Peck corrected him. 'I was just a rather poorly paid part-timer.'

'. . . to see if it's suitable for use as an incident room.'

'I think you'll find it is.'

'You may have . . .' Todd meant to say 'read'. For some reason, he used '. . . heard that offender profiles are on our agenda. Are you available to discuss it?'

So available, it turned out, that he could be there in under half an hour from his home near Gainsborough where Todd had crossed the swollen River Trent on the way here.

Todd suggested in an hour at the motel Harvard had mentioned to give himself time for a closer look at the stable block before it got too dark.

Britain's forty-something wealthiest man was washing up at a double white sink when Todd returned to the kitchen. Out of force of habit, Em's training, he picked up a tea-cloth and started to dry the cups and plates.

They looked out through the sash window into a long veranda and on to wide lawns that rolled into paddock with outhouses and greenhouses beyond. The rain had started again.

'Nice grounds,' said Todd enviously.

Yes, Harvard agreed sadly, but without the flower beds the old hall had. 'Wife's department.' When they lost her, they moved here. 'We got shot of the old place.'

It was a humble way of confirming that he had given it to the regional health authority to use as a cottage hospital, Todd acknowledged admiringly. 'But you hung on to the stables.'

'We had a vague notion that we'd breed horses one day.' His face lit up. 'Ah. Here's Toby.'

Approaching across the wet grass was a man who looked as though he was on his way back from the Haxey Hood Game. His blue boilersuit and green wellington boots were caked in black slime. He wore a black woolly hat that reminded Todd of Benny, the country yokel from *Crossroads*, a TV soap his grandma used to love and his grandad hated.

Harvard opened the kitchen door as Toby walked along the veranda. 'When you've tidied up, take Mr Todd here to view the stable block, will you, please?'

Todd stood at the open door, damp teacloth in hand. 'This is my son, Toby,' said Harvard, smiling warmly.

Toby beamed amiably and held up a hand to indicate it was too dirty to shake. 'Howdoyoudo,' he said in a rush and a cultured accent far removed from Benny's from *Crossroads*.

5

Toby had washed and changed, Todd noted with considerable relief, when he eventually came out of the black front door.

He had waved off Lord Harvard in the dirty Land Rover and had waited, sitting proudly upright behind the wheel of his pristine Volvo. He didn't want its cleanliness soiled by a muddy passenger, even a peer's son.

Head down, Toby turned left and started to walk in the rain, as if in a dream, up the drive towards the stable block. Todd pipped. Toby turned and walked back towards the car with befuddled features on his face.

Clumsily, he climbed in beside Todd, apologising for the delay. He'd been planting birch whips, he explained. 'They do well in this peaty soil,' he added expertly.

He was smaller but bulkier than his father. His woolly hat had been discarded to reveal mousy-coloured hair. He was mid-thirties, forty at the outside.

He had changed into faded denims and thick, dark blue polo neck. Over them was an opened wax jacket so stained it was difficult to tell its original colour. More worrying for Todd, it gave off a slightly composty odour that immediately masked the sexy smell of leathery newness inside the car.

Only mid-afternoon, but so dark already beneath the thick grey clouds that Todd switched on dipped beam and screen wipers.

Toby didn't ask if Todd knew the way, just assumed he didn't, and rattled out directions – 'left at the larch fence ... left again at those conifers' – all needless, because Todd could see their destination.

Not once did he comment – let alone compliment Todd – on his choice of car.

He had a weathered face and coarsened hands and Todd concluded he ran the estate rather than the frozen food business.

At the high black gates, Toby got out and rummaged, tutting, in every jacket pocket to retrieve a big bunch of keys. He unlocked and pushed the gates back. Todd drove in and stopped in a spacious, recently resurfaced yard.

'Plenty of space for parking, eh?' enthused Toby when he trudged up in black, ankle-length walking boots.

'Yes,' said Todd, eyes ranging through the streaming windscreen over buildings on all four sides, one of them double-storeyed.

All had sloping pantile roofs. A veranda ran most of the way round; paved walkways covered by corrugated see-through plastic. The doors leading off it had been coated in a watery green, all the rage on garden trellis these days. Flower pots, red clay, spring bulbs already shooting, were dotted along the open side of the veranda.

Todd stretched into the back seat to retrieve his long brown trench coat, not a good match for his Sunday best blue which was getting its second successive weekday outing.

Walking slowly, Toby led the way to a double door in the biggest building. As he fiddled again to open it, Todd got a close-up view of mature red brickwork with fresh pointing.

Inside was a U-shaped reception desk, light grey panelling at the front. A grey-blue carpet, reasonably new, respectable anyway, ran up a flight of stairs into a long room.

'The Hayloft,' Toby called it.

Big enough for the HOLMES team, Todd decided. 'A bob or two's been spent here.'

'Too much, I'd say.'

'Who by?'

'Three Counties.' He paused. 'They treated people from Notts, Lincs and Yorks, you know.'

I'd never have guessed, thought Todd, entertaining himself.

They climbed downstairs and Toby carefully locked the door behind him. Todd probed gently as the tour of inspection continued, interrupted as every door along the walkways was opened and shut. 'What happened to them?'

'The kitchen,' Toby announced. They viewed a steel sink with double drainer, hot water heater and flat surfaces round three sides.

The subject must be commercially sensitive, Todd decided. Try again. 'Were they here long?'

Toby opened lots more doors, but didn't open up conversationally until they had poked their heads into two lavatories, the Ladies getting the briefest of inspections.

They had signed a five-year lease, he said, which had two years still to run. Lawyers were arguing over what was owed under the contract.

'The Quiet Room,' Toby said, opening a door into a large lounge with restful lime-coloured walls. 'They spent a lot on it, didn't they?'

Odd, thought Todd, a touch disturbed. I've said that already. 'Why did they leave, then?'

'They're closing places like this, aren't they? Centralising.' Toby locked up and flicked his head in the general direction of the Cottage Hospital. 'That'll be next to go, you'll see.'

Todd decided to double-check on Dr Peck, needing more on him before meeting him. 'Did Mervyn Peck run it?'

A slow headshake and he named the tenant-doctor who, he added, had moved on to the State Special.

Todd knew it well. In his Special Ops days he'd run a search for a dangerous patient who'd escaped from the high security hospital. It was the job on which he'd met his wife. The media sometimes called it 'the Broadmoor of the Midlands'. He was rather fond of it. 'He won't be short of patients there then,' he quipped.

Toby didn't seem to find it funny. 'We look after the outside, the courtyard et cetera.' He swept an arm towards the gates.

'And the hospital grounds. You'd be responsible for keeping the inside clean.'

Todd wasn't expecting the services of Beth, the housekeeper, to be thrown in free, so he nodded.

'Is there room enough for you?' asked Toby.

They had looked in all the rooms now. They were very cold, but had white radiators beneath uncurtained double-glazed windows.

Walls in light pastel shades held back the ever-thickening gloom, except in one room with a heavy metal grille on its window. What Lord Harvard had jokingly called the padded cell, Todd assumed.

With a bit of nice furniture, even that could be made quite homely. Not too homely, he decided on second thoughts, earmarking it as the interview room.

'Plenty.' Roomy enough for Ben and Carole's squads of a dozen detectives each, as well as Deborah Thompson's HOLMES team. He could bus them over from Carole's station, cutting down on inflated mileage claims, protecting his budget. 'We'll take it. Thanks.'

Dr Peck was easy to detect sitting at a window table at the Seven Lakes Motel. He was the only customer; everyone else still down at Haxey for the Hood Game, Todd assumed.

A blue Merc had been the only other car parked before two blocks of smart chalets which stood at right angles to the long low main building with restaurant, bar and water sports shop.

Beyond it, street lights from the road to Crowle streaked the dark water of a wide lake with waves of orange.

Peck rose when Todd approached over a patterned deep red carpet through a small bar with a wooden ceiling and stylish interior brickwork. They shook hands and sat down opposite each other at a square table.

Tea and toasted scones were suggested. Todd opted for tea only. Peck called out the order towards the bar, then opened with, 'How was it?'

The former clinic, Todd knew he meant. 'Ideal, I think.'

In case Peck was still in touch with his ex-colleagues from Three Counties and not wanting to be embroiled in any cash wrangle over who was paying Lord Harvard, he revealed, 'He's giving us the run of the place – free.'

'He's very, very good that way,' said Peck in an affectionate tone.

'Nice place.' Todd probed gently. 'Pity the clinic went up the spout.'

Peck said he knew little about the reasons for its demise. The conversation drifted on to the weather, both looking out of a long window over a three-tiered terrace with flag-poles and a red lifebelt on a low wall. The rain was so heavy now that the lake seemed to be on the boil.

'Too wet even for water-skiers,' said Peck with a depressed sigh.

'Let's hope this Isle's much-vaunted drainage is up to it,' jested Todd, playing for time as he studied Peck.

He was tall and slender with fine facial bones, early forties, like Todd himself. His hair was blond, also like Todd's, but finer and with waves. His eyes were hazel. His suit was chocolate brown, three-piece, immaculate.

Bet he has trouble with emotional women patients, Todd mulled.

A pleasant woman in a pink blouse brought the tea. Peck poured carefully, then looked up expectantly.

Todd stayed with the subject of the clinic, sneakily checking up on Carole Waites, wanting to know if she had ruled out all ex-patients.

'Mine co-operated, certainly, I think you'll find,' replied Peck.

'What sort of problems are we talking about here?'

'A whole range. Depression, addictions and, yes, sexual.' The vast majority weren't from the Isle, he went on. Many had been referred there by outside courts requesting reports before sentencing decisions. The secure room had been for prisoners on remand.

'What about the clients of other consultants?' asked Todd.

Peck undertook to contact the clinic's ex-director at the State Special, to ask if he harboured thoughts about any of them. 'There are . . .' He worked his strong jaw, thoughtfully. '. . . ethical considerations here.'

A hard smile from Todd. 'Tell him we can always get a court order to see his old files.'

Peck nodded.

'Now . . .' Todd paused for his full attention. No need. He was hanging on to every word. '. . . We have to decide about profiling.' He wasn't going to make a firm offer yet. 'How do you feel about that?'

'More to the point . . .' Peck smiled, a clever smile, over the rim of his cup. '. . . how do you?'

Good question, Todd conceded.

Though he'd never teamed up with a profiler, he had worked with other shrinks, most notably on that break-out from the State Special. When he finally caught the escapee, he had to question him about serious sexual offences committed while on the run and could barely get a word out of him.

He'd consulted a staff doctor. 'He's blocking it,' he'd diagnosed. 'Don't be judgemental.' He suggested a question-line that cleared up three crimes. Todd told all of this.

'You're more enlightened than most,' Peck complimented him.

Must be thinking of Ben Nixon on the arsonist series, Todd concluded. He asked about his experience.

'A relatively new boy in the field.' In a light, easy-on-the-ear accent from over or near to the Welsh border, Peck admitted a few failures, blaming lack of data, claimed a few successes, finishing on the high note of Fish Finger Freddy and praising Carole Waites' work.

Todd heard nothing he hadn't already discovered from his ring round other forces. 'What are your ground rules?'

Annoyingly, as if they were in a therapy session, Peck threw the question back. 'What are yours?'

'Any reasonable request for access to confidential files granted, but I control the release of all info, including the profiles. I – and I alone – decide what should be made public and when. No wandering off on your own.'

Peck laughed lightly. 'None of us are Fitz from *Cracker*.' It was a dig about a TV series in which the profiler virtually took over every investigation, like a latter-day Sherlock Holmes, not nearly so poncey, but treating the police with the same disdain.

'Now,' asked Todd, firming his tone, 'what are yours?'

'I'd like a guided tour of all scenes of crimes, access to photos and statements, unescorted interviews with victims.'

'Why unescorted?'

'Little things their attacker said, how he treated her just before and afterwards, can sometimes provide insight – his background, the relationships he may have with others. Women will reveal things to a doctor they won't tell a police officer – '

Todd broke in, offended. 'We always have women officers doing those kind of interviews.'

'I know, I know. But sometimes a change of face...' Peck shrugged and left it there.

His handsome face, he means, Todd sensed. He fancies himself. 'But you'd tell us of anything extra they said?'

'Of course.'

Todd said nothing, uncertain.

'Some victims don't want to go through it yet again for a uniform, but they will for a white coat,' Peck went on.

Makes sense, Todd decided. 'What's your fee?'

A moment's pause. 'Five hundred, plus legitimate expenses.'

Five hundred? Todd repeated to himself. My wife can earn that in a morning. 'We're talking of two totally different cases here...'

'So I gather.'

From Carole Waites or the newspapers? Todd wondered. 'Two corpses in one inquiry, eight walking wounded in the other. A lot of work.'

'And a worthwhile challenge.'

Todd revealed a substantial reward was about to be announced without disclosing the source. 'Police officers and civvies engaged on the inquiry don't qualify.'

An earnest expression. 'I'd be happy just doing my bit.'

Can't speak fairer than that, Todd finally decided. 'Welcome aboard.'

They shook hands on it.

A good day's work, the new executive in Todd told himself as he drove back following the Trent south deep into Nottinghamshire, wiper on top speed, tyres sloshing through vast puddles nearly all the way.

A cheap day's work, the old on-the-road operator protested. A location scout finding free accommodation, an admin clerk fixing the office furniture, even a couple of camp beds, with HQ stores, a financial tight arse accepting reward money and signing up a consultant for next to nothing. You've caught no one. Call that work, real police work?

That's the way it's going to be from now on, the new executive sighed to himself.

The mobile phone clipped to the dash rang with home just a few miles ahead. 'Another incident, sir,' said Control. 'Non-fatal series.'

The saturated sergeant inspected his warrant card by torchlight at the road block, neither of them letting on that they had met seven hours earlier outside Haxey.

Todd didn't get out or invite the sergeant into the back; no point. Standing out in the swirling, incessant rain wouldn't make him any wetter than he already was.

Victim number 9 was a girl called Jennie, aged seventeen, the sergeant said through the half-opened window. He knew her family. 'Nice quiet lass.'

First reports indicated she had watched the end of the Hood Game. Then she'd started to cycle home towards the village of Westport on the banks of the Trent.

In a winding lane with high hedges, she'd been knocked off her bike. She came to and found herself on the other side of the hedge, tied hand and foot to a tree. A black shadow was cutting off her clothes so roughly that she'd suffered several wounds.

There'd been some conversation, if you can call it that, between them, but the sergeant didn't know what was said. The man vanished in the direction of the river as quickly as he'd appeared.

A villager walking home from the post-game festivities heard her cries, freed her, covered her with a coat, carried her some distance until he'd flagged down a car. He'd gone with her to the hospital.

The sergeant had put on a diversion to stop the scene being trampled over. He wasn't going to trample on it himself, but wait for Forensics. They'd decide whether to start their examination by floodlight or wait till dawn.

He'd asked the crew of a patrol car to inform the girl's mother and take her to the hospital. He'd also fetched out constables from their homes to knock on what few doors there were between the two villages.

He'd been through it before, too many times, Todd realised. Had the drill off pat. At first, he could think of nothing to say, except, 'Stick with it. And thanks.' Then a small idea came. 'I'll get the river patrol to scout the banks tomorrow.'

Carole Waites was already at the Cottage Hospital in the Casualty Department, not much bigger than the first-aid post at police HQ – just a brightly lit side room off the terrace with a couple of curtained cubicles.

She was wearing a dark suit, no make-up, and looked her forty years tonight; tense and drained.

The girl had been admitted to a private ward overnight, she reported. Her injuries weren't life-threatening, the usual knife slashes plus concussion from being knocked off her cycle.

She'd been found before hypothermia could set in, but her shock was deep. According to the doctor attending her, she couldn't remember much, timings and so on, just wanted to be with her mum.

Carole had already spoken to her rescuer, the motorist who drove her here and the nurse who'd initially treated her. Taken together, the girl described her assailant as short and broad, wearing a black balaclava with eye holes, dark, possibly black, tracksuit. During her ordeal, he'd asked in a tight, local accent, 'Good, is it? Enjoying it, aren't you? Love it, don't you?'

Todd had read it all before in the files, variations of it anyway; gut-churning, chilling. Neither used that old line, 'Same MO.'

They knew; all too obviously knew. And Todd knew, too, that nothing, absolutely nothing, he'd done all day was going to find the attacker and stop him.

A feeling of helplessness and impotence overwhelmed him.

6

'No overnight leak,' PR Pam said brightly, entering Todd's office at HQ after a single tap. 'Oh, sorry.' Her stride slowed when she saw he was talking on the phone.

He wrapped up orders to the inspector of the Trent river patrol. 'I don't know what you're bloody well looking for,' he said, tetchily. 'Anything out of the ordinary will do.' A rendezvous was fixed. The phone went down with more of a clank than a click.

Pam had reached his desk and stood before him, repeating, 'No leaks.'

There were no news cuttings pinned to her board, Todd's tired eyes noted. Neither had there been anything about the latest attack on the kitchen TV set or radio on a flick around stations during breakfast after four hours of fitful sleep.

'It looks as though you've plugged it,' she added.

At last, he thought, grumpily, she's read between the lines and rumbled the reason for ditching Ray Trench.

He told her to check with Carole Waites and release only what she wanted the media to know about the new case. Then he briefed her on the reward. 'Announce that too, but not the source.'

'Terrific.' Her round face lit. 'Most outlets . . .'

Makes 'em sound as fresh as mountain streams, he mused.

'. . . will lead on the reward and just tack this new job on the end; more upbeat.'

After all the grim news that had been coming out of the Isle for the last eight months, he realised. He'd learned from his Em that editors like a balance between what she called up and down stories.

'They'll want an on-the-spot conference,' Pam added.

'Let Carole do it.'

That raised eyebrow again, querulous. 'Not you?'

'It's her case.'

'What about the reward? They'll want top brass . . .' A stern look. '. . . preferably in uniform, fielding questions.' She eyed his back-in-business workaday grey suit and matching pullover.

All this fucking packaging and presentation and marketing for outlets, fumed Todd. His temper often mirrored the amount of sleep he'd had, both on the short side this morning.

He leaned forward, shoulders squaring up. 'I've no wish to appear on screen more often than a bloody weathergirl. You've more experience at it than me. You do it. And while you're at it, tell 'em we've established an incident room.'

'Not until I've got the phone numbers for it.' Huffily, she turned on her flat heels, on her way, the cow, to complain to the Chief about lack of co-operation, he speculated. Well, in this mood, he could fuck off, too, the old fart.

'Yes,' snapped Todd, snatching up the phone that had been ringing nearly all morning, mostly with piffling queries from Stores about furniture for the incident room.

'Ben Nixon.'

Speaking to someone doing real police work settled him. 'Oh, Ben.'

He'd ruled out the kerb-crawler as his double murderer, Nixon reported, but Debby Thompson on the HOLMES desk had passed on another tip that had resulted from the publicity. A woman down south had shopped an ex-lover over kinky sex games with a knife. He suspected she was just getting even after he took off with another woman, but he might as well check while he was this way.

'OK,' Todd concurred. He broke the good news about the incident room and the reward, then the bad, from Nixon's point of view, about engaging Dr Peck.

He took it like a real policeman, said nothing, but groaned loudly.

To make doubly sure he missed the media, in no mood for diplomacy today, Todd dropped in on the Isle's police station down a narrow street in Epworth.

In a modern building, the size of a bungalow, Sergeant Reith sat behind a small desk in a small office, looking so weary that he didn't attempt to get up. Todd knew the feeling and sat down heavily.

Normally, he'd have suggested Reith put a civvy raincoat over his uniform and that they go together to the Red Lion in the square for a pint and a chat. But he hadn't sussed the sergeant yet, wondered why he'd described the Hood Game as 'a rough and tumble' instead of coming straight out, as Lord Harvard had, with 'piss-up and punch-up'. He suspected he might be . . . well . . . religious, a bit narrow-minded.

Anyway, the dreadful thought that had troubled Todd during a restless night was highly confidential and, besides, both of them were clearly bushed. Better to talk here, he decided.

Forensics had been and gone, Reith reported, after taking the usual photos, measurements and plaster casts.

'If they found anything significant, like a dropped Stanley knife with fingerprints, they haven't told me.' A bleak smile suggested he was often kept in the dark by CID. 'A real will o' the wisp, this fella.'

'What's your feelings about him?' asked Todd.

'He's from around here, definitely. Not just because some of his victims say he's got a local accent. He knows his way round, the fields and footpaths, picks his ambush sites carefully, and his escape routes.'

He'd obviously given the crimes deep thought and Todd wondered if any senior officer had bothered to tap his local knowledge before.

'All of 'em happen on the east of the Isle,' he went on, 'so that's where he comes from. He gets away very fast, must be reasonably young and fit.'

'What about transport?'

'Concealed somewhere away from the scene unless he's always on foot which I doubt, 'cos we always swamp the area after every attack; cleverly concealed because we never get reports of vehicles parked in farm gateways. A bike in a hedge bottom maybe?'

'A real countryman, you mean. A poacher, perhaps?'

Not a poacher, Sergeant Reith said firmly. He knew them all and had checked them all. 'Someone like that, though. He always ties them to strong trees or fences, nothing weak or rotten. He's got field craft.'

More than troubled now, heavy doubt descending, Todd got round to the real reason he'd dropped by. 'Do you know Lord Harvard's lad Toby?'

A cautious nod.

'He's an expert on trees and I left him alone late yesterday afternoon with his father and housekeeper out at the game.'

Reith gave this long thought. 'Doubt he's our man, though.'

Oddly, Todd felt a touch of relief. 'Why?'

The first ambush happened on the night of an agricultural show in May, one of the Isle's big social events, he said.

A young stallholder from off the Isle celebrated a bumper day for orders for his garden furniture. In the beer tent, he said something offensive to a teenage girl, made her cry.

Toby overheard, intervened and a bit of a brawl ensued. He cracked his right hand, had it put in plaster.

'The victim surely would have noticed that. He wouldn't have been able to hold a knife anyway.'

Would if he's ambidextrous, Todd demurred, and lots of field craftsmen are.

'Surely she would have smelt fresh plaster of Paris,' Reith added.

Not if she was so terrified she lost most of her senses, Todd argued with himself. 'What happened to the other fellow?'

'Broken nose.'

'What was the outcome?'

'Neither would press charges.' Reith wasn't finished yet. 'Anyway, he's too slow.'

'Mentally or physically?'

Reith gave him a long look, but no answer.

'What's his problem?' Todd insisted.

'Both,' Reith finally replied. He'd never been well, he went on. He'd been privately educated, but hadn't gone to university or into the family business. His father put it about that he was the estate director, but they had a manager who really ran the place. 'He's more or less the groundsman.'

'So what's his problem?' Todd repeated.

'Head injury in his teens.' Reith shook his head very sadly. 'Finished his mother. She died quite young.'

Todd sensed that he cared for both Harvard and his son. Reith seemed to realise he'd reinstated Toby as a suspect. 'He's very polite and gentle, painfully shy with ladies.'

'No wife or girlfriend?'

A headshake. 'Neither has he any convictions. There's never been a breath of scandal about him.'

Well, thought Todd cynically, there wouldn't be, if his rich dad pays off everyone he's thumped.

He was unimpressed now. The one occasion when he needed fearless impartial eyes and ears and he'd got a local man who probably doffed his helmet to Harvard; lots of officers do to the aristocracy, including top brass.

Come to think of it – and perish this thought – especially top brass in debt to the tune of thirty grand and free accommodation, Todd admitted to himself as he drove the few miles on to Grey Green.

Too late to change things now, he accepted with deep foreboding. The news about the reward and the incident room would be out.

No rain all morning, much colder, occasional glimpses of sun and patches of blue in the sky, but now, in the afternoon, the sky was bruised by dark clouds and another depression was gathering above and within him.

Next to a huge removal van parked in the old stables' courtyard was a white truck, almost as big, with a grey metal mast twenty feet high.

Inside the mobile command post Carole Waites looked up from the keyboard of a laptop. 'Welcome to Starship Enterprise.' She was wearing last night's outfit but her make-up was discreetly back in place.

Todd flipped down a tip-up seat, sat and glanced around a cubicle, smaller than one of those compartments in old railway coaches. An array of new technology – fax machine, printer, VDUs – had been added since he'd used one of these posts in his Special Op days.

There'd been a smaller turn-out for the news conference than at HQ, but it went OK, Carole said in a bored tone. PR Pam had been and gone. Forensics had so far drawn a blank. She'd interviewed Jennie at length. Dr Peck was still with her.

'He's quick off the mark,' Todd observed drily.

'We might as well get on with it.' She gestured to the small black screen on which a white cursor pulsated silently. She was just about to transmit Jennie's statement to Debby Thompson on the HOLMES desk at her station, she explained. 'Do you want to read it?'

She tapped a key. The cursor flew upwards, dragging line after line behind it. She slid the machine at an angle across a plastic worktop.

Cycling home alone down a country lane after dark had not unduly concerned Jennie because most of the other attacks had taken place much later at night, Todd read.

She was certain no one followed her from Haxey. As she passed a copse, she felt the back wheel go, as if it had hit an obstruction on the road surface. She had just a fleeting glimpse of a dark figure as she fell sideways.

She came round to find herself tied by her wrists to a tree, bathed in yellow light, feeling perished and wet. Her anorak, sweater and jeans had already been removed. She'd been gagged.

She struggled violently, but vainly, against her bonds. A man's voice said, very quietly, 'Keep still and I won't hurt you' – an impossible order to obey, so uncontrollably was she trembling with shock, fear and cold.

She did move, often, and felt searing pains in both sides as her blouse came away. The straps of her bra were cut without her feeling further injuries.

She was certain the weapon was in his right hand and a torch in his left. When he moved towards her its beam shone full in her face.

He came so close to her that she could smell beer on his breath and feel his clothing on her bare skin – fleecy, not a stiff material.

He put his cheek on hers. His mask was soft, like wool. 'I'm going to take off the gag. Don't scream and you won't get hurt.'

He pulled her own scarf down to her chin. She was so weak now, almost fainting, that she didn't call out.

Then he started murmuring the usual things like, 'Good this, isn't it?'

She didn't say yes or no, just begged him not to hurt her any more. He stepped back, shone the torch on and then below her navel.

He sliced at the elastic of her pants, a tiny bit at a time, far slower and more carefully than he cut through her bra, asking all the time if she was enjoying it. She felt her briefs fall away.

He bent forward towards her feet. The beam went out and he went, too, just vanished. She waited for what seemed a long time to make sure he was out of earshot. She cried, screamed for even longer.

Todd looked up from reading about her rescue as Dr Peck slid in, filling up what little space was spare.

'Anything fresh?' asked Carole with a yawn.

'Dreadful, wasn't it?' He looked shocked. 'A ghastly experience.' Then he answered the question. 'I'll know more when I've talked to the rest and compared accounts.'

Todd finished reading and looked up at Peck, still standing, no place to sit. If he was wearing a white coat, it was hidden under a long, navy blue one with a velvet collar.

'She's sleeping again,' said Peck. 'I'll try for more in a day or two.'

'If there's more,' said Carole in a deeply depressed tone.

'There's always more,' said Peck stiffly.

'Looks like he's changed clothes.' Carole nodded at the screen. 'That sounds more like a tracksuit.'

Todd knew that other victims had identified material like a boilersuit.

She looked urgently up at Peck. 'He's becoming more dangerous. She could have fractured her skull or she could have frozen to death if she hadn't been found so soon.'

Todd had read on to the medical report. 'These knife wounds are deeper.'

'Yes,' said Peck, 'we're going to have to get on with it rather urgently.'

Not crediting the sergeant for his information, Todd pointed out that the first attack had happened after an agricultural show and the last after the big game.

Carole got the message, undertook to obtain details of the local social programme and double the guard for special events.

'Do it tomorrow,' said Todd, firmly. 'Go home and get some sleep now. Bring Debby and her team with you and we'll all operate from here.' He flicked his head in the general direction of the removal van. 'I'll make sure it's all ready.'

Dr Peck looked down, addressing Todd anxiously. 'Now I've made a start on Carole's series, would you mind if I stuck with it, chat to her witnesses first, get that out of the way before the double murderer?'

Carole summoned up enough energy to nod, almost enthusiastically. So did Todd. He didn't mind one way or the other, and he was sure Ben Nixon would be delighted.

The fog lamp of the police launch picked out Todd standing on a concrete quay stamping his feet. He'd been waiting half an hour in a misty dusk with the temperature dropping rapidly.

The operators of two cranes behind him had stopped lifting whole tree trunks from a huge imported stack into timber works next door. It was the only industry Todd had seen in Westport, a straggly village with a pub at either end of a long street and no view of the Trent behind a high grass bank.

From the vantage point of the quay, he could see that the river was about eighty yards wide here, brown as milk chocolate and fast-flowing.

On the other side, beyond a mile or so of flood plains, trees covered the gloomy skyline, acre upon acre of them, enough to rank as a forest.

The engine cut and the squat dark blue boat glided smoothly alongside, hardly a bump as it touched the rubber buffers.

'Nothing, sir,' the inspector called from the white deck. He threw up a thick rope which Todd caught and wound round a cast iron bollard before realising that ACCs shouldn't really be asked to do such tasks.

Scrambling up a metal ladder fixed vertically to the quay, the inspector added, 'There was a big tide, not predicted, not quite an aegir – '

'What's that?' interrupted Todd, handing over the end of the rope.

'A tidal wave, like the Severn bore.'

Todd wished he'd never asked as he stood, close to shivering, through a boring little lecture about high tides from the Humber funnelling into the Trent from its confluence with the Ouse.

'And what with the floodwater going the other way, a rowing-boat was ripped off his moorings on the east side and finished smashed up and well downriver,' the inspector went on. 'Anything, even a bike, left on the bank would have been washed away.'

'Thanks for trying,' Todd said, smiling. He switched off his smile as he turned and headed for his car parked beyond the quaykeeper's green cabin.

Waste of time, he chuntered. In future, he promised himself, he'd do what the Chief recommended when he promoted him – stop playing detective and just supervise.

Supervising the finishing touches at the incident room took so long that he set off for home later by a couple of hours than the night before.

The mist had thickened and rolled in from the river to the east and the peat bogs to the west. Coming out of Grey Green he stopped at a mini roundabout with a war memorial and wondered which way to go. M180 to M18 and A1 was longer but faster. Too fast if this turns into fog, he decided. He'd return the way he came.

Soon the lights of Epworth were behind him and Haxey's were coming up.

About twenty-four hours ago, he told himself, Jennie crossed this main road on her bike to be confronted by a sick pervo.

Blast, he cursed himself. Should have ordered that kowtowing, time-serving sergeant to nose around, check on who used the lane regularly, see if they spotted anything or anybody last night.

Do it yourself then, the old operator within suggested. You know the way to Westport.

I'm a manager, not a player, replied the new executive.

Be a player-manager then. Go on. Just for ten minutes.

He turned left into the lane.

A waste of bloody time.

Head craned over the steering wheel, his eyes moved left and right to the timing of the windscreen wipers. His dipped beam picking up nothing. Not a single red light. Not a car. Not a bike.

Then . . .

What's that? A beam. A beam flashing.

He flicked his car beam up to full.
Standing in the middle of the lane was a dark-hooded figure.
Gotcha, you sick pervo.

7

In full beam, the figure took full shape, short and broad. The right shape, Todd thought, more than excited, thrilled.

Calm, son, calm. His grandfather seemed to be talking to him as clearly as if he was in the passenger seat.

Study, size it up.

He calmed himself, slowed to a crawl and studied his target.

From left gloved hand weak torchlight shone. OK, that will be overpowered by the car's beam. Means he can't see me.

He's graduated from cyclists to motorists and may think he's stopping a woman driver. Don't disappoint him and turn on the interior light.

Oh, wonderful. He's a rabbit in my headlights. Not very good field craft, this. Is this dumb country boy in for a surprise? Terrific.

Steady, son. And study.

His right hand was held up, like an unmoving point-duty cop, something round in it.

A Stanley knife? Don't want that struck through an opened window against your temple. Check that window's fully up. Check and study.

His face wasn't hooded, just looked that way, with a dark Benny-type hat pulled down to the eyes and a thick, black scarf up to them.

Todd stopped just a yard or so away from him. Keep the beam on and dazzle him.

The masked man touched the car's silver bonnet with what looked like a smallish tree branch, certainly not a knife.

Slowly, he began to walk along the offside of the Volvo.

He's not going to give himself up, Todd knew, not with a club in his hand.

I'm going to have to take him.

True, but wait.

His own hand dropped to and hooked the silver door handle in his fingers. He waited.

Take a deep breath, you'll need it.

He took one.

The man moved cautiously down the offside.

Wait.

Alongside the door, he bent forward, as if about to tap on the window.

Now.

Fingers tugged on the handle. Shoulder charged the inside of the door. It flew open. The figure let out a piercing yelp, doubled, vanished from view.

Shoulder first, Todd rolled on and out of the car.

In the back light from the beam, he could see the man was on his knees on the grass verge, whimpering in agony.

Todd got to his feet first, crouching, moving nimbly, like the old days. He sidestepped beyond flaying arms and hooked both of his round the man's neck at the throat. He pulled his head hard into his groin and held it there.

Easy collar this, he thought joyfully.

'Help,' came out a muffled mouth. Then, 'Only . . .'

Easy as piss. Got him. He's mine. Todd freed one hand to pull the scarf away. Terrified eyes and an off-centre nose looked up at him. A tight mouth worked out, 'Easy, mate, for fuck's sake.'

Louder, no longer muffled. 'Get him off.' A pleading, pained cry. 'Do something, for f – '

Something behind Todd moved. Something passed over his head and in front of his face. Every muscle tensed.

Something cold and hard was at his throat. His head was yanked back.

An accomplice? Not so easy. Wrong, wrong, wrong. Something's wrong. Both his hands flew from his captive upwards and caught hold of two gloved hands each side of his chin.

Bright lights and loud shouts from across the lane, a different voice. 'Go. Let's go.' An engine spluttered, stopped. 'Out of it.'

A gang job? Impossible.

Yet more lights, a different engine sound, another vehicle approaching, more screamed, 'Quick. Out of it. Now. Come on.'

Help's coming. Thank Christ.

Todd's head was freed. Coughing, he fell back on the grass, rolled over on one side.

A kick sent pain, like an electric shock, from the base of his spine to the top of his skull.

Two dark figures were above him. One was doubled up and being helped away.

Breathless, Todd peered beneath his car, could make out two wheels heading his way, then four as a vehicle turned in a blue cloud of exhaust fumes into the lane.

Shit. They're getting away.

Four boots, one of them being dragged, clattered on the tarmac. Two boots vanished upwards. The wheels shrieked and skidded. Another boot went. Tyres spun and moved. The fourth boot didn't. A wheel ran over it.

Screams filled the dark, dank air. The boot disappeared. The wheels sped away, leaving the smell of rubber behind.

Todd sat up in grass, wet to his underpants.

A beam lit the lane to Haxey. Two red tail lights came on. So did the bulb above the number plate.

He read the number, repeating it to himself over and over again as he scrambled up. Lights were coming from the direction of Westport.

A blue Escort pulled up, nose to nose with his Volvo. Sergeant Reith got out and walked in measured strides towards him. 'You, sir.' He sounded only mildly surprised.

Todd ignored him, sat sideways in the driver's seat, feet on the tarmac, pulled a notebook and pen out of an inside pocket, reciting the number out loud as he wrote it down.

'Yes,' said Reith, quietly, 'I know, sir.'

Mrs Reith motioned to a sofa in front of a glowing log fire.

'Are you sure you want me to sit?' Todd queried. He looked down at his grey trousers, mud and grass stained as well as wet.

'It'll dry and brush off,' Mrs Reith assured him. 'Tom won't be a minute.' She closed the lounge door on him and returned to the snug kitchen where Todd had removed his jacket and dirty shoes, Em's training.

Left on his own, he didn't sit, but stood on a half-moon sheepskin mat, bending forward, with his backside to the fire, imagining the steam starting to rise.

He had followed the police Escort to this isolated stone cottage. 'Nearer than the station for a chat,' Reith had explained. And he felt at home as he looked around a cosy, cluttered living-room – the old furniture, lovingly polished, the family photos on the upright piano, the spring flowers forcing through moss-topped bowls.

Reith returned, his tunic top removed and blue braces hanging behind his black serge trousers. 'Jim Maddox, Tony Ivers and Chas Adams.' He sat heavily in a well-worn fireside chair with plenty of cushions.

'Not that I'm complaining . . .' Todd walked in stockinged feet from the mat and sat on the sofa. '. . . but what were you doing there?'

He always kept observations on scenes twenty-four hours, then a week and exactly a month afterwards, Reith explained, just in case someone or something aroused his suspicions.

Todd felt deep discomfiture, blamed the dampness spreading from him on to Mrs Reith's cushion rather than his earlier critical thoughts about her husband.

Following that routine, Reith had gone down the lane tonight. In a farm gateway, he'd spotted Maddox's truck; knew it well, an ex-army lorry, drab green, canvas-covered back.

Ivers was standing next to it, face visible; knew it well, too. He'd nicked him often enough. Ivers was dressed for the cold, but not masked.

Reith drove on, closer to the scene of Jennie's ambush, ready to note anything and anyone who passed by.

Through his rear view mirror, he saw dipped lights approaching from the main road, then stop on full beam. He'd wound down his window and heard shouts. He'd seen the gateway light up, realised something was amiss.

'Sorry I took so long,' he concluded with a stony face. 'Had to do a six-point turn, the lane's so narrow.'

Mrs Reith reappeared with two plates of fried potatoes and legs of cold pheasant. Todd wondered if the game was a back-door gift from a poacher, decided not to ask.

She pulled a square low table into position between them. She made more trips with cultery, pickles, salt and pepper, bread and butter, paper napkins. Finally she brought two mugs of hot instant coffee, left and didn't return.

'Who are they?' asked Todd, leaning forward to begin his meal.

Maddox was twenty-two, Reith told him, had been apprenticed to his father and taken over his garden furniture business when he died.

'Not the stallholder Lord Harvard's son thumped at the farm show, is he?' asked Todd.

An astonished look crossed Reith's face, as if Todd was some dumb cadet who'd suddenly surprised him.

'He was the one who stopped me.' Todd put down his fork and ran a finger up his nose. 'A break here.'

Reith nodded, chewed, then got back to Maddox. He lived in a caravan next to his workshop on the other side of the river, but spent a lot of time on the Isle. 'Sells his furniture in the summer and logs in the winter.'

Ivers was older, twenty-six, maybe twenty-seven now. He'd worked almost everywhere – pits, steel foundry, peat plant, timber firm, docks – but never for long. 'A hard man, leader of the pack.' He lived on and off with a teenager, a real tart, in Westport. 'Anyone who even looks at her is asking for trouble.'

Adams was younger, not yet twenty, also out of work. He helped Maddox on delivery runs now and then, but mainly just dossed around. 'He's walking sideways, I'm afraid.'

Todd frowned over a forkful of fried potatoes.

'Straying from the straight and narrow,' Reith explained. 'A Methodist phrase.'

And a nice one, Todd reflected.

'His parents are good folk. Broken-hearted, they are.'

'Members of your chapel?' Todd asked, mischievously.

A solemn nod. At least I got one thing right about him, Todd complimented himself.

'Their lad gambles, boozes, takes drugs these days; out of it a lot of the time,' Reith continued. 'Totally led astray by Ivers, he's been. Ivers just uses them both – Maddox for wheels 'cos he's off the road, banned; Adams as a dogsbody.'

Reith picked up his pheasant leg and started gnawing at it. Todd followed suit.

Between mouthfuls, he asked about criminal records and heard that Ivers had convictions for assault, possession of soft drugs and drink-driving twice, Maddox for motoring offences.

'Adams?' A sorrowful face. 'Only a matter of time.'

'You can put Ivers at the scene,' Todd pointed out. 'I can identify Maddox from his nose. How do you know the third man's Adams?'

Reith looked stunned even to have been asked. 'I've been on to the Cottage Hospital. Two casualties, just in – Adams with a crushed foot, Maddox with a smashed knee.' He got back to stripping the bird's bone.

Todd was sorry now that he had asked but managed a warm smile, then sank his teeth into what was left of his pheasant.

'The way I see it is this,' Reith said, wiping his mouth. 'Maddox held you up. Ivers went to his aid when you were getting the better of him. Adams sat in the truck. That's his style. An onlooker, weak character. He flapped when things got out of hand and stalled the engine. Ivers ordered him out to help Maddox, took over the wheel, but was in such a panic himself to get away he ran over Adams's foot.'

Todd was still eating, so the sergeant carried on. 'You've guessed what this is about?'

Todd had and, with a mouthful, hummed a Yes.

'It's more than do-it-yourself Neighbourhood Watch this; much more.' There was disgust on Reith's face. 'Vigilantes.' He shook his head fiercely. 'We can't have that, can we?'

Not really, Todd conceded, still eating, privately recalling that awful case when a toddler was snatched while out shopping with his mother and brutally murdered by two school truants.

Before their arrests the police picked up another kid for questioning. The news spread. A crowd gathered, banging on the side of the prison van, demanding his head; almost a riot.

Next day, the kid was released, cleared, totally innocent. Soon afterwards the culprits were caught. The crowd gathered again, baying for blood; all of it on TV.

They were so inflamed, so self-righteous, that it never entered their lame brains that they'd have lynched an innocent boy if they'd got their hands on him. There they were, large as life, doing it again, and on TV.

'No, we can't,' he said, his mouth finally empty.

'They weren't doing it out of good neighbourliness,' Reith said emphatically. 'They were after the reward.'

'How do you want to play it?'

Go for assault occasioning actual bodily harm on a police officer, namely ACC Todd, Reigh began.

The pain at the base of Todd's back had almost gone and he was far more worried about the state of Mrs Reith's cushion. 'Whoever came to Maddox's aid will claim he was acting in his defence,' he argued. 'And I didn't reveal my identity.'

Threatening behaviour then, Reith came back, and possession of offensive weapons. The clubs, Todd ventured, would be among the firewood in the back of the truck, making it difficult to prove.

Obstructing the highway, Reith offered. He was sure Ivers must have been at the wheel and was therefore driving while disqualified. 'I'll get 'em for something.'

Todd smiled. This was his patch. He was the law here. He could decide.

Personally he'd have had them on the mat for a bollocking, but he wasn't going to interfere. 'When you've finished with them, bring them up to the incident room. I want to quiz them about the night of the Hood Game.'

Reith lifted up his broad bottom and eased a bent notebook out of the back pocket of his uniform trousers.

'Now.' He rested it on his knee. 'I'll need your statement and to see if that kick's left a bruise for a bodily harm charge.'

It occurred to Todd that it would be the first time his bare arse had been viewed at close quarters by a village bobby since he'd been caught red-handed scrumping apples. 'Lend me a pair of dry underpants while you're at it,' he said.

They appeared before Todd next morning, looking more like a wounded trio in the Retreat from Moscow than the local branch of the Guardian Angels.

Maddox and Adams were pushed in NHS wheelchairs into the Quiet Room which Todd, having first choice, had bagged as his office-cum-conference room.

Each had a leg in sharp-smelling, gleaming white plaster stuck out horizontally in front of him. They were in the standard issue maroon dressing-gowns of the Cottage Hospital where they'd been detained overnight.

Only Ivers was able to stand, but hardly upright, handcuffed to a much shorter Tom Reith.

Ivers had been snatched from his woman's bed at eight. A donkey jacket over his stained crew-neck sweater and dirty jeans, he'd been bundled into a police car and then into the Padded Cell.

All had bleary eyes, unshaven faces and greasy uncombed hair – Ivers' black, Maddox's mousy and Adams' ginger.

Ivers was six foot plus with a powerful physique. Maddox was thickset and short. Inside the borrowed dressing-gown, Adams looked an eight stone weakling.

'Right . . .' Todd was in a fouler mood than yesterday, having discovered after breakfast not only a scratch on his new car's bonnet but a deep dent in the driver's door. '. . . the sergeant has told you why you're all here.'

Sitting at his desk, in his third choice brown suit, he ran through the caution and their rights to representation.

A knock came on the door as he was completing the formalities. In walked Dr Peck in dark pin-striped suit and shiny black shoes. 'Oh, excuse me.' He looked around the room. 'Is Carole about?'

Todd thumbed in the direction of the Hayloft where Deborah's team was being installed. 'She'll be here in a minute.'

Peck shut the door quietly and stood with his back against the lime green wall, ignoring a line of black, moulded chairs, all empty, facing Todd's desk.

Todd resumed. 'First, I want to talk about Tuesday night.' He looked at Ivers. 'Where were you between six and seven?'

Ivers regained some lost height. 'In me bed wi' me bird.'

An accent from further south, Fenlands perhaps, Todd guessed. 'At that time?'

'Any time.' He grinned salaciously, showing off.

'That's not much of an alibi,' said Todd stroppily.

'Wot's that mean?' A sullen silence. 'True. It's true.' Ivers looked sideways and down at the occupants of the wheelchairs. 'They'll tell yer.'

'Yeah, we dropped him off at his place about six thirty,' affirmed Maddox offhandedly.

'Right,' said Adams.

Todd's eyes stayed on them. 'And you two?'

'Sleeping it off,' Maddox replied.

'Sleeping what off?'

They'd been round the pubs since eleven, then to the Game, not playing for any particular side, taking a few cans with them, joining in the mêlée on behalf of any team that seemed to be winning. 'There's free drinks, see, at the end of it,' Maddox went on. They'd got wet through, he explained, and had gone to his truck where they stripped off and slept it off in the back on piles of dry sacks.

Carole walked in without knocking and stood next to Peck, just in time to hear Reith say to Maddox, 'You said you drove him home.' He tugged hard on the handcuff, making Ivers scowl.

Maddox looked behind him, curious, Todd assumed, about his audience.

'You.' Reith raised his voice. 'I'm talking to you.'

Maddox turned back. 'I weren't pissed,' he stammered. 'Just tired.'

Todd came back, incredulous. 'So you slept together . . .'

Ivers guffawed. 'They often do. They never pull.'

Find women, he meant, Todd knew.

Reddening with embarrassment, his confidence gone, Maddox began to stutter. 'Only an, an hour, just a nap, then w-w-we . . .'

Adams helped him. 'Went back to our local at Westport.'

'At what time?'

Adams shrugged, unsure or indifferent. 'Landlord there'll tell yer.'

Ivers wasn't grinning now. 'Wot's this all about?' He pulled on the cuffs. 'Told us, he did, it was about last night.'

'It's to eliminate you from our inquiries.' Todd smiled evilly. 'Or otherwise.'

'We're not that nutter with the Stanley knife.' Ivers glowered, offended. 'We were out to get him, bring him in. We're not nutters.'

'That's a matter of opinion.' Todd smiled. 'I'm certainly not satisfied with your explanations so I shall be turning you over to Chief Inspector Waites here . . .' He nodded towards the back of the room. '. . . for fuller statements.'

Todd paused while Carole and Peck departed. 'Now, since you mention it, about last night . . .' He let it hang there.

'We were only trying to help,' said Ivers, sulkily.

'Yer,' piped Maddox. 'I tried to tell you that.'

'Yer,' echoed Adams.

'We don't need help like that,' said Todd.

'You need it all right.' Ivers was tugged sideways but he pulled Reith's hand back, defiantly. 'You've been running around like blue-arsed flies since May, getting nowhere. Place ain't safe for young girls to walk out.'

On the way up from HQ, Todd had practised a little lecture about citizenship, duty, public co-operation and all that PR. Manfully, he delivered it, but knew he was wasting his breath. He looked at Reith. 'What's the situation, sergeant?'

'I'm reporting them for threatening behaviour, obstructing the highway and this one . . .' A sharper tug brought Ivers closer to him. '. . . for driving while banned and Maddox for aiding him.'

He's had to scale down, Todd realised glumly. He longed to add malicious damage to his car, knew it would never stick. He summoned up another smile, somewhat sadistic. 'And since he'll be reporting to me, I do assure you that you'll be appearing in court.'

He looked at Ivers. 'Third time round so it could be jail for you.'

Todd looked at Adams rather sadly. 'Bang goes your clean record. Your parents will be very upset.'

'Fuck 'em,' he almost spat back.

Reith shut his eyes tightly.

Todd phoned Pam in PR and requested a media release, cautioning against citizen's arrests, unofficial road blocks, unilateral action and stressing the need to go through proper channels.

'It's a bit boring,' she complained, still cold on him.

He told her three men were to appear in court and for what and briefed her on the background.

'I'll drum up something,' she promised, half-heartedly.

*

Todd ended the week in London, with his Chief Constable, baiting a trap to set up an arrest in an outstanding Complaints inquiry, a miscarriage of justice case that had taken weeks to unravel.

He took the weekend off, the only senior officer in the incident room to do so. Carole and Debby worked through, catching up on a backlog of processing for HOLMES that had built up during the move. Ben Nixon was on his travels.

The week that followed produced only dashed hopes as the leads and tips from the publicity out of the news conference and the reward announcement collapsed one after the other.

Nixon travelled on, undaunted, and reappeared only briefly. He'd adopted Post Mortem Morton's tag of Scissorhands, gave it its full film tile, Edward Scissorhands, shortened it to Eddie and then 'My Ed'. Because of the weapon used, Carole's quarry became 'Stanley' and then 'Stan'.

Distasteful, Todd acknowledged, but useful as shorthand.

Dr Peck went home with a pile of dossiers and a heavy schedule of appointments with Stan's victims.

Sergeant Reith called in. On Todd's desk, he slapped an evening paper which had carried the release about his arrests. It was opened at the letters page.

A reader, a prominent businessman, had written in to condemn the police as 'overbearing'. He had been stopped earlier on the same lane and had contributed a tenner towards the expenses of 'their worthy crusade'.

'It makes me want to weep,' said Reith, genuinely hurt.

The letter writer, Todd mused, would be most unwise to drive home even one sip over the limit when the sergeant was about.

During the following fortnight Todd was back in London making his arrest and then at HQ compiling his file for Crown Prosecution. The evidence was damning, the case so strong, that he felt right on top of the job; a champion.

Dutifully, he phoned the incident room twice a day, mostly speaking to Debby, who never had positive progress to relay. Every time he replaced the receiver his spirits went down into the dumps again; the pits.

8

With an admiring headshake that didn't disturb her permed fair hair, Carole Waites looked up from Dr Peck's profile on her man Stan, and all but gushed, 'Super.'

Sounds like a ten-out-of-ten school report on her two sons, chuntered Todd, eyes coming up momentarily to catch a modest expression on Peck's face.

Head down again, Todd read through it for a second time to make sure he'd missed nothing. He was hardly able to contain comment on one paragraph, intrigued and irritated at the same time.

'Why do you think...' Carole stopped in mid-question when Todd looked up again with a sharp, silencing glance.

He'd decreed when Peck handed around the copies in the Quiet Room that they'd go through it together chronologically, the three of them, Ben Nixon having found a reason not to be present.

The very first line disappointed Todd deeply, because he couldn't shake Toby Harvard free from his mind, especially now, after rereading that perplexing paragraph.

Obeying his own orders, he took it from the top, reading out loud. 'He will, I predict, be in the age range of eighteen to twenty-two, no older.'

Peck didn't wait to be asked, 'Why?' 'Speed of movements as recounted by victims and, more importantly, immature efforts at conversations with them.'

'Such as?'

'His wanting to know if they were enjoying the experience, sharing his pleasure. At the point of a knife, that's a naïve, juvenile thing to expect.'

Carole read out the next line. 'He'll have a history of, though not necessarily a conviction for, sexual misbehaviour – flashing, peeping, clothes-line thefts et cetera.'

Peck had an immediate addendum. 'All I'm forecasting is that you will not necessarily find him in your criminal records.'

Carole paused, thinking. 'Will he be in medical records?'

Peck hesitated, too. 'Possibly.'

Todd picked it up. 'Since he takes their pants as trophies, a clothes-line nicker must be favourite?'

Peck nodded, very positively.

Carole read on. 'He lacks social skills with females, suggesting a fairly strict upbringing, probably by a lone parent.'

Yes, Peck confirmed, and he favoured a single father without a steady, loving partner in his life. 'What relationships the father establishes might well be casual and, from his son's point of view, disruptive.'

Fluently, as if reading himself, he added, 'I doubt he has an immediate close family or intimate friends in whom he might confide this unhappiness.'

Todd noted that Peck also doubted that he had been bullied at school, rather the reverse, and he queried it.

'I don't want to give the impression you are necessarily dealing with a wimp,' said Peck.

Todd read silently on. 'He may well have been one of the gang, all-male, because of his lack of success in relationships with the opposite sex. He is extremely unlikely to have a girlfriend.'

Carole read the next line. 'In lonely adolescence, he probably turned to pornography which has become increasingly sadistic.'

Peck told her he expected examples of it to be found when she made her arrest. 'Plus, of course, the pants he takes as trophies.'

Todd scanned a rather long-winded section. 'His failure to interact with females and normalise his social life, along with his interest in hardcore porn depicting abuse of women, has resulted in an in-built, long-standing resentment of the opposite sex resulting in fantasies in which he causes them pain and humiliation.

'Inwardly, though not obviously, he might wish to be in a relationship. This would be impossible to attain, let alone maintain, because of the control he would seek to exert and the deviant demands he would need to make of them in order to get satisfaction.'

Goes without saying, thought Todd. It might help when we've caught him, but it ain't going to help us catch him.

Carole asked, 'Is he likely to use prostitutes?'

'No,' said Peck firmly. 'I doubt he has the social skills even to enter into negotiations with them.'

And they'd need too big a fee to go along with all this lot, Todd agreed privately, quite apart from the bill for replacement panties.

His eyes moved on to another cumbersome paragraph: 'Several victims report their last sight of him was of him bending forward, almost doubled up, which indicates he climaxes in the final act of removing the last item.'

Carole also reached it. 'Does that mean he's unlikely ever to rape?'

Peck answered indirectly. 'He targets teenagers. In his mind, he doesn't want to hurt them. He wants them to willingly participate. Some, like Jennie in the last case, were knocked out and dazed. Others had been drinking and were not fully aware. The rest, fearing for their lives, were submissive. He was able to kid himself they were enjoying it.'

Never say never, Todd realised he was saying, but didn't say so himself.

'What I think ... what I'm trying to say ...' Peck began struggling for the first time. '... should he ... by mischance, encounter a more mature woman who, perhaps fuelled by anger or ... maybe drink ... who fought back and verbally abused him ... then ...' He shrugged heavily.

Enough said, thought Todd with a shudder. He read out the next paragraph. 'His first offence in May bore the hallmarks of an impulse crime, not in any way planned, resulting from an inner explosion of rage at some slight, real or imagined.' He looked over his copy. 'Why do you think that?'

'Because he was extremely clumsy with her ...'

Toby Harvard, arm in plaster that night, flashed through Todd's mind again.

'... the wounds she received were the most severe,' Peck went on. 'He hadn't rehearsed it. It was a sudden explosion of rage.'

Wouldn't Toby be wound up after his punch-up at the farm show? Todd asked himself.

He skipped through the next bit. 'Having succeeded in escaping detection, he has set out on a deliberate course to repeat what was, for him, a pleasurable experience which can, unfortunately, be expected to occur more frequently.'

Todd didn't want to cause Carole pain or humiliation. She had been in charge of the inquiry since that first attack nine months ago. The failure to catch him, despite the long hours she put in, worried and depressed her.

Carole had skipped it, too, and read out, 'Educationally, he is a young man of few academic qualifications and below average IQ, but may have manual skills.'

They had reached the paragraph that so bothered Todd, but it was Carole who picked up on it. 'You suggest he may be engaged in some sort of forestry work.'

'Because of the pine-like smell Jennie reported after last month's attack.'

Todd took it up, looking from one to the other. 'I didn't know that.'

'Sorry?' said Carole absently, head down, not looking at him.

'I didn't know that Jennie mentioned that her assailant smelt of pine. It wasn't in the statement you took from her which I read on your laptop.' Todd yanked his head in the direction of the courtyard where the mobile command post had stood.

Carole was looking at him now, worried. 'She told Merv and he passed it on.'

'As agreed,' said Peck, somewhat ingratiatingly.

'It wasn't passed on to me,' said Todd, very sharply.

'Sorry.' Carole looked it. 'It should have been.' Without naming her, she was blaming Debby for not briefing him properly on his check-in calls in the two weeks he'd been away. 'Do you want it adding to his description?'

Todd shook his head, needing time to think.

Peck sought to defuse the tension that had arisen between them. 'It is safe to assume he is in work of some kind. Many of his victims smelt drink. It can remove inhibitions.'

Todd ignored him, regarded that theory as nonsense. Many criminals, sexual offenders or property thieves, booze on their benefits, no interest in work, the parasites.

Silently he read, 'He will live on or in close proximity to the Isle which he knows extremely well.' Sergeant Reith had already forecast that. Todd didn't comment.

Instead, he read out, 'Although he departs on foot and victims heard no motor engines and witnesses report no vehicle sightings, it is my belief he has available transport.'

He asked, 'What are we talking about here – vehicle, bike, boat?'

'I think you should bear in mind all modes,' Peck said, eyeing him intently.

They tossed it around without getting much further until sudden doubt stabbed at Todd. Cautiously he sought to quell it. 'On the one hand you forecast that he's unlikely to use the services of prostitutes. On the other hand, you suggest he's in work, earning and mobile.'

He got to the point. 'Are we right in our theory that...' He nodded at Carole. '... her Stan and Nixon's Ed are different people?'

'Haven't a clue.' Peck replied brightly, giving Todd no comfort. He was hoping to make a start on the scenes of those crimes tomorrow and would know better then. He smiled. 'If Mr Nixon is available.'

'I'll take you,' offered Todd.

It was not that he dreaded assigning Nixon to the task of chauffeuring Peck, he tried to tell himself.

It was more that February had started as January had ended – early white frost giving way to brilliant sunshine and blue skies, cloudless and windless; beautiful. He fancied a bit of a trip, some fresh air, after an office-bound fortnight on the miscarriage of justice papers. And now that was out of the way, he had nothing better to do.

When Peck had gone, Carole continued to enthuse about the usefulness of his profile. 'I'm going to take a closer look at Maddox and Adams. One or the other could fit this bill.'

Todd felt compelled to caution. 'It's not written in stone, you know. Keep all options open. Don't get tunnel vision.'

When she had gone, he wished he could follow his own advice over Toby Harvard. He could almost smell that composty odour he brought with him into his car when they drove here in the rain on Haxey Hood day, talking about planting birch trees and identifying larch fences.

Apart from age and that bit about being one of the boys, it could have been written with him in mind.

The woman who opened the plain pine door at Dr Peck's rambling residence was mid-forties, maybe a little older, wore a blue smock and pink gloves and said, 'Yes?' in a tired tone.

Todd wasn't sure if he was addressing wife, housekeeper or live-in patient. The place was certainly big enough for several residents – three or four whitewashed cottages knocked into one within a stone-walled garden with its own birch copse.

He played safe. 'I'm collecting Dr Peck.'

'He's in the surgery.' She gestured with gloved hand towards an ivy-clad building which stood apart from the house down a flagstone path. Net curtains were drawn across two upstairs windows above wide green doors with wood rot eating at the bottom edge.

He followed her hand, then looked back to say, 'Thanks,' but the pine door was already closing. He turned and walked along the path.

Peck emerged from behind a big green plastic water butt. He was wearing a sharp grey three-piece, thick dark blue coat over one arm, pink files tucked under the other. 'Ah.'

Todd, in his grey two-piece with matching sweater, turned again and walked back towards his Volvo, dawdling, to allow Peck to catch up. 'On time,' he said across his shoulder. 'Excellent.' He seemed full of enthusiasm, raring to go.

Todd opened the passenger door. Peck tossed his coat in the back and climbed in. Todd shut the door and walked around the scratched bonnet to the driver's side, glancing, as he nearly always did, at the dent Maddox's smashed knee had left.

He got behind the wheel and started up, moving in first gear down a shrub-lined driveway.

Peck patted the files which lay across his knees. 'You won't think I'm rude if we don't discuss these yet.'

Todd said nothing, concentrating on a blind turning into a country lane glassed over with patches of ice here and there.

'It's just that I don't want to subconsciously take on board other opinions, want to come to my own independent conclusions.' Peck smiled anxiously. 'If that's all right?'

'Fine,' said Todd, moving through the gears. Not really a clubbable man, he accepted he was none too hot on polite conversation, but he'd give it a go. 'Nice place you've got.'

'Hmm.'

'Live there long?'

'Some time, yes.'

'Got a surgery there, then?'

'Sorry?' Puzzled.

He's worse than me at small talk, Todd grumbled to himself. 'Above the . . . that ivy-covered building.'

'Ah.' Peck saw what Todd was talking about. 'The den. Everyone should have one. Got one yourself?'

'The small bedroom,' replied Todd, and gave up.

They travelled some miles slowly and in silence on narrow roads through heavily wooded countryside, lovely on another cold, bright day. Todd realised Peck's home was in that vast belt of trees he had seen on the east side of the river from the quay at Westport.

In one clearing, edged with snowdrops, itinerants had set up a camp of battered caravans. Todd wondered where Maddox lived, but didn't ask. Peck was looking straight ahead, as if psyching himself up for a big game.

They'd be spending most of the day on motorways, so Todd decided on a more restful route across country, heading south to, then west from Gainsborough, ignoring the signs to Epworth and the Isle.

Round about Retford, half-way into the first leg of their journey, it occurred to Todd that he'd never have made a shrink.

When a limping conversation did get going, Peck, by batting back almost every question, had learned far more about him than he had about his passenger.

Todd had chatted happily and openly about his policeman-grandfather, his Em, how they'd met, their daughter, their between-the-wars home. He'd run through his career – beat bobby, young detective, Special Ops where he got his leg wound and the mainly tedious desk jobs since.

In return, the only personal fact he'd gleaned was that the Pecks had two teenage sons away at boarding school. He'd dwelt much longer on professional matters, including a longish list of academic qualifications beginning at university where he'd met his wife. 'She's a doctor's daughter,' he added, finally giving something away.

'So . . .' Slyly, Todd returned to his original question. '. . . what is it above that building – a den or a surgery?'

His father-in-law had been a physician, Peck was virtually forced to explain. In semi-retirement, he'd seen private patients in consulting-rooms above what was once the woodshed. Having had central heating installed, it was now a winter store for garden equipment and furniture. After his father-in-law died, Peck took it over, used it as a study, though his wife still called it the surgery.

So it was his wife who opened the door then, realised Todd, slightly surprised.

'I have my computer up there, building a database,' Peck went on. He was convinced that patterns would emerge into which most crimes and criminals would fit. He was working on what he called 'templates for detection'.

On professional topics, there was no stopping him. He complained about chief constables who had declined to co-operate in collecting research material. 'All it would entail is completing a form after an arrest, giving background, potted history, modus operandi et cetera of selected offenders.'

Todd countered that an arresting officer spent too much time already filling in forms for prosecuting and welfare authorities. 'We need 'em back on the streets making more collars.'

'You disappoint me.' Peck looked downcast. 'I thought you were an ally.'

He argued that his templates would result in more arrests than beat bobbies could ever make. He complained about the lack of funding from the Home Office and the cost of hiring researchers to trawl records and conduct prison interviews with convicted offenders.

Special pleading, Todd decided dismissively. Everyone wants bigger budgets. Beyond Worksop, he steered the conversation round to the Harvards. Though the son was uppermost in his mind – and wouldn't shift – he began with the father. 'The old boy's been very good to us, I must say.'

'Now he,' said Peck with emphasis, 'is enlightened.'

'Do you know him well?'

'Quite well, yes.' Harvard had been in on the planning of the assessments Peck conducted on his company's executives and had personally followed the hunt for the extortionist.

'He's got a nice place, too,' said Todd idly. 'Ever been?'

'Temple Hall? Yes. Lovely. Just the once for dinner after the blackmailer's arrest, a small party of us. A bit of a thank-you. Debby, Carole and a few more but, unfortunately, it ended rather abruptly.'

Did Toby misbehave? Todd wondered. 'Why was that?'

'The ladies were called away. An attack that night, number 5 in the series.'

As casually as he could, Todd introduced the name of Toby. 'Ever met him?'

'Naturally.'

'Was he at that thank-you dinner?'

'He was about the house somewhere, his father said, but he didn't join us. Why?'

No independent alibi then, Todd realised. 'What do you make of him?'

As usual, Peck bounced it back. 'What do you mean?'

'Well, he doesn't work in the company, potters about the estate all day.'

Peck saw what he meant. 'He was in an accident at his school's swimming pool. Almost drowned. Suffered oxygen starvation. Irreversible, I'm afraid.'

'Is he a patient of yours?'

'Lord, no.' He gave a name and address of some professor in Harley Street.

Both were silent again for a while, then Peck began to speak very slowly. 'I know what you're thinking. He's not Carole's Stan. He was in hospital with a broken hand when it all started, wasn't he?'

Todd nodded agreement towards his windscreen. Sergeant Reith's reason for ruling him out, too, he acknowledged. Theories were bouncing around his head.

In his profile Peck himself had pointed out that the first attack was different in that the injuries were more severe than those that followed.

So, could that have been a one-off? Did that attacker stop then, afraid of the consequences of his crime? Did the series really start with the second assault? A copycat crime that he's gone on copying?

Have Peck and Carole Waites grown too close to Lord Harvard to see it? Has the whole bloody inquiry become incestuous?

More and more he was regretting accepting Harvard's largesse. He decided against voicing such doubts. He wasn't ready for counselling by a shrink.

Soon, perhaps, unless they got a break, but not yet.

9

Dr Peck stood in the packed lorry-park at a service station on the M1 sniffing in clouds of diesel fumes as though they were sea breezes.

Just why he was spending so much time wandering, head up, among lines of goods vehicles puzzled Todd.

Peck had thrown no more than a cursory glance over the car-park where they got out, declined Todd's suggestion of a coffee, and headed for the lorries beyond a lawn with three flags limp on poles on a windless morning.

On his own, Todd had climbed a flight of steps into a cafeteria with a sharply angled roof whitened by thick frost. He had a quick coffee. When he came out, he could see Peck amid a maze of lorries of all sizes and colours.

Todd stood on the top step, cold without his topcoat. Nothing he'd read in the pink file indicated exactly where Patsy Evans was picked up by Edward Scissorhands.

A dumpy bottle blonde, she'd been working the motorway for three years since she left school at fifteen without a single qualification, but with a baby on the way.

What clients Superintendent Trench's team traced more than a year ago had all been HGV drivers who'd had sex with her in squalid sleeping quarters behind their cabs. Twenty quid a trick, she charged; half a dozen tricks on an average working day.

A long distance driver had been her last known customer, a quickie at another service station some twenty-five miles south.

Then he'd given her a lift towards her home in a rundown former pit village in Derbyshire.

He'd dropped her off here at the fuel pumps and had last seen her walking towards the cafeteria.

No staff or customers had come forward to say that they had seen her inside, but the post-mortem examination had established that she had drunk a cup of coffee an hour or so before her death. She could just as easily have been chatted and picked up over that drink as in the lorry-park, in Todd's view.

Her last known punter had been cleared because the mileage on his vehicle's tacograph proved he couldn't have made the detour necessary to dump her body.

Ben Nixon had carefully established that he was allergic to coffee, only ever had tea in his thermos flask. What was good enough for Nixon was good enough for Todd and he'd ruled him out.

Anyone who had read the statements knew that there was no evidence in the file that she had set foot that day in the lorry-park. As Peck had said at the very outset that he didn't want his opinions, Todd wasn't about to offer them.

He wandered down the steps as Peck reappeared from among the lorries and they walked together back to the Volvo, neither talking.

Peck climbed back in the passenger seat, rummaged in the file and brought Patsy's photo to the top. 'This was at the centre of her regular beat, as I understand it.'

'Her home base,' Todd agreed, slipping behind the wheel.

'She seldom operated much further south than Nottinghamshire...' Peck looked left and north. '... or much beyond South Yorkshire that way.'

Todd nodded.

Peck gazed down on Patsy's chubby face and shuffled up another photo of what looked like charity shop clothing she'd been wearing. 'I read somewhere in the file there was a fiver on top of her usual fee to remove all of these.'

'Yes,' said Todd.

'OK,' said Peck, seemingly satisfied with what he'd seen. Todd started up.

They had come on to the M1 at a junction south of the service station and Todd had been surprised not to have been asked to stop at the roundabout there.

At the end of a good day – and she'd had a six-trick day – Patsy's routine had been to thumb a lift to that junction. There she would catch a bus home to relieve her mother of babysitting duties. She could have hitched a ride to her death from the southbound side of the service station or that roundabout.

It's a massive assumption that the fatal pick-up was here, Todd thought, driving beyond the fuel pumps to rejoin the three-lane road.

Five miles on through gently rolling countryside Todd couldn't really appreciate in such thick traffic, and a big blue sign announced that the motorway was about to divide – north-west to stay on the M1, north-east for the M18. 'Do you want to see the top end of the patch she patrolled?' asked Todd.

Peck indicated to the signs to the M18. 'Let's take the route they took.'

Twenty more miles on dual carriageway in lighter traffic and Todd put on his hazard warning lights and pulled into the hard shoulder just beyond the start of the M180.

There was a good view from here of the western side of the Isle, an area of special scientific interest with its skylarks and nightjars and rare fungi, flat moors with straw-coloured grass, only a few trees, mainly lines of poplars.

Not much to look at, admittedly, but worth a glance across to the desolate Chase where Lynn Dawes was found in December. He pointed it out. Peck didn't even follow his finger. 'Later. Let's focus on Patsy, shall we, for the time being?'

Unoffended, Todd pointed to a power station several miles further on, its cooling towers looking no bigger than paint pots on the horizon. 'Up there's where she and the bag were found.'

'We'll get to that,' said Peck rather stroppily.

Todd shrugged unhappily. 'Your guess is as good as anyone's on their route from here to there.'

Peck turned in the passenger seat and looked through the rear window. 'So this stretch was virgin territory for her?'

Odd thing to say, in view of Patsy's profession; nothing

whatever to do with the point he was trying to make, but Todd answered anyway. 'In that she always shuttled between service stations on the M1 and there are none between her last port of call and here, and, indeed, all the way to Hull.'

Peck looked about him, not mentioning the wild moors, the distant power station, the grassed-over slag heaps or the twin winders from an old pithead. He just lapsed into another of his long silences, some sort of trance.

'As I was saying . . .' Todd broke into it, looking ahead. '. . . no one is sure if he stuck to this motorway or dropped down to that A road.'

Peck placed a road map on top of his folder, studied it for a moment or two before making up his mind. 'Stick to the motorway.'

The blue and white tapes that marked the spot where Patsy Evans was found had long been removed, but the photos in the file told the story.

When they were taken, the grass verge just off a roundabout a few miles from the M62 had been trampled on only by the passing motorist who spotted her among a clump of broom and the emergency services he summoned. No attempt had been made to hide her body.

The lack of blood was a sign she had been killed elsewhere. She'd been stripped to her briefs, hands tied behind her, and was lying on her face so the motorist hadn't seen the knife wounds all over her front.

Looking at the photos again, Todd thought that the final fatal blow to the throat must have come as a merciful release. He said nothing. Neither did Peck.

Todd drove another mile to reach the spot where her black shoulder bag had been found five days after her body.

Close to, the power station's ten or a dozen cooling towers were massive, much higher and much, much thicker than the biggest of gasometers, white clouds rising above each one, hanging in the still cold air, as if unwilling to escape.

Todd stopped again. Engine idling, he buttoned down his window.

Peck undid his belt and craned across Todd's chest to look at a trimmed hawthorn hedge that marked the power station's roadside boundary.

He pulled himself upright, delved into his pink folder and held up his copy of the postcard addressed to Superintendent Trench with the picture of Chesterfield's crooked spire.

He didn't comment on the +'s and the i's dotted with o's in the message, read it out: 'You have made a mistake. The wages of her sin will be found at the power station.'

He paused. 'Did it take you long to find her bag?'

Todd was almost as new to the case as Peck, and didn't take the 'you' personally. 'The tracker dogs were given a scent from clothes her mum provided. They sniffed it out within the day.'

'Was the money intact?'

'One hundred and twenty; her average.'

'No odd five-pound notes?' Peck smiled rather sickly.

No bonus for undressing, Todd knew he meant. The pathologist believed that she hadn't had intercourse immediately before her death. He couldn't be absolutely sure after such a full day, but was certain there had been no rape.

Todd assumed Peck had read all of this for himself and replied factually. 'All tenners.'

Suddenly talkative, Peck asked, 'Have you a view as to why he addressed his postcard personally to Superintendent Trench?'

Patsy's mother reported her missing when she failed to collect her small daughter, Todd answered. As she lived on Trench's patch, he initiated the original search for her.

Then the body, but not the handbag, was found on the East Ridings beat of DCI Nixon. They liaised. At one press conference, Trench speculated that robbery may have been the motive. Some newspapers quoted him, but didn't name Nixon. Todd nodded at the copy of the card. 'That's to put Trench right, I suppose.'

'Tell me . . .' Peck stopped for a second or two. '. . . I don't know Mr Trench. He's no longer on the case . . .' To partially turn it into a question, he added, 'Apparently.'

'No,' Todd confirmed.

'Is that wise?'

Yes, Todd angrily but privately replied, in that there had not been a single leak of info for over a month now. 'Why?'

'Well, in the second murder, although the handbag was found in Mr Nixon's area, the killer wrote to Mr Trench.'

Todd wanted to say, 'Because Trench keeps a high profile in the press and Nixon is publicity shy,' but stayed silent.

Peck seemed to sense he was meddling in police politics. 'Having established this line of communication, he may get in touch with him again.'

He didn't add, 'When he strikes again.' Didn't have to. Todd knew what he meant.

Dr Peck seemed mesmerised. They'd driven to the waterfront east of Hull, and looked across the brown river, almost two miles wide here, a magnificent sight.

Seagulls wheeled and cried overhead. Great cranes, cream warehouses, pylons and a huge car ferry with white superstructure stood high behind them.

He appeared not to notice any of it – only lorries, their cabs, their trailers and multi-coloured containers.

He'd asked to be driven back to a roundabout where ferry and docks traffic converged from five roads. Now he stood on the circle of grass, fascinated.

What is this thing he has for lorries? Todd was asking himself, sitting in the driving seat of his Volvo, not invited to join in this particular muse, and not wanting to.

Dr Peck walked slowly off the grass and back to the car, head down, deep in thought.

Todd drove back to the main road and on towards the city. Cloud had come in from the sea and the afternoon was dull, but warmer.

Peck waved a hand. 'And nowhere here, none of these shop assistants or customers, people in pubs, no one, saw her getting into a vehicle?' he asked again, almost incredulously this time.

'No one saw her at all; at least, no one that Ben Nixon and his team located,' Todd repeated patiently. Passing a jail, built like a Victorian fort, he added, 'Not even the guards on duty there – and they were asked.'

Each left the other to their private thoughts and Todd let it all run through his mind again.

Lynn Dawes was thirty, lived with her pimp in a damp two-up, two-down on the west side. Two weeks before Christmas, he'd dropped her off in the old town. That evening, the weather and trade had been so bad that all the other girls had knocked off early.

Lynn couldn't afford to. She and her pimp had heroin habits that cost a hundred a day between them.

The last mug shots of her taken by the Vice Squad were testament to what hard drugs and the beatings she took when she failed to reach the cash target had done to her. Her thin face ravaged, her dyed blonde hair falling out, she looked closer to fifty than thirty.

The last person to speak to her, apart from her killer, told Ben she intended to try her luck down towards the docks. There was no eyewitness who said she got that far.

They were passing a gold-plated statue of a man on horseback, arse-end of both towards them, that marked the entrance to the old city, with its monuments and church spires and fine old pubs, one of which they'd lunched in, surrounded by framed photos of great Rugby League stars.

Todd jerked his head towards the statue. 'We have to turn right at King Billy for the Wilberforce monument. Want to take a look?'

Peck didn't even answer, still wrapped up in his private world. 'She charged twenty-five a time and took her clients to waste ground where?'

Todd took that as a No. 'A retail park on the old fish docks, near to her home. Have a look at that if you like.'

'But you found nothing of note there?' Peck patted his file.

'Forensics ruled it out as the scene of the crime.'

'So the probability is that she was picked up, unseen, between the docks and there?'

Todd toned it down. 'It's a possibility.'

'And she was driven out of town,' Peck continued. He paused. 'Let's do that then, shall we?'

Todd took that as another No. Soon they were on a fast road inland.

A copy of a postcard was shuffled to the top of the file on Peck's knee. He studied a photo of the Wilberforce monument he'd declined to see for himself. He turned it over. 'To save me looking it up, this arrived how long after she was reported missing?'

Todd frowned, surprised. 'She was never reported missing.'

'Oh, sorry, yes, sorry.' A flustered headshake. 'That was Patsy.'

To make sure the sequence was clearly fixed in the doctor's mind, Todd reiterated that Lynn never returned home. Her pimp assumed she had run out on him again and didn't tell the police. Her body was found next day on the Chase. She was identified from fingerprints in Records. The postcard arrived in the second class mail four days later, franked in Hull.

'Yes, I follow,' Peck muttered. He read out the card. 'The wages of her sins are at the golf course north of the Humber Bridge.'

He looked up and round. 'Let me get this right.' He fingered the copy. 'This didn't lead you to her handbag?'

No, Todd confirmed. By then, it had been found by a member on the roadside hole they had just passed. He handed it in at the professional's shop.

An assistant looked inside for documents with a name matching a lady member's. Instead he found Lynn's benefit book and less than thirty pounds. Meantime, Nixon had released her identity with an appeal for information. The shop staff had read it in the *Hull Daily Mail* and reported the find.

'It was a bit of luck, really,' Todd went on. 'There's another one or two courses off this road. We could have been searching for weeks.'

Peck flicked his copy sharply with a fingernail. 'But for that happy chance, this would have led to finding her bag.'

'Eventually,' Todd agreed.

They were sitting side by side in the car-park of the golf club beneath a bare, but handsome chestnut tree. In front of them was the imposing clubhouse, Georgian-style, with long narrow windows and covered entrance. Behind was a manicured putting green. 'What now?' asked Todd, a bit bored.

'Which way back, you mean?' Peck smiled slowly and thoughtfully. 'Not easy, is it?'

Todd knew what he was driving at. The north end of the Isle of Axholme was encircled by fast roads.

The Chase, where Lynn Dawes was found beside the M180,

could be reached by two routes from here – west from the Humber Bridge to the M62, then south on the M18 to join the M180 east-bound. The other way meant a toll charge on the bridge, and due south to the M180 west-bound.

Peck took some time to make up his mind, head over his map. 'Her body was found on the south side which seems to indicate he was travelling east to west.'

Peck having made the choice, Todd drove out of the club grounds and back along the lane with the fairway of the road hole on the left behind a fence, shrubs and trees, one of which, ironically, had a 'Private. No Dumping' sign nailed to it.

On the main road again, the bridge soon came into view suspended in the air by mile upon mile of wire cable from twin towers – another stunning sight that failed to draw any remark from Peck.

At one of half a dozen kiosks, Todd paid the £1.90 fee. The sun suddenly re-emerged from behind the clouds turning the water below from brown to a bluish-grey, giving the coast ahead a thin haze and reflecting off the wet black surface of the long bridge, making Todd concentrate on his driving, happy not to be talking.

About twenty miles and twenty minutes later they crossed the calm River Trent, a stream compared with the Humber. They were back on the Isle.

A few minutes and a few miles more and the Cottage Hospital, the stable block and Lord Harvard's home came up on the left, but Todd ignored the turn-off and drove on.

Just beyond a vast holding depot packed with dully waxed, imported cars, he pulled into the hard shoulder.

Both got out and looked over the same bleak motors Todd had viewed from a different angle this morning. He pointed to a bank between a ditch and three-bar fence where Lynn Dawes had been found by a tractor driver gathering peat.

'Again no attempt at concealment,' Peck observed. He studied the scene silently, then, very slowly, 'We came the right way. He'd hardly carry her across four lanes of traffic to throw her down there, would he?'

Back in the car, Peck said. 'Give me a moment.' He rummaged

through his folder. 'Let me refresh my memory.' He sorted through copies of news stories about the Lynn Dawes case. 'You see, I don't recall a single mention of Superintendent Trench in any of these.'

'That's right,' Todd confirmed. 'Our PR released the news of the discovery of her body, but East Riding force shouldered most of the early donkey work because she came from there and so, obviously, would any leads. Media matters were left entirely to Ben Nixon.'

'And yet . . .' Peck flicked the photostat of the postcard again. '. . . this was addressed personally to Mr Trench at force HQ.' He looked at Todd. 'You see what I mean?'

Todd saw all right. He seemed keen to get Trench back on the case, far too keen for someone he claimed not to know.

10

Every time Todd drove over the River Idle on to the Isle he had to resist the temptation to stir guiltily in his leather seat.

Idle all too accurately summed up his work rate. Apart from the hundred-mile round trip from home, he'd hardly turned a wheel for two weeks.

No need to fight off a cringe today though as he crossed the river on a cold grey morning. He had something to do. Dr Peck was emerging from the solitude of his den to deliver his profile on Scissorhands.

Todd pulled up alongside a grimy Escort that wasn't often seen in the courtyard of the stable block.

Good or bad? he asked himself. Good in that Ben Nixon had obeyed his three-line whip and come in from his travels. Not so good if Ben argued his way, with his usual truculence, line by line through the report. His antipathy to profiling bordered on outright hostility.

Nixon was lounging in the easy chair, his grey suit looking as though he'd slept the night there. He was reading a tabloid.

'Good morning,' chirped Todd, walking to his desk in the Quiet Room.

Nixon looked up with a peeved expression. 'Morning.'

Todd reminded him of his instructions when he ordered him back for their meeting with Peck, due to arrive in a few minutes. 'No questions till we've had a chance to study it, then we'll go through it with him together.'

Nixon nodded glumly. In this sort of mood, he might opt to say nothing at all, Todd reasoned; good on the whole.

Great, thought Todd, hugely relieved, as he read Peck's wordy opening sentence. 'I fully concur with the policy decision to treat the two murders as the work of one offender unconnected with the series of non-fatal, though serious, knife attacks on the Isle; a conclusion reached on the basis of the weapons carried and the methods used in targeting victims.'

An inner purr remained as he read, 'Logistically and economically, it makes sense to pursue both inquiries from the same centre of operations for cross-fertilisation of ideas, leads through Records and assessing incoming information, with the strict proviso that both investigation teams accept that they will not find common linkage between their entirely separate cases.'

The feel-good warmth cooled as he read on. 'The murder squad is undoubtedly faced with an infinitely more difficult task. Homicides involving prostitutes and hitch-hikers are statistically among the hardest crimes to solve and, in the Patsy Evans case, there are elements of both.'

When he had gone all the way through it twice, Todd took the first three paragraphs as read and began with, 'He'll be about forty, you say.'

Peck nodded. 'A couple of years either side, I estimate.'

He headed off the obvious 'Why?' by hurrying on. 'He's mature enough to talk experienced women into his vehicle which suggests he is articulate enough to discuss terms and conditions beforehand. As you'll have seen, there's evidence he is a careful, if not avid, newspaper reader.'

He wagged a finger to tell Todd to read down. 'And you'll also see he is capable of holding down a driving job that we know has lasted for at least a year.'

Todd read further down. 'It would seem he has a home or a

job that takes him to or from Humberside, which suggests stability in his lifestyle.'

Peck waited until he finished, then, 'All of that, taken together, is indicative of early middle-age rather than, say, the twenties.'

Todd was on the wrong side of forty and he estimated Peck was too. This morning he looked almost dandified in a jet black three-piece with gold fob chain that made Todd's grey job look shabby.

He guessed Peck would not be overjoyed to be described as of early middle-age. Neither was Todd, but he bit his tongue as he read on. 'His movements and knowledge of the road network point to employment in transportation, most probably heavy lorries.'

He took issue, very bluntly. 'Why lorries and not vans or cars?'

'Er...' Peck ruminated for several moments. 'I wouldn't entirely rule out close-sided vans, but, on the whole, favour a much larger cab or the sleeping quarters of a lorry as the scenes of crime. It's a question of ergonomics...'

He glanced anxiously at Nixon who wasn't looking at him. '... space, if you like. There would be more room available for the stripping, binding and the rituals that took place before the killings.'

Eyes back on Todd, he said, 'Read on.'

Todd did as he was told. 'He will of necessity have his weapon close to hand to immediately control, dominate and finally kill his victim. He will therefore have a valid excuse for possession of scissors, e.g. for cutting ropes or string on parcels which points to a delivery driver.' He looked up.

Peck's eyes were still on him. 'No such reason exists for a motorist to carry scissors. The sight of a readily available weapon would immediately arouse suspicion and fear in any passenger, particularly a street-wise woman.'

Todd hoped not. When he drove to the Peaks to place flowers on his grandfolks' plaque – admittedly only twice a year at most – he always took scissors with him to shorten the stems. He decided not to reveal it.

Peck again. 'What I'm suggesting is that delivery records to and from Humberside might be a fruitful source, lorry drivers on regular runs and...' He seemed to modify his original theory and accept Todd's view. '... van drivers, too. And if the records of runs match your records ...'

Hitching his shoulders, he left it at that to allow Todd to continue reading. 'It can be anticipated that his name will be in Criminal Records for a sexual offence or offences, most likely involving prostitutes.

'There is reason to believe he may well have been caught and convicted for kerb crawling and this led to either financial or domestic difficulties.

'The fact that he now takes pleasure in taunting the police with postcards may be an indicator that he was caught in a special anti-Vice operation by an undercover policewoman posing as a prostitute.'

Todd felt he had to object. 'That's a quantum leap of imagination, isn't it, doc?'

Peck smiled again. 'In one, or rather two, fell swoops, he has avenged himself on both prostitutes and the police.' He seems to lose a bit of confidence. 'Alternatively, of course, he could have contracted a venereal disease which led to difficulties at home. It's a thought worthy of exploration. I put it no higher than that.'

'But he's not screwing them.'

'Not now, no. The humiliation of arrest and public exposure...' He paused and added a modification. '... or VD treatment would be very off-putting sexually, I'd have thought. Maybe he's now impotent.'

'You see...' Todd flicked back a few pages, but couldn't find what he was looking for straight away. '... you talk about a stable home – '

Peck broke in. 'Or job.' He relented. 'Or both, yes.'

Todd looked over the top of his sheet, deciding to call it what it was. 'Yet you speculate about the possibility of domestic difficulties arising from associating with prostitutes.'

'What I'm keen to emphasise is that you shouldn't be concentrating entirely on men with a low or itinerant lifestyle. He could well be married or in a stable relationship.'

Todd raised his eyebrows. 'With a partner who knows about his visits to pros?'

'Many women will overlook the breadwinner's conduct to protect the status quo, especially if they have children.'

Good job Carole Waites and Debby Thompson – and certainly my Em – aren't present to hear that, Todd mused, slightly shocked.

'Look at what Lynn Dawes put up with from her man in order to retain their relationship,' Peck went on.

Todd remained unconvinced, thinking: In that squalid set-up, she was the breadwinner – or rather drugswinner.

His silence forced Peck to continue, 'Their marital sex may appear normal, he achieving ejaculation via fantasy. She may, of course, have left him or be insisting on separate beds. It's not unknown in early middle-age.'

Todd sneaked a look at Nixon, wondering if Peck knew that he was sleeping in a single bed, his marriage having broken up because of the hours he put in on the job – the police job, that is. He had his head down, reading.

Peck backtracked. 'What I'm saying here is that, to the world at large, the offender could give the impression of normality and stability in both his working and married life.'

Todd's head went down again. 'And you're also recommending that we should treat as significant this odd style of handwriting – the plus-marks and the i's dotted with o's.'

Peck nodded energetically.

'A computer buff, for instance?' Todd suggested.

'Or he may even have worked with computers until professional and/or domestic disaster overwhelmed him because of his uncontrollable urges to haunt red-light districts.'

He began to talk very urgently. 'He is not at the lowest end of qualified skills. Something in his background, something connected with prostitutes, is the key here, I'm sure of it.'

'On the other hand . . .' Nixon spoke for the first time and very languidly, too. '. . . he could have read it up.' He recalled a widely reported murder case where detectives received a confession written in similar computer-style fashion. The case was never solved so no one was sure if the confession was genuine or a hoax.

'As you've already said,' Nixon went on, 'he reads newspapers and he could have remembered that case and copied the style to cause confusion.'

Peck looked blank, seemed not to know about the case and didn't respond.

Todd had to resume. 'This wages of sin business. You doubt that he's suddenly found religion? Then how did it come about?'

'This way, I think.' Peck leant back and closed his eyes. 'He picked up Patsy at or near the M1 service station. He abused and killed her in his cab or sleeping quarters.'

He paused, then added, somewhat sheepishly, 'Or in the back of a van. He dumped the body without deviating far from his route on the motorway.

'Later, he found her bag in the cab. He threw it out the window. To do this, it's possible he did make a slight detour or his normal route may have been past the power station, hard to say.'

He opened his eyes. 'He then read in the papers that robbery was the motive for his crime. He was deeply upset and offended. Revenge, pure and simple, was his motive. He wrote that card to correct and, perhaps, embarrass Mr Trench who, in his eyes, made the mistake.'

'But,' said Todd slowly, 'he did things differently on the second occasion.'

'Exactly,' Peck said with a 'well done' beam. 'He picked up Lynn, again tortured and murdered her. With the body still in his vehicle, he then secreted her bag at the golf course. He doubled back to buy, write and post the card. Only afterwards did he drive on and dispose of her.'

A pleading expression. 'Don't you see? He enjoyed making mischief with the police on the first occasion, so much so that it's become part of the – for want of a better word – fun.'

'And dumping Lynn there . . .' Todd flicked his head towards the Chase. '. . . knowing that we have a knifeman independently running loose on the Isle, added to his enjoyment and our confusion?'

'Yes,' said Peck gravely. 'He's having fun at your expense. He clearly reads the papers. He's beginning to like the publicity, even courts it.'

Doesn't nearly everyone these days? Todd brooded.

'He doesn't see women as objects of sex any more, but objects to destroy. I'm afraid you may not have heard the last of him.' Peck concluded with a very solemn expression.

Todd was afraid of that, too; kept him awake nights.

*

'Crap.' Mercifully, Nixon only gave his verdict after Peck had closed the door of the Quiet Room. 'All bollocks.'

He dropped his copy of the report on the carpet beside his chair as if the paper was soiled. 'Half of it is teaching your grandma to suck eggs. The rest is guesswork. Every time you raised a query, he shifted his ground.'

He shook his head in rejection. 'I was half expecting him to suggest we treat the crooked spire and the monument on the postcards as fucking phallic symbols.'

Not quite that bad, but certainly more speculative, a lot less factual than his profile on Stan, Todd privately agreed.

He decided to give Peck the benefit of considerable doubts. 'Yeah, but, on Carole's jobs, he had survivors to talk to. They gave him a fuller picture. In your Ed's case, no such luck, unhappily. It's bound to be more difficult.'

'Yer, but . . .' Nixon's protesting tone still. '. . . we are looking at kerb crawlers and delivery drivers. Spending all hours that God sends on them. We don't need him . . .' He pecked his head at the closed door. '. . . to tell us how to do our job.'

All Todd could think of was repeating what he'd said to Carole Waites. 'It's not written in stone.' Then he cautioned, 'Don't ignore it, that's all.'

He sensed from the dismissive shrug that Nixon would do just that. He changed the subject. 'Are you looking at the transport department at Lord Harvard's frozen food company?'

'We're concentrating on the north side of the Humber.' Nixon frowned. 'Why?'

Because, Todd replied, he needed a valid reason to approach Lord Harvard again and, more particularly, his son. For the first time he gave his reasons for his suspicions about Toby.

'I can spread the net,' Nixon volunteered.

'Don't make a big production out of it,' Todd instructed. 'Just a couple of officers for a couple of days. Don't restrict them to lorry and van drivers. Get them to have a look at the records of company car drivers and the mileage claims of executives.'

'OK,' said Nixon, helpfully.

In the days that followed, Todd had plenty of idle hours to hone his approach to perfection. He rehearsed it one last time as he walked in misty rain from the stable block to Lord Harvard's house.

He would say, 'I've come to apologise for the administrative inconvenience my men are causing in the necessary task of going through your firm's travel records. It's at the suggestion of Dr Peck who, as you know, has a good track record in these matters.'

Being a gentlemen, Harvard would say something like, 'Anything to oblige.'

The master-stroke next. 'It would be good industrial and public relations if we let it be known that we had gone right to the very top, excluding no one.'

Another 'Anything to oblige' and he would pointlessly take Harvard through his movements on the days of the murders.

Then he would turn to Toby and ask him if he minded telling him where he was on the days of the non-fatal attacks.

He anticipated some protest which he'd counter with, 'We are asking every male between fifteen and fifty on the Isle to account for himself. I thought it best that, as I'm technically your tenant, albeit non-paying, I should conduct this interview.' Any flannel like that would do.

With luck, his father would democratically agree with something like, 'We seek nor want any favours, only to be treated like our neighours.'

Should work, Todd hoped as he knocked on the black door.

It was opened by a woman of about forty, with an attractive, rather over-made-up face, neat blonde hair and trim figure in denims. Beth, the housekeeper, he guessed.

She smiled pleasantly through his introduction, then said, 'They're away.'

'No trouble,' said Todd, easily. 'I'll call again later.'

'But they won't be back till the end of March or the beginning of April.'

Todd could feel his mouth drop.

'They've got a place in the Caribbean,' she went on. 'They've gone to do a bit of sailing and watch some cricket.'

A smile rose on his face as he walked back.

He began to think, hope, believe – no, expect. Somehow, he didn't expect Stan to strike again until the spring.

11

SPRING

Another month gone by, towards the end of March now, and neither Stan nor Ed had struck again.

Todd assumed that PR Pam would be pleased; quite the reverse. 'A very bad press,' she whined.

Sitting opposite her at his desk at HQ, he flipped back through a sheaf of cuttings from that morning's newspapers with headlines like 'Have-A-Go Hero Jailed' and 'No Tolerance Cops Slammed'.

Beneath were pictures of Maddox and Adams wearing hurt expressions and leaning on walking-sticks outside the magistrates' court where moderate fines had been imposed on them.

Their solicitor had successfully pleaded that they had already suffered physically from their leg injuries and financially through being off work.

Ivers missed the photo opportunity, having been jailed for two months, the lawyer unable to talk his way out of a third offence of driving while disqualified and uninsured.

What should have been an up-story for PR Pam had been turned upside down with quotes from the local businessman who'd expanded on what he'd written in his letter to the paper. 'Ham-fisted policing' was one quote.

'It's got the fingerprints of Post Mortem Morton all over it,' Pam grumbled on.

So what? thought Todd. They had made public the news that the trio were to appear in court. All Morton had done was to get the date of the hearing and sweet-talk the businessman into beefing up his anti-police views; routine journalism. 'There's no leak involved,' he reasoned.

'Don't suppose so,' Pam agreed, almost reluctantly. She eyed him steadily. 'Has Morton ever approached you?'

Todd eyed her back, hard.

'Not waving an exclusive contract and lots of lolly, I don't mean,' she sped on, 'but for background for later use, a promise of a nice write-up blah, blah, blah.'

Todd decided not to tell her that if the cases were cracked he'd get a nice write-up anyway from his mate Jacko Jackson in one of his books, with names and locations safely changed. 'Why?'

'That's his style. He'll try to sign up somebody with the inside track, mark my words.'

Todd wondered who she had in mind. Ben Nixon, he assumed, because Carole Waites was more Pam's style from an image point of view.

Debby Thompson walked into the Quiet Room, Dr Peck tagged on behind. She sat in Nixon's usual seat and crossed quite shapely legs at the knee. Peck perched himself on an arm of the chair.

'Sorry,' she mouthed.

Todd sneaked a look across his desk at her legs and knew she was apologising for being a minute or two late. 'OK then,' he said, addressing no one in particular.

'Not yet,' Carole Waites blurted. 'Ben's sidekick's still on the blower.'

In no hurry, Todd sat back, letting his mind wander.

In the first quarter of the year, the incident room had received forty-two memos from police officers in response to the New Year circular and 126 calls resulting from *Crimewatch* in which super-cool Carole had made her national TV debut.

Between them, officers from the two squads had actioned 1,137 inquiries. Twenty-one names remained in Ben Nixon's frame for his Ed. Seventeen had been designated 'not cleared' by Carole in her hunt for Stan, Toby Harvard among them, at Todd's insistence.

All this quite useless information was available to him whenever Debby Thompson pressed one of HOLMES's many buttons.

For some weeks, he'd been aware that he'd made a mistake about her on their first meeting after the news conference; must have caught her on a bad day.

She seemed to have blossomed like the spring bulbs in the pots along the outside walkway, all fully out now, gorgeous.

Far from being frumpy, she was a poised lady. Her big specs had been replaced with contact lenses that made her brown eyes sparkle. Her face was pale but interestingly mobile, with make-up always understated. And what he read into it was that she was someone either in love or happy in her work.

She didn't sit in the Hayloft with her fingers hovering over her keyboard like a concert pianist, posing, like Todd at HQ. She played the thing like a virtuoso. She could find a file, a name, a date, in a second or so and bring it up on screen for him.

She worked longer hours than Carole, and much longer than Todd. She had even won Ben Nixon's heart, producing for his team a pro forma which they dutifully filled in on the history of every suspect they quizzed.

Todd had grown so reliant on her that he invited her to most of these team talks, along with Sergeant Tom Reith, who was sitting next to Carole against the pale green wall.

Today both women wore suits, Carole's dark, Debby's mustard-coloured, with a pleated skirt that showed more leg. Todd sneaked another look.

She was smiling and chatting with Peck, appearing for the first time at this sort of get-together at Carole's invitation.

Todd's eyes came away when Nixon's number 2, a burly inspector in a shiny suit, walked in. 'Sorry, boss. Ben's just been briefing me. Could be promising, this.'

He sat alongside Carole and Reith, looking down at his notes. 'A tip from South Yorks Vice,' he began. 'A call girl operating as an escort agency hostess. Told a pal about a customer who'd hired her to go to his hotel.

'Spiked her drinks, she's alleged to have claimed, and she came round to find herself stripped to her briefs and tied to the bed-head. He was running a knife over her flesh. Not expecting her to come to her senses so soon, he hadn't gagged her, it seems. She screamed. He untied her, ordered her to dress and bustled her out without paying her. Her pal's a Vice officer's snout. She tipped him. He tipped us.'

The DI kept the best to last. 'Her client's a professional golfer and there were tournaments in the right places on the days of both murders.'

Todd felt that familiar *frisson* of excitement shudder right through him.

'Ben's gone across to Sheffield to turn him over,' the DI ended.

Todd grinned at Peck. 'Interesting, eh?'

Peck looked dubious. 'Let's hope so.'

Hope not, you mean, Todd wagered. A pro golfer would totally bugger his profile on Ed.

He swivelled towards Carole, who had called this meeting. 'I'm far from satisfied about Maddox,' she said, straight in, 'and, to a lesser extent, Adams.'

Peck perked with interest on his chair arm. Reith leaned forward, concentrating. Todd, having heard her on the subject before, sat back.

Carole had devoted much time and effort on the vigilante trio after Todd turned them over to her following their arrests. She'd quickly discounted Ivers. From what all the victims had said, he was far too tall to be Stan and his accent didn't fit.

Maddox and Adams were the right height. Only Maddox was stocky enough. That, she accepted, hadn't totally ruled out Adams because padding can be worn under loose outer clothing like boiler and tracksuits.

They alibied each other for the night of the Hood Game, but Adams had been so befuddled with drink and, she suspected, drugs that she didn't trust his recollections.

They'd claimed the clothes they wore that night had been so soiled in the mudbath of the game that Adams had taken them home for his long-suffering mother to launder.

She'd revealed to Carole that she had also washed a black fleecy tracksuit and a grubby pair of underpants that didn't belong to her son.

On the nights of half a dozen other attacks, they were each other's sole alibi, claiming to have kipped in sleeping bags under sacks in Maddox's truck, but again their timings were vague.

'And,' she continued, 'having worked with wood and sometimes slept among logs, both smell.' She glanced at Peck, whose eyes had never left her.

'To say nothing of the fact that the assaults have ceased since both have been on crutches,' added Reith.

'Promising.' Peck had sat almost bolt upright. 'Any background?'

Adams, Carole replied, had good GCSEs, but had never found a regular job. He helped out Maddox occasionally on his logging round. Mostly he drank.

He lived more off than on with his parents, both caring, honest people at their wits' end over the way their youngest son was wasting his life in bad company.

'I'll vouch for that,' Reith chipped in.

Maddox had good qualifications, too, from an agricultural college his widowed father had sent him to.

They'd lived in a caravan on the east side of the Trent, north of Gainsborough where they had a concession to collect wood from a forest.

They had their own workshops in which they turned out high quality garden furniture. Maddox had continued the business after his father collapsed and died three years ago. He lived and worked on his own.

'Now he is interesting,' Peck almost purred.

Fits his profile to a T, he means, Todd realised.

'What's the problem then?' Reith asked.

Carole covered some old ground first. On the night of the first attack, she recalled, Maddox had been punched by Lord Harvard's son at the agricultural show. Toby had gone to the Cottage Hospital with a broken hand.

Todd transferred his eyes to Reith who was smiling to himself, vindicated.

Maddox, she continued, had set off for home. Half-way there he'd checked into hospital at Gainsborough where an X-ray revealed a broken nose.

'What was the altercation about?' Peck asked.

'Maddox offended a young local girl in the beer tent,' replied Reith.

'Sure it wasn't the other way around?' asked Todd, double-checking.

'No,' said Reith emphatically.

Since no complaint was filed and, therefore, no statements taken, Todd wondered how he could be so sure, but didn't ask.

'The problem . . .' Carole finally got round to answering. '. . . is that the hospital staff insisted he left his vehicle behind when they discharged him after treatment. He was too woozy to drive. A porter saw it there several times during the night.' She paused. 'Which means he was without transport to return to the Isle and commit the first offence.'

'Available transport,' Peck pointed out immediately. 'Has he no alternative?'

'Not that we've discovered,' said Carole unhappily.

Todd addressed Peck, raising a doubt he'd so far shared with no one. 'Is it possible that the first case was the work of someone else who's now gone to ground and . . .' He flicked his head at Carole. '. . . her Stan's series really started with the second attack?'

Peck gave his answer some thought. 'The fact that it occurred after Maddox had been publicly belittled over a girl suggests not.'

He's convicting Maddox already, making the facts fit his profile, Todd thought, deeply uneasy.

'Also,' Carole went on, 'Maddox's truck was in a garage overnight for repairs when one other attack took place.'

Get out of that, thought Todd, watching disappointment flit across Peck's face.

'But, as for the rest, I'm not happy with the alibis,' she went on. 'Maddox is at ease in the company of blokes, but he was very uncomfortable, shy even, talking to me.'

'Oh.' Peck beamed. 'Couldn't you get a search warrant to look for other modes of transport and, more important, the panties taken as trophies?'

Tunnel vision, Todd realised. Both have got tunnel vision; dangerous.

Todd floated a compromise without thinking it through. 'Why not announce we have discovered a DNA trace at one scene and intend to ask males in their early twenties to give samples for elimination and knock on his door first?'

'He'd be within his civil rights to refuse,' Reith advised, legally correct.

'No point.' Peck's objection was even more forthright. 'Our man climaxes in what he wears. He knows he leaves no semen behind at scenes. He could volunteer a sample with impunity.'

With a casual shrug, Todd accepted rejection of what wasn't a very bright idea in the first place. 'Take out a search warrant then and turn his place over.'

Carole looked uncertain now. 'Can it wait a week?' She'd been summoned to attend the trial of Fish Finger Freddy which was expected to last five days, she explained.

She smiled at Peck, who did not smile back. She switched her attention to Todd. 'There's no great rush, is there, if he's out of action still hopping about on one leg?'

No, Todd agreed but, playing safe, he ordered her to assign members of her team to continue to probe Maddox's background in her absence – 'especially this question of other transport.'

He paused, looking up at the restfully coloured ceiling. 'Get Surveillance to stick up a camera near his caravan so we can keep an eye on him.'

Don't you get tunnel vision, he ordered himself, still looking up. The Harvards will be home soon from their long Caribbean holiday and Toby's absence could be another reason why Stan has been inactive.

He looked across at Reith. 'While they are at it, get them to put up another camera in a position where we can track Harvard's son.'

'But – ' Reith was given no time to get out his objection.

'Just do it,' snapped Todd, making it plain it was an order.

Nixon came into the Quiet Room next day and flopped into the easy chair, exhausted. 'Trouble.' He issued a long, low sigh, heartfelt. 'Big trouble.'

He seldom sought advice, just got on with it, so Todd leaned back in his seat, pleased, almost proud, that he'd brought his problem to him.

His suspect was Raymond Chivers, aged thirty-seven, golf pro. He was based at one of those big expensive complexes with squash, swimming and other fitness facilities as well as a golf course and driving range; a sporting club, not just a golf club. Nixon had arrested him at his widowed mother's home near Sheffield.

While being escorted to the car, Chivers had collapsed – feigned, Nixon suspected, to buy time. Taking no chances, Nixon had made a detour to the hospital for a check-up. His mother insisted on accompanying them because she knew his medical history. 'A severe migraine,' doctors diagnosed. They released him.

All this took time at the hospital, which Nixon had used by dropping in the odd sly question when they were on their own. Yes, Chivers admitted, he made regular use of prostitutes when he felt randy. He was divorced. What business was it of anyone else?

Yes, he may well have been on the M1 and in Hull on the days of the murders, and may have hired girls on his way home. He couldn't remember, but, if so, he left them alive.

His mother had used the time even more profitably. When they finally reached the police HQ, a solicitor was waiting. On tape, it was 'No comment' to every question. Not only that, the call girl complainant who'd started the hare running had done a runner herself; bought off, Nixon was convinced.

'Chivers' mum's a blowzy bitch from the back streets, but rich and shrewd. Her old man struck it big in property, actually built the club,' he went on. 'The only way Ray could break into the game, I suppose, because he's not much cop. Not in the rankings or on the big tours, only earns a few quid from teaching and piffling pro-ams.'

Nixon kept Chivers in overnight and had brought him to the incident room that morning. His solicitor was with him in the Padded Cell. In half an hour, Nixon would have to charge him or let him go. 'Will you come and size him up?'

Raymond Chivers was difficult to size up. He had the frame of a man in the prime of life, six feet tall, slim and athletic in sharply pressed grey Farrah slacks and dark blue lambswool sweater. He had the face of a much older man, weathered and wrinkled, with a full head of short hair that had already turned grey. His blue eyes were pale and pained, as if he'd been looking into the sun.

Beside him at a table in the Padded Cell sat a middle-aged man, dark-suited, with bright, alert eyes behind thick, black spectacles.

Theatrically, he inspected a gold wrist-watch. Since another ten minutes had gone on a fuller briefing and discussing tactics with Ben, Todd knew he was telling them: Twenty minutes.

Nixon switched on a tape recorder on the table, announced the time and the fact that ACC Todd had entered the room.

The solicitor gave Todd no opportunity to speak. 'Now that you have been put in the picture by your colleague...' He flicked his head at Nixon, but penetrated Todd with his eyes. '... I take it you will be releasing my client.'

Todd ignored him, looking at Chivers, who wasn't looking at

him, head hanging. 'Mr Chivers, you engage the services of prostitutes, I understand, and – '

The solicitor broke in. 'Not from anything said on tape and under caution, you don't, so please don't play games.'

Todd slipped the photo of Patsy Evans across the table. 'Make use of her services just over a year ago, did you?'

Chivers didn't even look at it as his solicitor said, 'No comment,' repeated when the date and place were put on record.

The same response came to Lynn Dawes's photo, the date before Christmas and the place.

When the call girl's allegation was raised, the solicitor replied again. 'There is no complaint, never was, all a misunderstanding.'

'Up her fee, did you, Ray?' asked Nixon, chummily.

'No comment,' snapped the solicitor.

Todd soldiered on. 'Were the cuts her friend describes to her body a misunderstanding?'

'Hearsay,' snapped the solicitor. 'Produce her. Let her pick him out at an identity parade.'

Todd went back to the murders, placing the postcards in front of Chivers. The lawyer went back to No Comments. He held up a hand, fingers outstretched. Five minutes, he was saying.

They were filled with desperate questions like: 'The handbags you dumped...' 'The scissors you used...' None were completed as 'No comment' was remorselessly repeated.

Finally, Todd made an offer. 'Would you like to stay and talk to your pen-pal, Superintendent Trench?'

And finally a variation from the lawyer. 'He wants to talk to no one and he isn't staying. Time's up.'

When the tape was switched off, the solicitor said, very dourly, 'I know your game. You wanted a holding charge while you build your case on the murders.' A defiant expression. 'Build it then.'

Todd knew his game. Defence lawyers, the smart ones anyway, and this one was very smart, don't ask a client, particularly a rich one, 'Tell me the truth. Did you do it? Yes or no?'

They don't want the truth. They want proof, absolute, uncontestable proof, against their client. Only then will they even consider a scaled-down charge or a medical defence. Meantime, they won't help to provide that proof, seek the truth, not with a single fact, not a solitary word.

He didn't hate them any more. He understood them now. That was their sworn duty under the law.

What he couldn't understand was how they could live with themselves when a killer they'd shielded went out and killed again.

12

'Twenty Years For Poisoned Food Terror', ran a typical headline, but what turned an up story for the force into a downer for Todd was an article beneath the court report.

'The Crackers', by Harry Morton, featured thumbnail photos of several of what he described as 'top profilers', Dr Peck among them, along with the chubby-faced actor who played Fitz in the TV series *Cracker*.

He'd used Fish Finger Freddy's trial as a peg on which to hang a rehash of old clippings about the successes they'd notched up.

Surprisingly, the piece ended with a laudatory quote from Detective Chief Inspector Carole Waites: 'Dr Peck's insights were invaluable to us.' Unsurprisingly, the piece didn't feature his failure on the serial arsonist.

Sitting at his desk in the Quiet Room, Todd read the article again and then asked himself: What do I read into this?

Dr Peck wasn't a witness. Hunches, intuitions, educated guesses – call them what you will – aren't admissible evidence in court. So Morton must have had an inside tip about Peck's involvement.

It wasn't your investigation, he reminded himself, so what's it to you? And when a case is all over, no longer *sub judice*, does it matter?

Well, yes, it does if there's a danger of an eventual leak on this job. Is Carole too close to Peck? A much darker thought now. How close?

He'd have a quiet word with her, he resolved, just to warn her of the danger. Not today, though. There was too much on the agenda for a meeting so sensitive that Debby Thompson had not been invited. Police service ears only, he'd decreed, officer rank, which meant that Reith wasn't attending either.

Todd folded up the newspaper when a knock came on the door. Carole came in first, almost step-dancing in a tartan dress with frilly white collar and cuffs. She glanced at the papers on the desk and smiled, a radiant smile, basking in the afterglow of her rave reviews.

Ben Nixon trudged in behind her, so preoccupied that he looked as if he hadn't slept. Last in was the reason he was so harassed – the director of the regional police authority's legal department; a nit-picker.

'We'll begin with potentially the most damaging and expensive,' said the legal director. A small, neat man, approaching sixty, he pulled up a chair to a corner of Todd's desk so he could spread out his files.

He put on a mournful face as he disclosed that Ray Chivers, the golfer Nixon had pulled in, was suing for everything from wrongful arrest to slander and demanding a heavy pay-off.

'I went by the bloody book,' grumbled Nixon.

'They say the questions you've subsequently been asking around the clubhouse are defamatory.'

'How else am I supposed to get his background?'

The director rounded on him. 'Your call girl has retracted any allegations and we're up the creek without a paddle.'

'He or his mum have bloody well bought her off,' Nixon came back.

'Well, we can't very well pay her more in order to top his offer and to prove it, can we?' the director fired back. A deeply depressed sigh. 'Is he your man?'

'Top of the list.' Nixon rattled through the background he'd gathered, most of it gossip, all of it no more admissible as evidence than profiles. He admitted as much. 'We need time.'

All eyes fell on Todd. He swung round in his swivel chair and gazed out of the window across the parklands around the stable block, grass growing long in April's mix of sunshine and showers.

Got to back Ben, he knew. OK, he can get a little heavy at

times. He's dealing with dregs after all. He's working or travelling double shifts most days, only ever takes a day off when he's got access to his two kids.

Can't let him down. Work is all he's got. I must back him. How?

Todd swivelled back, no real clue yet about what to do. 'His mouthpiece is anticipating that we'll cave in and quickly, isn't he?'

The director put more gloss on it. 'I think our insurers are minded to make an offer rather than contest it in civil court.'

Typical, thought Todd angrily, his fighting spirit rising. Insurers weigh up the odds. If they estimate defending a case, however justified, will cost more than the likely damages in the event of losing, they throw in the towel.

All too often these days police forces pay out unnecessary damages rather than fight for the reputations of their frontline cops. He couldn't let that happen to Ben.

Slowly, an idea was forming. 'And his lawyer wants an out-of-court settlement, presumably, without publicity?'

The director nodded briskly.

'OK.' Todd was so deep in thought now that he barely noticed Nixon slump lower in his chair as if trying to make himself invisible. 'Write to them saying the officer in charge of the inquiry . . .' He tapped his chest. '. . . mention my name, is deeply upset about any embarrassment and inconvenience caused to their client.'

A few seconds' contemplation. 'So much so . . .' He stopped and gave a little absent wave with a hand. '. . . put this in your usual jargon, but say I'm so angry that I'm proposing to charge the lady complainant with wasting police time and stick her before the magistrates.'

Warmed up now, he went on fluently, 'Tell 'em I shall require a statement from their client for the court detailing the upset it's caused him.'

He smiled rather sadistically. 'And also from his ex-wife to say that such conduct in the bedroom by her former husband is totally unthinkable et cetera.'

He was smiling broadly now. 'Tell 'em we'll circulate the date of the court hearing to ensure that the press are present in number to clear his good name.'

'That's blackmail,' the lawyer declared delightedly. 'Should do it.'

Nixon, sitting up straighter in his easy chair than Todd had ever seen, grinned happily.

'Let's hope the next item can be resolved just as effectively,' the legal director resumed ominously.

The solicitor who had defended Maddox before the magistrates had served a writ on the force and Todd for personal injuries over the manner of his arrest which resulted in pain, suffering and loss of earnings, he announced.

'It's another try on,' protested Todd, in the hot seat himself now.

'Maybe so, but you didn't identify yourself as a police officer when you opened the car door on him with, he claims, unnecessary force.'

He flicked through his file. 'Nor, does it seem, did you claim on police insurance for repairs.'

'It was a fifty quid job. I paid it myself to protect my no-claims and save all that red tape at HQ.'

'Yes, but it makes it look like you're accepting responsibility as an individual.'

Infuriated, Todd almost began to gabble. 'It was at the scene of a bloody crime committed twenty-four hours earlier, and I do mean bloody, and he was dressed like the attacker. If I'd popped my head out of the window and said, "Nice of you to stop by. I'm a police officer," he'd have either hit me over the head with his club or run away or both.'

He sat up fully and slapped his thigh quite hard. 'And with this leg I'd never have caught up with him.'

The lawyer became just as rambling. 'His case will be that he was doing what he saw as a public duty as a result of which he's received injuries for which he wants compensating and, in view of the circumstances, the insurers are keen to settle for a modest amount.'

'Just hang on a minute.' Briefly, Todd held up a hand. 'I'm named in the writ, did you say?'

'As second defendant.'

'And, you say, I could be deemed to have acted individually – i.e. not as a police officer on duty.'

The director pecked his head in affirmation.

'Right.' Todd threw himself forward, one elbow on the desk. 'Well, you can tell your authority and their weak-kneed insurers that if they want to settle that's up to them. I, as an individual, shall hire my own solicitor and fight it all the way.'

'Is that smart?' A startled expression. 'After all, unlike in his case . . .' The lawyer flicked his head at Nixon. '. . . Maddox will be untroubled by publicity. He's already had plenty and appears to enjoy it.'

'I don't mind explaining my conduct in public either.'

'It could be costly.'

'I'm not going to bottle it.' An evil thought occurred. 'We've got surveillance cameras on his place. If he's caught on them hopping around like a spring lamb, can I use it against him?'

'You could subpoena any useful film, I suppose.' The director looked away in thought. 'I'll make your views known, suggest we stall for a while.'

Carole Waites spoke up for the first time. 'Where does that leave me?' All Nixon's earlier woes seemed to have been transferred across the room to her.

The legal director asked what she meant and heard that Maddox was her prime suspect in the hunt for the knife attacker. 'I was planning to take out a warrant to search his place,' she explained.

'What reasonable grounds do you have?'

Carole lent heavily on Peck's profile, adding nothing that Todd didn't already know. He assumed her team had dug up no new leads in her absence at court.

The director was shaking his head. 'You can't pray in aid a psychologist,' he said, lapsing into legal jargon. Off pat, he quoted a High Court precedent in which a judge had ruled such evidence as unscientific and inadmissible.

'What are you telling me?' Carole grumbled.

'Quite simply, that if you raid him and find nothing, you're merely adding harassment to his litany of claims and upping his damages.'

She slumped back. 'Shit,' she groaned.

*

Debby Thompson was summoned by phone for the regular team talk after the legal director had left.

While they waited, Nixon cheerfully complained about being held up on his travels by luxury coaches taking tourists from Scrooby, from where the Pilgrim Fathers departed, via Wroot where Wesley was a curate, to his old family home in Epworth.

Many who journeyed through the black peat bogs on narrow roads with drains each side were Japanese. 'Nips that pass through the shite,' he called them.

Racist, most certainly, Todd accepted, but he laughed. Carole kept a po face. But then, he reasoned, she didn't drink with Nixon occasionally at the Red Lion in Epworth, as he did, and might not know, as he did, that he'd lost both his grandfathers in PoW camps in the Far East. In such circumstances, he'd grant any grandson his prejudices.

Debby knocked and entered. As Nixon had reclaimed his easy chair, she sat next to Carole, who was glowering rather than glowing now.

Nixon's expression suddenly became serious. 'Do you think,' he asked, eyes down, 'that my Ed could be a tourist?'

'With his crimes nine months apart, he's been here on holiday a sodding long time,' said Carole, sulkily.

'No. No,' said Nixon, unfazed by her rudeness. 'Do you think he travels abroad?'

No one responded, forcing him on. 'For someone with his sort of bloodlust, nine months between crimes is a long time.

'Are we talking golf tours here?' Todd queried, knowing that Nixon was thinking about Chivers.

'He goes abroad now and then, not on the tournament circuit, taking parties on package trips to pricey hotels.'

'No harm in bouncing it off Interpol, I suppose,' Todd said, hardly enthused. 'Ask for a list of unsolved vice murders in golf destinations like Spain and Portugal.'

'He could be a sex tourist,' Debby put in.

Mmm, thought Todd. It's not as though a golf-club is the murder weapon. Keep an open mind. Widen the inquiry. 'OK, Amsterdam, Hamburg, Bangkok, sex hot spots like that, too.' His eyes stayed on Debby. 'Is that on?'

'Absolutely. Shall I put your name and rank on the message? It will give it a bit of weight.'

Since he always started his day at HQ, he suggested she gave that address as well.

Debby wasn't finished yet. 'How about sending a précis to the FBI Unit of Behavioral Science in Quantico, see if they can come up with anything similar?'

She's read or watched *The Silence of the Lambs*, too, thought Todd, amusing himself, nodding, smiling.

'This case summary of yours.' An American voice over a crystal clear line to HQ. 'Cuba have a similar job.'

Cuba? thought Todd, caught off guard. 'I didn't know it was a sex centre.'

'Plagued with it since Castro let the mighty dollar back in when his Soviet paymasters went bust,' said the FBI man, a touch gleefully.

Cuba? Todd repeated. Hadn't the USA boycotted it since the missile crisis and that fiasco at the Bay of Pigs? So how does the FBI know what's going on there? Must have informers; better not ask.

Back in mid-February, he heard, monitors in Miami reported that a teenage girl had been picked up in Havana and found dead off a major highway more than a hundred miles out of town. 'It's been written off as a hit and run so as not to upset the tourist trade, their biggest dollar earner, but our info is that her throat was slashed.'

Todd tried not to gulp. 'Was she a prostitute?'

'A sports star of some sort, out of action because of injury. They throw grants at anyone who might win medals and glory for them. But when they're on the scrapheap, your guess as to how they earn a buck is as good as mine.'

Sex crimes like this are common the world over, regrettably, Todd accepted. 'Did the killer communicate afterwards in any way with the police?'

'By postcard, apparently,' he replied.

But that was unique as far as Todd knew from his research; taunting letters, yes, but postcards were unheard of. That *frisson* of excitement ran through him.

'Some police chief called Nadel's in charge,' the FBI man went on. 'An old revolutionary. He plays things close. Naturally we haven't had sight of the exhibit.' He paused. 'Shall I forward what we've got?'

'Please,' Todd almost sang.

'How can I help?' A posh voice, old BBC-style, had introduced himself as commercial second secretary after Todd had been bounced around several departments by the switchboard at the British Embassy in Havana.

From his days in Special Branch, Todd guessed second secretary meant MI6, but didn't pursue it.

'Yes, indeed,' he said when he was told how he could help.

He more or less confirmed what the FBI had said. He'd also heard that there had been communication with the police – 'handwritten in an odd sort of English.'

He'd got the tip on the diplomatic grapevine from a Canadian source, he went on, because the card had been posted in Quebec.

Todd was so thrilled he hardly heard him explaining that the Canadians led the field in putting two fingers up to the American blockade and sent more tourists to the island than any other country. 'What's happened?'

'Don't really know. Never made the papers as a murder investigation, not uncommon here. A road accident, they said.'

'Why drop it?'

'The presumption must be that if they think some homicidal maniac has gone home and is no longer running loose on their island they've lost interest. It costs money they haven't got to mount an international investigation on that scale. And they don't send investigators abroad in case they claim political asylum, like half their boxers, and don't come back.'

Todd hoped they were speaking on a secure line.

'I can try to fix up for you to talk to the infamous Capitaine Nadel if you wish, but be warned, he's an awkward sort and you may not get much.'

'Thanks,' said Todd.

'It would mean a personal visit. He's not one for saying much on the phone.' He laughed, confirming Todd's suspicion about his real role. 'And you'd need to send someone of rank. He's a stickler for protocol.'

A desperate need for new leads swept aside all budgetary considerations. 'We'll see you asap.'

Todd offered the trip to Nixon. 'And eat paella for days? Besides, I've too much on here. But bring back some cigars.'

He had his quiet word with a still subdued Carole about the show Dr Peck got after the Fish Finger case. 'The PR department cleared it,' she said, testily. She'd been short with him since the legal director vetoed a raid on Maddox, and he sensed she blamed him for causing her difficulties.

He offered her the trip, but she turned it down, too. Her husband was about to go away to a business conference and she didn't want to leave two teenage boys unsupervised at home.

It took an agonisingly long week for the embassy to fix the appointment and to find a seat on the overbooked scheduled services. 'We've had to bump off two Saga travellers and route them via Madrid, poor old buggers,' said the force's travel agent. 'Tourist class only, sorry to say.'

The afternoon before he left, Thai police responded to Debby's bulletin with a fax reporting that they'd had a prostitute abducted from Pattaya and dumped with throat cut on the expressway to Bangkok two years earlier, still unsolved.

'Get all you can,' Todd ordered her. 'Especially about any communication to the police from the killer.'

At home, Todd was interrupted by a phone call as he and his Em, hindered by their little Laura, packed a suitcase and a handgrip.

'*Our Man in Havana* and *The Old Man and the Sea*,' sighed Jacko Jackson when he heard where he was going. 'Do you think we're on for a Cuban hat-trick?'

Jacko, Todd knew, dreamed of joining Graham Greene and Ernest Hemingway in the top literary league. Cruelly, Todd told him, 'It's a Caribbean island, not Fantasy Island.'

Jacko always responded to affectionate abuse and laughed. 'Bring back a decent yarn; failing that, some cigars.'

13

For almost an hour, Todd had been sitting in what seemed like a huge cigar tube, the DC10 not revving up, never mind going anywhere. An overloaded luggage bay or something. He hadn't caught it fully over a muffled tannoy.

Add to that the compulsory check-in three hours ahead of the flight and the plane could have been almost half-way there by now, he calculated. He was untroubled. With the time difference, he had plenty of extra hours to play with.

He'd nodded at his next seat neighbour, a big black man, about fifty, in colourful loose-fitting casuals. Out of the politically correct politeness he always afforded blacks, but not always whites, they'd small-talked awhile. 'Holiday?' his neighbour had asked.

'Business. You?'

'Visiting friends. First trip?'

'Yes. You?'

'No.' Soon bored, the man went back to his *Guardian*.

Todd resumed the Lonely Planet guide started the night before in an over-heated, over-priced hotel in a room no better than the Padded Cell.

Take-off at last, very smooth, and his neighbour swapped the *Guardian* for a thin tabloid called *Granma*. Todd looked across at a headline in English about trade talks in Beijing.

His neighbour noticed his interest. 'You can get one from the stewardess if you like.'

Todd took another look at the dull headline and shook his head. 'Odd title, that's all.'

'In honour of the boat that brought Castro home,' came the reply in a Midlands accent, almost Brummie.

Todd smiled weakly and touched his Lonely Planet. 'I haven't got that far into my guide.'

The man lowered the paper. 'Where are you staying?'

'Not sure. I'm being met. You?'

'With friends. What line of business are you in?'

'Forensic science, a researcher,' Todd replied cannily. 'Off to a conference. You?'

He was a full-time official with a union in the motor trade, he said. He visited the island twice a year. 'Wonderful place and people.'

He'd been brought up on tales of Che Guevara and would be paying homage at the tomb at Santa Clara where he'd recently been reburied.

Todd aimed for a regretful expression. 'Doubt that I'll have the time.'

He didn't really need his guidebook as he sat through a potted history of the overthrow of the corrupt Batista regime with its Mafia connections and the social progress since with health and education second to none.

The man was taking bars of soap and pens with him, he said, because there was a shortage of such basics. He launched into a long diatribe against the US economic blockade.

Not a word, Todd noted, about the plea from the Pope on his visit a couple of months back for the release of political prisoners. He pointed it out only to himself, not wanting a debate, particularly with a *Guardian* reader.

Now Britain was being lambasted for kowtowing to the bullying States and holding back on investment. 'Miles behind the rest, we are. We're missing out.'

Todd was relieved when the film started, lunch was served and his neighbour dropped off to sleep. He got back to his reading over a can of beer.

Just west of Ireland they ran out of beer and the film broke down.

He looked around the crowded plane and wondered what other passenger had been bumped into the other Saga seat.

In place of the film, they screened a big map of their route across the Atlantic with a tiny plane that seemed to move about a tenth of an inch every half an hour or so until he, too, fell asleep.

Troubled now. Deeply troubled. Fifteen minutes from their destination, they had made some stop he didn't know about at a holiday peninsula he'd never heard of where they'd been turfed off and then back on to the plane at the cost of another hour.

At Havana airport, he'd been faced with a TV monitor that said 'Welcome' while he waited in a queue for three-quarters of an hour at Passport Control to get his visa stamped.

At Baggage Reclaim, another long wait for his suitcase that wasn't on the conveyor belt. Tired, hot and hungry, he walked beyond guards to look for an embassy driver in the Arrivals Hall with a placard saying 'Mr Todd', couldn't see one. They wouldn't let him back into Baggage to report his luggage missing.

The nine hours he'd budgeted for had become almost twelve and his old wound had stiffened because of restricted leg room.

Outside the airport, a long, low black and white building, touts surrounded him, offering cigars, rooms and cheap rides in cabs and with women.

He chose an official taxi, a black newish Toyota, and had to listen to the driver moan in good English about the peanuts he earned in pesos. 'Toilet paper,' he called it.

At first the roads were clogged with thousands of bikers, crowds of hitch-hikers, lorries belching black fumes and crammed with people standing in the back.

They drove into a stylish, much quieter suburb with banyan trees thicker in girth than the centuries-old Major Oak back home in Sherwood Forest.

The taxi pulled up on the corner of two very select avenues. 'You are here,' the driver announced. Todd topped up a ten dollar charge with a five dollar tip.

The embassy looked like a wedding cake with pink icing, pillared entrance, white grilles on windows, grass verges and trimmed hedges; very pretty.

There was another hold-up while a guard on the security gate phoned round to find the man Todd knew only as the commercial second secretary.

'Ah. At last.' He rose from a large under-used desk when Todd limped in. 'Almost given you up. Tea?'

'Please,' Todd almost gasped. For the trip, he had carefully selected a light grey jacket without lining, black cotton trousers and white open-necked shirt, yet felt both overdressed and underdressed in this company.

The so-called second secretary was wearing a brilliant white Cuban shirt, short-sleeved, beautifully pressed, no jacket, but a tie that looked clubbish.

They shook hands, his cool, Todd's clammy. 'Call me Harry,' he said. He didn't give his last name and Todd didn't ask. They sat opposite each other.

Harry listened patiently to Todd's travel troubles, but frowned on hearing about the missing case. 'Anything in it?'

'Only a week's supply of clothes, that's all,' said Todd, close to a whine.

'Important, I mean.'

'No papers, if that's what you mean.' Todd nodded down at the green grip he'd stowed in hand baggage and hugged on his lap in the taxi here. 'They're all in here.'

Harry looked relieved. 'I'll report it for you, of course.'

A dusky girl with a slinky walk served lemon tea and Todd began to cool down under two electric fans in the low, cream-coloured ceiling.

Harry gave him the name of the hotel where he'd booked a room for him in Central Park. The car that had returned empty from the airport would take him there.

He'd also arranged for him to see Captain Nadel at noon tomorrow. From a desk drawer, he pulled out and unfolded a street map on which he marked the way from the hotel to police headquarters.

He put down his pen. 'He's undertaken to give what assistance he can, or, rather, sees fit to, on the strict proviso that there'll be no publicity.'

Todd nodded.

'Note that, please. This sort of thing is commercially sensitive; national interests on both sides.'

Todd remembered what his fellow traveller on the plane had said about Britain dragging its feet in investments here and wondered if we were trying to catch up.

'Anything new on the grapevine?' he asked.

'He's playing it extremely tight, nothing leaking at all.' Harry's expression became solemn. 'He's a real son of the revolution, fighting in the mountains as a schoolkid, the Bay of Pigs and

Angola after that. He's shot more people than any other serving police officer, they say.'

Todd swallowed. He'd never shot anyone. On one infamous occasion, he'd fired, but, thankfully, missed. He wouldn't mention that tomorrow, he decided.

'He's a stickler for protocol.' Harry began to write on the map. 'These are his HQ phone and fax details. Any delay, contact him.'

Harry continued, 'If he takes a shine to you, the job should be easy. If he takes against you, you're in for a wasted journey and a hard time, I fear.' He gave him a rather anxious look. 'In which case, leave me out of it, if you would.'

The nose of the silver Humber came up and out of an underground tunnel and Todd viewed the finest seafront he'd ever seen.

To his left, the Gulf of Mexico looked purple and calm, yet white spray broke over the sea wall that seemed to stretch for miles. 'El Malecon,' said the driver rather proudly.

Todd looked to his right at prime site buildings that were faded and forlorn. Can't be so proud of them, he thought.

Behind them was a mix of the splendid and the seedy, elegant Spanish mansions and stark Soviet tower blocks, both colonial in their differing ways.

The magnificent prom was packed with cars, mostly American from the fifties, classic models when they were abandoned by their fleeing owners, clapped out now.

The driver nodded ahead. 'The meeting tomorrow is a small way in that direction.' He didn't take it, turned right instead into a tree-lined avenue and stopped in a wide square outside the Hotel Inglaterra. The driver obligingly translated for him. 'England Hotel.'

With its neo-classic façade, Hotel Inglaterra was hardly home from home. A gum-chewing receptionist had been slow to find his booking. Droning air conditioning had made the second-floor bedroom icy cold. He'd showered, couldn't shave, then changed back into travel-stained clothes.

Behind arched wrought iron railings, he'd dined alone. The restaurant was big, tables so far apart he couldn't eavesdrop on any conversations, a favourite occupation when he was on his own. All he could hear was a piano playing in a bar behind more railings.

A waistcoated waiter took an age to get around to him, time spent studying strange paintings, modern and, to his eye, vaguely obscene, on high cream walls. He ordered steak which took another age to arrive and was hardly worth the wait; small and tough.

He walked outside to a long terrace with a dozen or so cream columns and separated from the crowded pavement and noisy street by a line of potted plants with ribbed, two-tone leaves.

He sat in a cane chair at a round table topped with mock marble, ordered Cristal, a canned local beer with a pleasant barley taste, and looked out on Parque Centro; slabbed, not grassed. A Cuban flag, blue and white stripes with white star on red triangle, fluttered on a pole in a cooling breeze from the sea.

Every so often a female face, some disturbingly young, would part the palms and peer through. 'Hi. Where you from? Wanta come with me?'

Every time he looked away, concentrating on conversations at other tables. Two were occupied by trios with English accents.

One party was dressed in identical fawn trousers and floral shirts and he thought they were in a band. Wrongly, it soon became apparent, for they beckoned three girls in from the pavement. All wore skin-tight outfits more suitable for the beach. Negotiations began over the price of what promised to be a wild night out.

The other party were of Saga age, a few years either side of sixty, haphazardly dressed. *The Last of the Summer Wine* comes to Cuba, Todd decided, amusing himself.

A bearded man gave fairly short shrift to a thickset black girl with wild hair who broke through the screen of plants, undetected by a doorman in a fawn double-breasted suit.

She moved to Todd's table and sat down uninvited. 'Where you from?' She rolled her eyes, a bit like Carmen Miranda.

'England.'

'Ah, I have friend in London.' A disturbingly deep voice. 'Come with me. Fifty dollars.'

Only now did Todd realise the hair was a wig and the voice was male. Todd shook his head, finished his beer and got up. 'Hi, you, come with me,' the transvestite called after him.

Christ, he thought, safely back inside, walking between tiled pillars and beneath a chandelier, feeling quite shaken. What a crazy place.

A day away and already he longed for the certainties of Em and home. Going up in the lift, he thought about tomorrow.

Walking to his room down high, narrow corridors with lots of inlaid mosaics in pottery, he decided his limp would prove to the Capitaine that he'd seen action, too, and they'd get along just fine, old soldiers together.

Tomorrow, he was sure, would be a much better day.

14

Cock-a-doodle-doo.

Todd awoke, befuddled. A cockerel? In the middle of a capital city? Is there some joke alarm I should have switched off last night? He looked at his watch: not yet six.

The cock crowed again and again. No joke this, he decided, lying naked in a double bed. He'd silenced the noisy air conditioning before turning in. He was hot under a rust-coloured cover. He threw it off.

Two narrow windows were curtained with tan netting and the only dim natural light came from the bathroom. He climbed out and followed it across brown floor tiles. He switched on the light and showered.

He examined his face in the mirror as he dried himself. His blond stubble was very prickly and far too irregular to be described as designer. He rubbed an index finger on the small bar of soap and then on to his teeth. His mouth still tasted foul. And he'd forgotten to buy bottled water. Shit.

He'd have to get toilet things and clothes, no doubt about it. He sat on the bed, pinkly naked, not wanting to pull on his soiled briefs and stiff socks.

He rummaged through his pockets to collect and count his

cash. Hardly a dent had been made in five hundred dollars. There was another five hundred in travellers' cheques. In his wallet was an American Express card, unacceptable here, but a highly usable Mastercard.

Plenty, he realised. Compared with that cabbie, he'd probably rate in the top fifty richest in this land.

He looked at his watch again. Too early for breakfast, let alone shopping. A TV set on a brown chest of drawers was turned on and surfed until he found CNN. All the President's Women was still in the news; as boring as trade talks in Beijing, he decided, and turned it off again.

He forced himself into dressing and took the lift up to the top floor with a flat roof and breathtaking views of the old city.

Next door was a beautiful domed building, a ringer for the Capitol Building in Washington. Overlooking the sea were ancient forts and statues. Vehicles' horns blared in the streets below. The cock still crowed.

He went back to his room to collect the map Harry had given him. The bedside phone was ringing.

'Ah. At last.' It could only be Harry. 'Found your suitcase at...'

Somewhere that sounded to Todd like mumbo-jumbo. 'Say again.'

'Hemingway's hotel...' Harry slowed down, even spelt it out. '... Ambos Mundos. Half-way between you and police HQ. Ochre-coloured place. Lovely. Easy to find.'

'What's it doing there?'

'Some driver of a coach party took it from the airport by mistake.' Harry lowered his voice. 'Or so they say. Awaiting collection. Nip round. Must look smart for *el capitaine*, eh? Don't give him my regards, by the way.' He laughed lightly and hung up.

Todd strolled out of the hotel and across Parque Centro. The sky above was blue and cloudless. The straight narrow street he entered was crowded and warm. The cigar touts were already out, too early for the girls yet.

Harry was right. The Ambos Mundos was a lovely place with a friendly staff. He collected his case from the bellboy, slipped him a dollar and strolled back, slower still.

The old city fascinated him – old and new and falling down.

Here and there were beautiful squares shaded by tall palms with silver bark. Classes of small children, all neatly dressed, filed into some for outdoor lessons.

Round the corner was dereliction and decay, pot-holed roads and pavements. Parts looked like Bosnia as if Captain Nadel and his men had lost at the Bay of Pigs and not won.

Back at his hotel, he opened his case and studied inside it before he unpacked. If anyone had searched it, they'd been so careful as not to be noticeable.

He showered again, shaved, changed into clean underpants, socks, grey trousers, white shirt with striped tie and felt terrific. He retained the lightweight jacket for its pockets. Downstairs in the spacious restaurant, he brunched rather than breakfasted – lots of fresh fruit, scrambled egg and thick black coffee. He took a big bottle of water back to his room.

Now he was certain today would be a much better day.

His confidence began to wane when he'd been kept waiting for an hour.

He'd found the police station with ease – a grey-stone fort overlooking the waterfront, its dry moat littered with rubbish. He crossed what must once have been a drawbridge, concreted down now, but the chains were still in place.

Producing his warrant card, he'd introduced himself to a young, fresh-faced officer on the heavy-studded gate. They couldn't understand each other.

Another was called, then another. All wore grey shirts, mid-blue trousers and matching baseball caps. All carried a gun on one hip, a baton on the other.

A fourth officer was summoned, a veteran who spoke English. He didn't use much of it when he led him down gloomy corridors to a large, very scruffy room.

He was pointed to a wonky chair with a plastic rather than cane base and there he'd sat for an hour, nothing better to do than watch the fan in a low ceiling circulate stale air.

His fresh underpants and shirt stuck to him. It had to be ninety in here, he estimated.

Old bikes leant against one grey wall. Ill-matching cabinets stood against another. On top of one was an ancient sit-up-and-beg typewriter. Steel grilles rather than glass covered three windows.

One corner had been partitioned off, half glass, half wood painted dark brown. From within came the sounds of ringing phones and a voice that was often raised.

Next to the office was a much smaller room with black bars. Behind them sat a man on a bunk with his head in his hands, sobbing soundlessly.

No police station Todd had ever visited in more than twenty years' service had been more rundown. And this, he reminded himself, is the base of their top cop.

Finally the veteran officer marched noisily across cream and grey tiles, beckoned him and about-turned.

Todd exaggerated his limp slightly as he followed him into the office.

Behind a chaotically littered desk sat a small, swarthy man, head down over papers.

Todd limped before him. His escort stood at his shoulder and didn't say, 'Sit down.'

The man behind the desk had two rows of colourful medal ribbons stitched to his grey shirt just above the breast pocket. His black belt holstered the regulation gun, no baton. Tucked into it at the stomach was a Che-style black beret.

His balding head came up and Todd looked down into a creased, leathery face so ancient that back home he'd have been pensioned off more than a decade ago.

He pushed a single sheet of paper across the desk and said something in Spanish.

'Captain Nadel . . .' said the voice at his shoulder.

Todd smiled down at him, got blanked for his trouble.

'. . . requires you to read that.'

No please, Todd noted, unnerved.

He picked up the paper and turned it round. Black words in capitals leapt off the page. 'GLOBAL HUNT FOR M-WAY SCISSORHANDS.'

Already Todd was fearing the worst, hoped his hand wasn't trembling with anger as he read the smaller print on a fax of a cutting from an English tabloid printed that day. 'Detectives hunting the motorway mass killer are spreading their net worldwide.'

The very worst came into the second paragraph. 'They have called in Interpol and flown to Cuba seeking links with unsolved cases of the abduction and murder of two prostitutes.'

His eyes barely took in the rest that recapped his own two cases and lumped them together with ten other unsolved crimes near motorways.

Inwardly, he wanted to scream. A leak. Morton's got a new source. And he's fucked me, totally fucked me.

He looked over the top of the sheet down on Nadel. 'This has been written without my authority.' The man at his side began to translate. 'It is unauthorised. I am deeply embarrassed and sorry.'

Nadel spoke quietly and Todd got a message a few seconds later. 'It is not in accord with our agreement with your embassy.'

'I know. It is an unofficial report and a severe breach of our own security.'

Nadel tapped a brown file on his desk and raised his voice. It was some seconds before they were turned into sense for Todd. 'Rosa Melena is not a . . .'

A name, at least, I've got a name, maybe all I'll get, so note it, Todd ordered himself. In doing so he missed something about gin-something.

He looked over his shoulder and frowned. 'A woman jockey. A prostitute,' the interpreter explained.

His eyes went back to Nadel speaking words he was to hear a little later. 'She was a young, fine athlete, the flower of our nationhood. We were proud of her. You have defiled her memory.'

'Not me,' Todd blustered. 'I have said in public not one word about her or this country and promise I never will.'

Nadel pointed at the sheet in his hand. 'Your press has. Your public will think she was a . . .' gin-something again '. . . and she was, in point of truthfulness, a very fine young lady. She represented her country with pride.'

Todd tried to calm him. 'I accept what you say entirely. I would never dream of suggesting she was engaged in vice.'

Far from being calm, he was infuriated. 'But you have – '

'Not me.'

The flood continued. 'She comes from a good family who have served us well. Her sister is with broken heart.'

Todd tried again. 'I am desperately sorry – '

There was no stopping Nadel. 'They never lived here in this place. She never walked or worked these streets. She was only here for a short stay to witness her sister from . . .'

A place that sounded like Cure Hotel Something and Trinidad was added. Todd assumed Nadel was not talking about the island in the West Indies because he had read in his Lonely Planet about an ancient town on the south coast called Trinidad. He decided not to check, just noted Cure Hotel Something and tuned back into '. . . and she was returning there for more treatment.'

'I understand,' lied Todd. 'Was she killed on the way?'

'By a foreign motorist.'

'Did he molest her?'

Nadel rested a hand on his oft-used gun. 'She died unspoilt by sex.'

Not raped then, Todd realised. The same as our two cases.

Though they were speaking through the interpreter, their eyes locked on each other as Todd pushed. 'Was it a road accident or was she murdered?'

'That is our business to decide.'

'But, you see, we have had two ladies killed in similar mysterious circumstances.'

The captain nodded at the sheet in Todd's hand and repeated, 'Gin-something.'

Not proper ladies, prostitutes, he means, Todd told himself; ignore it. Press on. 'My hope is that by working together we can catch this foreign motorist. I believe he lives in England.'

'How do you know our circumstances?'

Todd couldn't answer, 'From the FBI.' Instead: 'Can we not share our information? Did the man responsible for it send a *postal* . . .' From his reading of the guide he'd remembered the word for postcard. '. . . to the police?'

'If so, it will be in our files and will take time to find. Why should I take such time for you so you can use what I say in your papers? We have kept our inquiries secure, private. Now you and your press have spoilt the operation with false information. Can you not control them?'

Todd didn't want to debate freedom of the press, not here, not now, but he was desperate. 'I will try to put it right, correct this untrue item. Now perhaps – '

'Then . . .'

'Sorry?'

'Not now.' He pointed to the fax. 'When you have corrected this item of shame, told the truth, then we might talk.' He looked down and waved him away.

Todd had no need to exaggerate his limp when he retraced his steps across the tiled floor. He was so weak in both legs he could barely walk.

'I can bloody well read. I'm not bloody blind.'

The line from his hotel room to the headquarters of Eastmids police had broken up twice during Todd's briefing, but was working well now. There was no need to shout. Nonetheless, he was shouting. 'I know who's behind it. The question is, what are you doing about it?'

PR Pam shouted back. 'I tried to warn you. You dropped the wrong man.'

Or Post Mortem Morton had found a replacement snitch for Superintendent Trench, Todd suspected. 'I'll sort that when I get back. Now, what are you doing about it?'

'What can I do?' Pam sounded plaintive.

'Get it corrected.'

'They won't do that. It's not as if they have named or libelled anyone.'

'You've got to find a way to put it right or I'm buggered. This captain knows a lot and I need him on side.'

'It's well past knocking-off time, but I could sound out Morton tomorrow . . .'

'Today. Now.'

'. . . invite him for lunch . . .'

'You're always on about networking with the media so make that dinner tonight.'

'No need for that.' Her icy tone. 'Let's think it through. Now . . .' A thoughtful pause. 'What . . . exactly . . . do you want?'

'Another piece saying we've ruled out Cuba.'

'You're not listening. That's just a correction and they won't buy it. Now, please, let's think.'

Todd thought. 'OK. Get hold of Debby Thompson. She'll still be there. Tell her to get back to Bangkok and ask for more details on their case.'

Pam was catching on. 'What if I ask her to get details of any other unsolved vice murders?'

'Why?'

'Then I can say we are examining X number, the more the merrier.' Into the swing of it now, she went on, 'Can I say you've ruled back in those other unsolved motorway murders?'

Todd was too astonished to speak.

'Just hint at it. Open mind and all that.'

'Why, for christsake?' he spluttered.

'Because Morton's obsessed with them, got that book deal to write them up.'

Todd was about to curse obscenely, stopped himself, recalling the advice he'd once been given by his grandad. 'A small fib is OK in pursuit of a greater truth.' He sighed. 'OK.'

'What have we got?' Pam started to sum up. 'Police investigation into a total of a so-and-so number of murders at home and abroad and a bit at the end quoting Assistant Chief Constable Phillip Todd as saying what?'

'Something like, "We have categorically ruled out any connection with Cuba. We are absolutely satisfied that the death of a well-respected girl athlete was not vice-related but the result of a roadside incident."'

'Say accident...'

'It may not have been.' Privately, Todd clung to the hope that it was anything but an accident.

'... because "incident" is catch-all. They'll start making their own inquiries.'

Don't want that, Todd decided. 'OK then.'

'The day after tomorrow is the earliest we can hope for and I can't guarantee that. It may not work.'

'It's got to work.'

'I may have to level with him and, if so, he'll want something in return.'

'Such as?'

'First bite at the next really big juicy one.'
'Promise it to him then.'
'Have I your authority for that?'
'Yes.'

'Calm down,' Em ordered. 'You never perform properly when you're tensed up.'
He was so stressed he didn't pick up the ambiguity. 'What can I do? I can't chase people for results for three months and return with nothing to show for around five hundred quid spent already. I can't hang around here doing nothing for days on end. Every other local wants to sell me sex or cigars.'
'And you don't smoke,' mocked Em. 'Is there a Press Club there?'
'Dunno. Could find out. Why?'
She told him why and handed him on to Laura, already dressed for bed.
They talked toddler talk for a couple of minutes, at ten dollars a minute, and he was calm again.

15

Someone finally answered, 'Club Prensa.'
Todd gave his name and hotel, and asked if anyone there spoke English. Eventually someone did. He gave the same details, adding that he was an English researcher at a medical conference and desired to talk to any English-speaking journalist who specialised in sport.
Another wait, another voice. 'I will attempt my help.'
'You are most kind.' Todd ran through everything again and added. 'I am preparing a paper for my journal on the treatment of sporting injuries in which, of course, your country leads the way. I have heard you have a very fine establishment near Trinidad.'
Kurhotel Escambras, came the reply, in the mountains not far north of the town. His English was far from perfect, but good

enough for Todd to gain the impression that it was something like a spa hotel, not just for athletes, but anyone who had served the state well and was in need of treatment or a rest.

He took the plunge. 'Do you know of the Melena sisters?'

'Field sports champions,' he answered immediately. 'Dolores is javelin, Rosa high jump. But you know she is dead?'

'Rosa! No!' Todd feigned shock. 'I am so sorry.' He had heard about Kurhotel from colleagues, he lied on, and that Rosa Melena was among the sports stars being treated there.

Yes, the journalist confirmed. He tried valiantly but vainly to explain what her injury had been and Todd was left to guess at a snapped Achilles tendon.

'What a tragedy. What happened to her?'

She had come to Havana by special bus with other athletes sidelined by injury to watch a big event, he replied. She had to return to Kurhotel before the rest of the party to see a specialist. 'She obtained a ride with a tourist and there was an incident on the way.'

Incident, not an accident, Todd noted. 'How tragic. What sort of incident?'

'She was with throat injury and she could not be saved.'

A throat injury in a road accident; unlikely, Todd decided. 'A crash?'

'No one sure. Tourist drove away.'

'Did the police not find the car?'

'No.'

Can't have been a crash, he told himself. 'Or the driver?'

'No.'

'Was it reported in newspapers like *Granma*?'

'A big ... what you call it ... o ... o ...'

Todd helped out. 'Obituary. Did it give details of her career?'

'Oh, yes.' He named some of the honours she had won which Todd didn't take down in his notebook opened on the bedside table.

'Where did she live?'

'She came from Santiago.' He didn't know her home address, only her school which was affiliated to the national athletic authority. He spelt it out and Todd noted it down.

School, he thought? 'How old was she?'

'Fifteen.'

Fifteen? Jesus. His stomach tightened. If it is Edward Scissorhands, he's now killing indiscriminately. 'Did the obituary say precisely how she died?'

'A traffic incident only. No proper . . .' He corrected himself. '. . . full explanation of the cause of her death.'

'Do you think she was murdered?' Todd asked point-blank.

'It is possible.' Stronger. 'I think so.' Stronger still. 'Yes.'

'Why did the papers not say so?'

'Better you ask the state police.'

Better not say that I already have, Todd concluded with thank-yous and goodbyes.

He'd missed another tunnel at the east end of the Malecon and finished up in a maze near the docks – tiny single-storey houses, breeze block hovels really, in unmade streets that had turned into brown rivers when clouds he hadn't even noticed gathering suddenly burst.

He had stopped at a garage and filled up with twenty-five dollars' worth of obviously black market petrol and they had put him on the right road.

Now the sun was out again and he had found the *autopista*, four lanes each side, big and straight enough to land a DC10 on, but he had hardly seen any other vehicles. Apart, that is, from ox carts being driven the wrong way down the hard shoulder which wasn't hard at all, just a dirt track.

He'd been annoyed when all the car rental firm could offer was a little red French car at sixty dollars a day, plus fifteen insurance which he'd put on plastic. They'd demanded he signed but left open another Mastercard docket to be torn up when the car was returned unscathed. He never signed blank cheques, so he lodged two hundred dollars in cash as a deposit.

He was pleased now with a 1.4 engine, fast enough when driving on the wrong side of the road on a surface that was crumbling into holes deep enough to bury bodies in. With all the lane-hopping entailed, it was just as well there was so little traffic.

Plenty of pedestrians though. Here and there, they lined the central reservation, no more than a baked verge, holding out items for sale – strings of garlic, cakes and, bizarrely, a small crocodile he hoped was dead.

Even more people sat in the shade of bridges reducing the motorway to just the outside lane as they ran forward to thumb lifts.

He felt pangs of guilt every time he passed them by, eyes front to avoid looking into their disappointed faces. On the back seat sat his handgrip. He had divided his belongings to avoid losing the lot again. Half were back at the hotel. The rest and his toilet bag were with him. Don't want that bag squashed by a carful of passengers, he kidded himself.

Fifty miles into his journey, he came across a girl on her own and no longer had an excuse. She had a rucksack on one shoulder and a sleeping bag tucked under the other arm.

He pulled in and she ran loose-limbed in long, flowing floral skirt, pink off-the-shoulder blouse and sandals on the dusty hard shoulder towards him.

He opened both offside doors. She placed her sleeping roll on the back seat, taking care to avoid his grey jacket which lay over the handgrip.

She got in beside him, very gracefully, clutching her rucksack to her lap. She was mid-twenties, dark and beautiful. Across her bare shoulder, she flashed him a heart-stopping smile.

'I am going to Trinidad,' he said very slowly, wondering if he was doing the right thing. Back home, he'd never pick up a girl on her own in case she cried rape.

'You are English,' she almost trilled.

'Yes.'

'Oh, this is my lucky day,' she said breathlessly. 'My home is on your way.'

He drove on, hearing that she was an English lecturer at a university on the west side of the island and was going home to Cienfuegos, a port on the south coast.

'Are there no buses or trains?' he asked, disbelievingly.

'Very few and they cost money one cannot afford on fifteen dollars a month.'

Everybody here almost boasts about the pittance they earn which means there's a catch coming up, thought Todd on his guard.

'Even those who can afford a car can get little petrol because of rationing.' She motioned at the windscreen and the empty road which disappeared ahead into a heat haze. 'So short is transport that the police can compel vehicles to stop and give lifts to children of school age.'

To earn more dollars, she often took a break from college to go home and act as a guide for tourists from Varadero, that peninsula where Todd's plane had made the stop he hadn't expected. She had been on the road since yesterday and had slept overnight beneath a bridge.

So, Todd mused, hitching is a way of life here. Maybe Captain Nadel's hot denial about Rosa being on the game was the truth.

The hinterland was very flat, but the trip was no longer tedious as she chatted about English replacing Russian in schools and quizzed him about the English way of life.

He talked for a long while about his family, told her he was a sports researcher and where he was going.

He tried the name of the Melena sisters on her. She knew Rosa had died, but no more.

When she spoke about her own country, every sentence started 'before' or 'after' – meaning the revolution. On the whole, Todd decided, 'after' sounded a much better life.

Billboards displayed no adverts, only slogans that proclaimed the revolution. She translated one. 'The Nation before all.' At least he could make out the words, even if he couldn't understand them, more than could be said for direction signs with lettering that had all but peeled away.

An hour on, she pointed ahead to a rather ramshackle cafeteria with petrol pumps on the opposite carriageway and said, 'Servico Aguada. Turn off there.' Without her, he would have missed it.

The road he took was much narrower, slow traffic, mainly lorries and tractors, both ways. She identified the crops in the fields – banana plantations, orange groves and mile upon mile of sugar cane in red soil.

She named the birds that fed in or flew over the fields – black frigates that glided, carrions as big as vultures, snowy white egrets.

On tight corners, horsemen in wide straw hats reined in their mounts and motioned them through with machetes. In villages, schoolchildren in lemon trousers and skirts waved. Every hamlet had a brilliant white clinic adorned with a red cross and a small shop from where, she explained, free rations were distributed.

All too soon for Todd cranes from a distant port appeared on the horizon. She asked him to pull up in front of a clapboard farmhouse a few miles from the town. All around it horses and cattle were tethered and pigs and chickens roamed free.

'Please come into my home and meet my family and eat and drink with us,' she said with an earnest expression.

Watch out, Todd cautioned himself. 'I am sorry, but I must get as far as I can by nightfall. I may have to go on to Santiago.'

She looked aghast. 'It is many, many miles. The *autopista* runs out short of Santa Clara and the road is often like this all the way. It will take many hours.'

The fastest and safest way, she advised, was to drive on through the mountains from the Kurhotel to Santa Clara, leave the car there and catch the Havana–Santiago express at around midnight.

Heads close together, they bent forward over his map and she told him the way in great detail.

She began to open a pocket in her rucksack. 'I have a friend . . .'

Here it comes, the catch, Todd anticipated. He was disappointed, because he had already decided to tip her five dollars, wouldn't now.

'. . . in Cambridge.'

Still rummaging, she said, 'We have never met, but he sends me books I cannot obtain here.' She found what she was looking for – a white envelope. 'I need a book very urgently for an examination. Would you please do me the favour of mailing it for me when you get home?'

'With pleasure.' He took the envelope and felt the thin, poor quality of the paper. He glanced down on a name and an address of a college in Cambridge. 'Do students and other young people ask this often of tourists?'

'All the time, I am afraid. The post from here can take three months or more to arrive.' She resumed her rummaging. 'What will the cost of that be?'

'Please. No.' He raised a staying hand. 'I should really be paying you for the guided tour.'

'Oh, no. I enjoyed your company very much.' She got out of the car and bent back inside to retrieve her sleeping bag. She stood up and smiled radiantly. 'This has been my lucky day.'

Mine, too, thought Todd, driving on.

He had worked out how the killer could have mistaken a virtuous hitch-hiker for a prostitute and how he'd talked an innocent tourist into posting a card to the police.

Night fell suddenly, barely any twilight, and he was on a road that kept rising and twisting through dark forests.

The smell of pine was powerful and he thought of Maddox and Adams back home, and Toby Harvard who'd returned at Easter after more than two months away.

Concentrate on the road, not on Stan, not even Ed; eyes on this bloody road, mind on nothing else, or you'll be off it, he ordered himself.

More hairpins and ahead the tallest hill seemed to be bathed in a pale yellow light, and not from the moon hidden behind clouds. Rounding the next bend a strange building came into view above the treeline.

The closer he got the bigger it became, as big as an ocean liner, all lit up. At the top of a steep driveway, he stopped in an almost deserted car-park.

He got out, put on a tie and his jacket, stuffed his map in one pocket, patted others with his warrant card, notebook and pens, the policeman again.

He walked up wide steps to a well-lit entrance. Closer to, he could see the building was clad in green stucco streaked with algae, eight storeys high, more in keeping with central Moscow than the mountains.

In an echoing foyer, he put his warrant card on a long desk and asked a male receptionist for any duty official who spoke English.

Several phone calls were made before a tall, lithe man in a lime green tracksuit came up to him. He introduced himself as a member of the coaching staff. 'I will try to help.'

'Good,' said Todd, crisply. 'I have already spoken today to your Captain Nadel . . . You know of him, of course?'

A grave nod.

'I wish to speak to you about Rosa Melena.'

'Please.' The coach held out a hand towards a tiled staircase. Climbing two noisy flights Todd explained he had travelled all this way because the man responsible for Rosa's death also came from England.

'Does Captain Nadel know you are here?' asked the coach anxiously.

'He gave me this address.'

Only then did the coach say, 'We thought he was from Canada.'

Her killer, he means, Todd knew. I'm getting somewhere at last. 'No.' He shook his head firmly. 'From England where he has taken the lives of two more ladies.'

He was shown into a bar and to a formica table with red-cushioned chairs. The coach went on to a sparsely stocked counter.

Todd fancied another Cristal and sandwiches because he hadn't eaten since that brunch. He was disappointed when the coach returned with two small, black coffees.

'You see ...' Todd took out his notebook and began to talk urgently. 'This man killed our two ladies on *autopistas* like the one I journeyed down from Havana.'

A hesitant nod and Todd guessed he was indicating understanding rather than confirmation.

'He cut their throats.' Todd drew an index finger across his own. 'He removed all their clothing, apart from their briefs.'

Another nod, firmer, which Todd took as agreement.

'He left their bodies by the side of the *autopista*.'

A frown, no nod this time. 'Rosa was found on the road around Cienfuegos.'

Todd remembered driving down it. 'The fast road with two lanes? It is a similar sort of highway to ours.'

The coach's face was puzzled. 'We were told the man responsible went to Canada.'

'He wants people to believe that. That is why, we think, he had a Canadian tourist mail a *postal* for him from there. To confuse us.'

The coach looked more than confused, utterly baffled.

'Did you not know that?' asked Todd.

'No.'

'He always sends a *postal* to the police. Twice in England, once here. It is to taunt us, boast of his deeds. He is a sick and evil man. In them he tells us where to find his victim's handbag.' He took the plunge. 'Rosa's handbag was recovered, was it not?'

'At Aguada.'

Todd pulled the map out of his pocket. 'Show me, please.'

The coach studied, then pointed to the junction where the girl hitcher had indicated the turn off the *autopista*.

Todd took another gamble. 'Near the cafeteria?'

'Behind it.' The coach's expression became suspicious. 'Did not Captain Nadel tell you of this?'

Todd tried to shrug it off. 'There you are, then. How do you think the police knew where to look?'

The coach looked as if he hadn't a clue.

'The *postal* told them. He does the same in England. It is the same man, trust me.'

His face was anything but trusting now, and Todd hurried on. 'Rosa was here for treatment for an injured ankle. Correct?'

A cautious nod.

'How then did she get from the centre of Havana?'

The coach wasn't following.

'She had an injured foot,' Todd pointed out. 'Most people have to reach the *autopista* to get lifts. How did she get from the centre of the city to the *autopista* when she could not walk far?'

'You do not know?'

'I am asking you.'

Suddenly the bar, the whole building, the floodlit mountain were plunged into darkness. 'Power cut,' the coach said. 'Usually they do not last long.'

A minute or so later, the lights were restored and Todd saw a changed, more determined face in front of him. 'Did not Captain Nadel tell you?' he asked.

'I saw him today.' Waffle, Todd urged himself. 'He wants this killer caught as badly as me.'

'But he did not tell you?'

Oh, Christ, thought Todd. He's had time to think. 'I am double-checking information. How did she get that lift?'

A second or two of silence. 'Please.' He made a slow-down motion with both hands. 'I must speak to my superiors. You will wait here, please.' The coach made it sound like an instruction.

Todd only waited until he was out of sight, then scurried out of the bar and hotel to his car, feeling like a fugitive.

16

He awoke when the train lurched. His throat was desert-dry. Hunger pangs gripped him. He looked out of a filmed-over window on to a grey-black sky, then at his watch: not even six.

He was starving, hadn't eaten since that brunch, what? – twenty hours ago. The drive over the other side of the mountains had taken so long that there had been no time for a meal at Santa Clara, let alone to pay homage at Che's tomb.

He'd left the hired car near the station. A street urchin approached. 'Crimewatch,' he thought he'd said and he'd queried it. 'Pardon?' The boy gestured at the red Citroën and said, 'Car watch.' He was offering to keep an eye on it for a dollar, a routine scam he'd read about in his guidebook. Todd gave him two, not knowing when he'd be back.

He'd bought a ticket at a booking hall which was more underfurnished than Captain Nadel's office. The train was already in, exceedingly long, with brown coaches so dirty he could barely make out the cream stripe running down the side.

He'd taken a brown seat, its man-made cladding still warm from the passenger who had just got off. A stewardess in blue waistcoat and short trousers informed him that there was no dining car or bar.

He'd reclined the seat, watched the cockroaches emerge from the woodwork round the window until exhaustion overcame hunger and he'd dozed.

Now, five hours on, the cockroaches were going back into the woodwork. A pink streak thickened and pushed at the indigo above, changing it slowly into sky blue.

A small inquisitive face popped up above the seat in front: a pretty girl, no more than four. A woman began to brush and replait the kneeling girl's black hair.

The grooming took a long time and the girl grew bolder. Chin on the top of the seat, she smiled and pointed at the Lonely Planet guide in which Todd had begun to read up on Santiago.

He turned it, showing her a map, the island coloured yellow on a blue background. It looked to him like an open-beaked, long-necked goose making a flat-footed landing on water. He worked his elbows and honked. She laughed, brown eyes sparkling.

He offered it to her. She took it and dropped from view. Her mother turned her head to smile.

Far from being an express, the train, in Todd's estimation, never topped thirty and now it came to a standstill at a place where there didn't seem to be much of a town or station.

A young man boarded at the far end of the carriage with a cardboard tray of rolls and worked his way slowly down the aisle.

Todd peeled a dollar from a damp roll of notes in his trouser pocket and held it in his hand, ready to ask for three and four, whatever the filling.

The girl's head reappeared and she handed back his book. '*Gracias*,' he said. 'Thank you,' she said, prompted by her mother.

The vendor's tray was empty when it reached Todd. He groaned, clutched his stomach dramatically and rolled his eyes. The girl laughed again, delightedly. Her mother's head disappeared, then the girl's. Words were whispered.

When the girl came back into view, she held something like a rusk in her small hand. She offered it to him.

He shook his head and smiled. 'Please,' she said with a pleading expression.

'*Gracias*.' He took it and ate what was thick dry toasted bread very slowly. She handed him another slice, watching him intently as if to make sure he finished. She gave him six slices in all, until he patted his stomach again and sighed contentedly.

He pulled a pen from his pocket, just a black, two quid retractable, and gave it to her. Her mouth opened and she put a hand to it, too thrilled to speak.

Her mother raised herself up in her seat and turned to thank him. They had a stab at conversing but got no further than the facts he was from England and they lived in Santiago.

He pulled his notebook from his pocket and pointed to the

name of the school he had written down. He'd learned that *'donde'* meant 'where' and tried it out.

He couldn't follow the reply. The mother hailed the stewardess. He handed her his guidebook, opened at Central Santiago. She pointed with a pencil to a shaded square in the middle of the town.

The girl sang several melodious songs for him. He sang a couple of Laura's favourite nursery rhymes, not nearly so well.

No wonder the square was shaded on the map, thought Todd, when a taxi from the bustling station dropped him off.

The canopy of a dozen or so trees spread over slabbed walkways with green benches and marble ledges.

On all four sides were stately buildings – a cathedral with cream plaster, stone columns, angel with trumpet and two brass domes, a grey brick museum, a quaint town hall with national flag flying, but nothing that looked like a school.

What attracted Todd most was the Hotel Casa Grande which had a long open terrace at first-floor level shaded by red and grey striped awnings and white shutters above.

He walked up a few steps from the street and to a small reception counter. Yes, said a smart black receptionist, they had a room. Yes, it was available now.

He showed her the note in his book. Yes, she knew the school. 'Most will have music lesson this morning there.' She pointed with a pencil to the terrace and the square beyond.

He was shown up another floor to a corner room with a slatted door, long windows, dark green curtains from floor to ceiling and a matching bedspread.

He shaved, showered, changed and went down again for breakfast. He helped himself to a plateful of fruit and asked for ham omelette which was cooked on a hot plate while he watched. He went back to the hot plate and asked for and got another.

Hunger satisfied, duty took over and he went to the receptionist to seek telephone codes to England. 'I will do it for you,' she offered, ever helpful.

Again it took some time, and then he was told the extension

was engaged. 'This,' he barked, 'is costing ten dollars a minute, so break in.'

A few seconds later he was talking to PR Pam. 'I've just put down the phone on Morton for the umpteenth time today,' she began.

The paper which had carried the story that so offended the Cuban police would run another piece tomorrow with his agreed quote, she said. 'He drove a hard bargain, wants that next big one. OK?'

'OK,' said Todd, very sullenly. 'Fax the correction here. Hang on.' He leaned across the desk to find a hotel letterhead.

Pam talked while she waited. 'Debby was marvellous, by the way...'

Todd read out the fax number.

After a pause, Pam continued. 'She pulled in vice murders from all over to give the article some clout.'

Todd wasn't really listening. 'And to Captain Nadel at...' He struggled to pull out and open up his map and read the number Harry had given him at the embassy.

What Pam had said finally registered. 'Tell Debby thanks, but to concentrate on the Pattaya job now. Any hired car involved, English connections and, above all, did the police get a postcard?'

Sipping coffee, he sat in a deep wicker chair on the terrace listening to a girls' choir making marvellous music. He didn't understand the words. In the more martial stuff he thought he caught the name of Che here and there, couldn't be sure. The harmony in the slower pieces was note perfect.

The accompaniment – lots of flutes and guitars – was of professional standard, higher than he'd ever reached, having studied music at university, but not hard enough to make a career of it.

He took another sip of coffee; also wonderful. Lord Harvard had good taste, he decided, stocking it at home.

When the class began to break up, he walked down the hotel steps, across a narrow one-way street, into the square and up to a plump middle-aged woman who'd been conducting. 'Do you speak English?'

'*Momento.*' Slightly flustered, she called across to a younger woman who had been playing a flute, said something to her.

The flautist joined them. 'I teach English.'

He fished out his warrant card. 'I am with the British police. I am here to investigate the homicide of two ladies in my country which may be connected with the death of your student, Rosa Melena.'

'Good,' said the flautist. 'It was a wicked thing.'

He pulled out his notebook and pen. 'Could you write down for me the address where I will find her family?'

She took them and wrote slowly on a blank page, handed them back and said, 'I wish you well.'

Sometimes, he thought, walking out of the shade into blistering sun to a taxi rank, this job's dead simple.

Not so simple now, he conceded, standing, sweating, outside the Melena home where he'd alighted from an ancient cab, red Chevy body with a Lada engine, he suspected, from the way it climbed hills.

He knocked on an ill-fitting blue-painted door in a side street, a single-storey breeze block terrace with wooden sloping roofs.

A sad-faced woman in a long black frock opened it.

He held up his card, said, 'British police,' expressed condolences he wasn't sure were being understood.

He was let into a room with three chairs at a bare table and two rocking chairs on a floral-tiled floor. On one sat a black middle-aged man in grey flannels and white shirt who ran mournful eyes over him.

On white-washed walls hung photos of two bright-faced girls of mixed race. They were in sports kit. Attached to the frames were rosettes and ribbons he assumed they had won.

The room was cooled by two fans – one in the ceiling, one on a chipped cabinet where a small statue of the Virgin Mary also stood.

The woman said something to the man, then called, 'Dolores'.

A broad-shouldered teenage girl with skin the colour of milky coffee came in. She wore blue blouse, denim jeans and white trainers.

He repeated all he had said at the street door. 'Sit down, please,' she said, politely.

He avoided the free rocking chair and sat at the table. 'I know this is very painful for you.'

Dolores began to translate for her parents.

'Two other families in England are in similar pain.' Picking each word carefully, he ran through all the other connections – hitch-hiking, motorway, fatal wound. Almost everything he'd learned was confirmed.

The man muttered something which Dolores turned into, 'It is the work of the devil.'

His wife said something which turned out to be, 'We must help you to find the truth.'

Prostitution wasn't mentioned and Dolores was unsure where her sister's shoulder bag had been recovered because it had not been returned. Questions about the postcard from Canada were met with blank expressions. 'We know nothing of such mail.'

He coaxed out of her details of the trip to Havana. She was competing at the stadium, Rosa watching because of her injury.

The championships last four days. Half-way through, Rosa had to return to Kurhotel to see a specialist she hoped would give her the all-clear to resume light training.

'Was she fit enough to walk to the *autopista* and get a lift?' he asked.

'An official drove her from the stadium to Parque Centro. The ride was arranged from there.'

'Who by?'

A cousin, she said. The day before, he had met a tourist planning to go to Trinidad. He agreed to give Rosa a lift and the cousin told Rosa where to rendezvous.

Dolores had not been present and didn't know more details. 'Our cousin has written from Havana with deep sorrow. He feels it is his blame but we do not think so. He was in much upset and did not come to the funeral and we have not seen him to comfort him and discover more of the circumstances.'

'Has he told all the circumstances to the police?' asked Todd.

A grave nod. 'That is why he feels so bad.' She shook her head sadly. 'He is with police, an officer.'

Todd swallowed to stop his mouth from dropping open, like the little girl's on the train, and closed his notebook.

He called at a travel bureau just off the square to book a one-way flight back to Havana and inquire about the flight on to London. It took the usual series of phone calls, two of them disconnected. They couldn't find him a seat to the capital until the following day and nothing was readily available for London. 'Try at Havana when you get there,' she advised.

Suits me, he thought. He'd have a relaxed night. He'd write a few postcards, though he suspected he'd be home three months ahead of them. He'd watch the sun set behind the mountains across the bay, try the grilled sea bass he'd seen on the menu and that Hemingway drink he'd read about – rum, lemon juice, lots of ice and a sprig of mint.

He asked the agent to contact the car hire firm to tell them where their Citroën was parked. More calls and another wait and Todd browsed around the adverts on the walls, wandering eyes stopping at a poster with details of day trips from Montego Bay to Santiago.

Montego Bay? Questions queued up. Jamaica? Where did England start their winter's cricket tour? When was that match abandoned in Kingston? February, was it? Could the Harvards have nipped across here?

He looked round at the woman hanging on to her phone. 'Do you need a visa for this?'

'But of course.'

'Do pleasure boats come into the harbour here from Jamaica?'

'Yes, but they also must have visas.'

He studied the poster. Come on now, he rebuked himself, you don't seriously think that Toby could be both Ed and Stan, do you?

The woman interrupted before an answer could form. Hand cupped over the mouthpiece, she said, 'Are you the policeman?'

He nodded automatically. Immediately different questions crowded in. I never told the car hire firm my job, so how do they know? From Nadel? Must be.

Was that union bod on the plane a fifth columnist? Was my case snatched and searched? And, learning nothing, was Nadel bugging my hotel phone when I ordered the car? Did he have it fitted with a tracking device to keep tabs on me?

If so, someone's spending a miserable day watching that 'car watch' urchin watching the car. Hope Nadel assigned himself to the job personally, the incompetent, corrupt bastard.

He'd covered up a brutal killing, the work of a globe-trotting multiple murderer, to safeguard the tourist trade and the millions of dollars it earned, and to protect a police officer who'd dispatched a teenaged relative on a ride to her death.

He pictured him sitting, hot and hungry, on the kerb with the urchin at his side, in the gutter where he belonged, smiled and went on smiling even when he was informed that the car rental company had decreed that he'd have to forfeit his deposit.

17

No hanging around for a suitcase when he got off the twin-prop Fokker. No need to search in Arrivals for a placard with 'Mr Todd'.

The veteran interpreter came to attention and fingered his baseball cap which matched his mid-blue trousers, gun and baton on its belt. 'Captain Nadel wishes to see you.'

No point in booking an onward flight, Todd decided, anxiety gripping his gut harder than those hunger pangs on the train.

Waiting outside was a white Lada, red lights on the roof already flashing. Police officers in raised boxes at every main junction waved it through. Nothing was said on a swift ride through the suburbs, under the tunnel and along the Malecon.

Todd felt a clamminess that had nothing to do with the afternoon heat. Must protect my sources, he instructed himself. No mention of the FBI or Harry at the embassy. He'd be searched, of course. In his inside jacket pocket, they'd find that letter to Cambridge, the writing on the envelope badly smudged by humidity, and he worried about the girl hitch-hiker.

Red lights still flashing, the Lada rattled over the old drawbridge into the police HQ that had once been a fort. He had a vision of the chains being wound up behind him.

He was about to be confronted by a cop with the reputation of shooting more people than any other police chief, someone he suspected of being incompetent and corrupt, a pseudo stickler for protocol he'd already angered and who'd be angrier still about him trampling uninvited all over his patch. He wondered when he'd cross this bridge again.

'Ah,' Captain Nadel stood. 'Sit.' He motioned to a wooden armchair beside his desk.

Todd stood his ground, grip in hand. I'm not a bloody dog to be ordered around, he fumed inwardly.

Nadel gestured again. 'Please.'

'You speak English then,' said Todd sarcastically.

'Forgive me.' Nadel beamed. 'I swear my oaths much better in Spanish.' He gestured yet again. 'Please.' He put on a pleading expression.

Puzzled, Todd sat, placing the handgrip on the brown lino. The veteran who'd met him at the airport had not escorted him in front of Nadel, but had left the door open. Another officer, black, mid-thirties, sat on a chair at the opposite corner of the desk. He looked like Todd felt – worried.

Nadel sat and picked up a sheet from among the piles of paper on his desk. 'A man of your word.'

Todd caught a brief glimpse of a faxed newspaper cutting he had seen at the hotel in Santiago over breakfast. Only the last paragraph in which he'd been quoted was pleasant reading. The rest made Ed out to be the biggest mass murderer since the Wests.

Nadel shuffled up another sheet which could have been a carbon copy of the fax. 'Received also from our embassy.'

Double-checking, Todd deduced, but then he would have done the same. 'I've seen it.'

'Thank you,' said Nadel politely. 'Now.' Pause. 'Did you have an enjoyable tour around our island, may I ask?'

'Thank you, yes.'

'And what do you think?'

Todd didn't know what to think, really. 'Very beautiful – and the people – '

'Please.' Nadel looked displeased. Had the phrase 'Don't

patronise me' been part of his vocabulary he'd have used it now, Todd guessed. 'About the case, please.'

Todd didn't reply.

Nadel rocked back in his chair. 'I know what you think.' He closed his eyes for a few moments. 'You think I have deliberately, how do you say, held fire, stalled, in my own or my country's interests or both, do you not?'

A panicky thought. Have I said something on those lines in any call back home and been tapped? If so, he couldn't bring it immediately to mind. Ah, well. Time for the truth. He cleared his throat. 'It's crossed my mind.'

A benign smile. 'You are wrong.'

Todd remained on guard, watching Nadel picking up a thick file and placing it in front of him. 'We have worked very hard; sadly, without success.'

He leant forward, elbows each side of the file. 'You wish to share information. Let us do so now.'

Todd bent forward to take his file out of the grip at his feet. His head felt dizzy at the sudden change in tactics, wondered when the catch would come.

Nadel cocked his hand and turned up his palm. You first, he was saying.

'It's possible that our Ed ...' Todd broke off to explain the codename the faxed newspaper article had used and the film it came from.

He began again. There was a possibility that Ed killed in Thailand two years ago, he said, same wound, same roadside disposal of the body. 'Can't be sure until we get more information.'

'Have you also been there?' asked Nadel mischievously.

'Not yet. I came here first because your case is the most recent and therefore the trail is warmer.'

'I wish it were so,' Nadel responded mournfully.

What was known for sure, Todd pressed on, was that he'd killed in the same fashion in Eastern England thirteen months and four months ago. 'On both those occasions he sent a postcard to the officer in charge of the investigations telling him where the victim's handbag could be found.'

Nadel opened and flicked through his file, sliding out a sheet with photocopying on both sides. He rose briefly to hand it to Todd.

One side showed a black and white photo, marked 'Museum of the Revolution', with a missile pointing to the sky. The other side was addressed to Capitaine Carlos Nadel, c/o Cuban Police, Havana, Cuba. It had a Quebec postmark and a Canadian stamp, the colour of which didn't show up.

'It was written in pencil,' said Nadel.

The message was in English and had those +'s and i's dotted with o's that Todd had come to know so well:

T+h+e ... w+a+g+e+s ... o+f ... h+e+r ... s+i+n+s ... w+i+l+l ... b+e ... f+o+u+n+d ... a+m+o+n+g ... t+h+e ... b+o+u+g+a+i+n+v+i+l+l+e+a+s ... a+t ... S+e+r+v+i+c+o ... A+g+u+a+d+a.

Todd stood, head swimming with excitement now, and passed over copies of both postcards addressed to Superintendent Trench, adding, 'He wrote these with a pencil, too.'

For some time, Nadel studied them with his hand over his mouth. Then he slid the hand down to his chin. 'The same man.' He threw himself right back, sighing wearily. 'We have been looking in the wrong place.'

He gestured to the officer who had sat silently and looking drained. 'This is the cousin of Rosa Melena.' Sad eyes flicked in recognition of the mention of her name.

'A very good officer,' said Nadel. Then, smiling affectionately, he spoke in Spanish and the cousin perked up a little. 'He speaks no English,' Nadel resumed in English. Then: '*Mais un poco français ...*'

That mixture of languages finally coaxed a smile out of both the cousin and Todd.

'... because one side of his family came originally from Haiti.'

Back in excellent English, Nadel explained that the cousin had visited the Melena sisters at the stadium while off duty, then gone on his beat round Parque Centro.

A tourist approached, pointing to a road map. He asked a question in English which the cousin didn't follow. They got no further in Spanish. In French, the tourist asked the way out of town because he was going to Trinidad the following day to see the old colonial sights.

In broken French, the officer managed to tell him that he had a relative who wanted to go there on that same day and she would guide him. A rendezvous was arranged at the flag-pole in the park.

He got a message to Rosa to tell her of the arrangement and described her volunteer driver.

Two days later her body was found on the ring road at Cienfuegos. A week after that, the postcard arrived.

'How did he know to address it to you by name?' asked Todd.

Nadel tightened his jaw and wagged his head into a Don't Know.

Todd persisted. 'Has your name been in any newspaper lately?'

Nadel shouted something in Spanish at the opened door, then he flicked his head at the officer and continued, 'He did not get the tourist's name, naturally. Nor was he told where he was staying, nor see his car. The man was on foot at the time. It is a busy and difficult place to park there, as you know.' He smiled slyly to tell Todd he knew where he'd been staying.

Todd smiled back. 'And it is the custom here for police officers to arrange lifts for schoolchildren.'

Nadel chuckled, impressed.

'What did the man look like?' Todd asked.

Another sheet came out of the file. 'Six foot – or feet, is it? – high.' He held a hand to the top of his head and said something in Spanish. The officer said, '*Si*.'

'Not thin, not fat, but fit, no facial scars. Less than average – how do you say – width.' More Spanish and another '*Si*.'

'Age of forty years, perhaps plus. Face that is pale to our eyes, but has seen some sun, certainly; blue eyes.'

Every line was being translated now and Todd was thinking of Raymond Chivers, Nixon's prime suspect.

'Wearing fawn trousers, check shirt of Scottish sort with short sleeves,' Nadel continued.

Every translation was being confirmed with '*Si*.'

'Blue baseball cap with "Labatt" written here.' He drew a finger across his forehead. 'Canadian beer.'

'Also widely available in England,' Todd put in.

Nadel looked downcast. 'I did not know so. You see, with the cap and the postcard coming from Quebec, we thought he was

Canadian. We have spent many hours searching through records for a car hired on a Canadian driving licence, hotels and airline passenger lists. We have expended our normal budget three times.'

'That's understandable,' said Todd sympathetically. He held a finger to his sideburns. 'Hair. Did he see any hair here?'

Nadel interpreted the question and reply. 'The colour of our palm trees.'

'Silver?' Todd cross-checked.

'Yes.'

'And his eyebrows?'

Nadel checked in his native tongue, then. 'The same.'

Not Toby Harvard on a day trip then, Todd thought, unless he uses dye.

The veteran officer came in, offering a newspaper cutting to Nadel. He waved it towards Todd who took it. He looked down on a group of police officers with medals on their chests. Among them was Nadel and he could make out his name in the story below.

'Decorations for work on the Pope's visit,' Nadel explained.

'When did it appear?'

'Early in February.'

'And this is from *Granma* of which there is an English edition?'

A grave nod. 'What do you think about it now, Mr Todd?'

Todd had been thinking of hardly anything else over a lonely dinner the night before and on the flight back and he began to speak very fluently.

'Let's forget Thailand until we have more detail. Our Ed's mad, insane. He killed his first English victim, took exception to what the police officer in charge of that inquiry said about robbery and sent him a postcard to put him right.

'He enjoyed the whole experience, all good fun. He killed again just before Christmas and had more fun at the police expense.

'But then we hit back by releasing copies of the postcards to the media.' He explained the news conference. 'Panicked him a bit, but he'd learned a lesson.

'He came here. Like it or not, I have to say he'd see lots of gin . . .' He stopped and looked for help.

Nadel gave it. '*Jineteras.*'

'His problem was to get one out of town on the road, to fit in with his homicidal fantasies of whisking them away to their deaths.

'Tragically . . .' He nodded at the cousin and prayed what he was about to say wouldn't be translated because he looked to be suffering enough. '. . . his good deed presented him with the opportunity. Ed no longer cares if his victims are engaged in vice or not. He just wants to kill. He also wants the added kick of making fun of us.

'He got your name from the paper. He had heard about your students asking tourists to post letters in need of urgent replies. Maybe he'd been asked by one – in which case, a male student, bound to be, or he'd have killed there and then.

'He believes that he . . .' Another nod at the cousin. '. . . thinks he is French-Canadian so he asks a French-Canadian to post the card to you from Quebec. It gave him time to get off the island.'

A question occurred that he should have asked earlier. 'Did you find Rosa's bag?'

A stern look. 'You have the answer to that, surely?'

The coach at Kurhotel had been on to him and he'd cross-checked with the Melena family, Todd suspected, shaking his head.

'Yes,' Nadel's face filled with regret. 'There was only thirty pesos in it. Not wages of sin, would you say?'

'No.'

'That is why I was very angry when you last visited. I was angry for her family.' He threw a hand out towards the cousin. 'For him, her school, her sport.'

'I am sorry,' said Todd apologetically.

Nadel bowed slightly. 'You have put matters right and we will say no more.'

Nothing was said for some time, Nadel in deep thought. Then: 'Can this Ed be caught?'

'Why not?' But, Todd accepted privately, it would have to be done the admin way, the boring way. 'Can you let me have a list of all Brits who came in, say, a week before your name appeared in *Granma* and who were still here when Rosa died?'

A pained expression. 'It will run to many thousands.'

'We can put them into our special computer . . .'

Nadel talked over him. 'I mean, to extract British-held visas only will take much work, many, many weeks and I have little manpower and none of your computers.'

'How about overtime?'

'I have little money also.'

Todd fell silent. Is this the catch? Is he angling for a backhander? Does he realise I've got much of the story under my own steam, so he's decided to sell the rest and pocket the cash?

Every round-the-world traveller tells tales of bribery in Latin America. But this is communist Cuba. Is he setting me up? If I offer a capitalist hand-out, will he nick me and win another medal for his incorruptibility?

Either way, I need that list. Tricky, this. He picked his words with care. 'Would two hundred dollars fund some overtime?'

Nadel smiled very thinly.

Todd hurried on. 'It is customary in my country for one police authority to compensate another financially for requested services.'

Nadel looked away, deep in thought. 'It would pay for many hours.'

Todd explained about the impounded deposit for the car he'd rented. 'One phone call from you would get it back, no doubt.'

It would be a cash advance, a down payment, he went on. The bill for the rest would be settled when the list was received.

What did it matter to him if the invoice stipulated some account in somewhere like the Cayman Islands? he asked himself. He had a multiple killer to catch.

Nadel took half of the next day off and picked up Todd at the Hotel Inglaterra. Their first call was at the car rental office. Todd handed the cash on to Nadel. He insisted on signing a receipt for it. 'To protect us both,' he added. Todd pocketed it, filled with remorse.

Then he was shown the sights. No one selling sex or cigars came within yards of them as they strolled round the lovely squares, but Nadel had them spotted. 'You will take back bad memories of them.'

'Balanced by the recollection of a mother who gave me breakfast,' Todd replied, and he told him the story.

Nadel noticed Todd's limp and heard that story, too. No tales of derring-do came from him. A modest as well as honest man, Todd decided.

At a shaded coffee shop, he bought three packets of ground to take home. At the airport he planned to get cigars for Ben Nixon and Jacko Jackson, Cuban shirts for Em, a T-shirt with Che on the chest for Laura and Havana Club rum for himself.

Music from highly skilled buskers followed them everywhere. It's in their souls, thought Todd, but if he heard 'Guantanamera' one more time Nadel might just have the first case on his hands of mass murder by a musical tourist.

They ate sandwiches and drank Cristals at a humble little café with open sides on the Malecon. At the old Presidential palace, an imposing white building, he saw *Granma*, the vessel that brought Castro home, and the missile from the picture postcard. He recalled Nixon's wisecrack about phallic symbols.

Splattered on the walls of the marble staircase were bullet holes from the shots fired when the revolutionaries stormed the palace. 'Any of these yours?' Todd jested.

Nadel smiled, very wickedly. 'I know what your friend Harry Armstrong . . .'

He even knows his name, more than me, Todd realised.

'. . . and the CIA – or was it the FBI? – say of me. I do not wish to spoil a legend by telling the truth. Let us just say that when I fire I never miss.' He looked down at Todd's gammy leg. 'That way you do not get wounded.'

Todd wasn't sure who was jesting now.

18

A box of twenty-five Romeo y Julietas, Ben Nixon's bribe, was handed over during breakfast, just the two of them, at the lakeside motel.

He was more excited by the description Todd brought home of Rosa's killer than the cigars. 'It could match Chivers.'

'Or, with a bottle of hair colouring, Toby Harvard,' said Todd. For the first time, he shared his suspicions.

Nixon whistled softly. He conceded he hadn't found any incriminating evidence, certainly not a Labatt's cap, when he searched Chivers' home while he had him under arrest on the say-so of the call girl before she recanted.

He'd tracked down his divorced wife, but she wouldn't dish any dirt; to protect generous alimony, he suspected. 'He just buys his bloody way out of trouble.'

'Our trouble,' sighed Todd, 'is that neither name shows up yet.' Nadel had a team of clerks working for thirty six hours non-stop, going through immigration records for both Chivers and Harvard without success. Now they were extracting all British names, but it might take a month or so.

Nixon ate another forkful of scrambled egg, very slowly. 'Do visas give home addresses?'

'Sure. Why?'

He'd been worrying about Chivers' passport, which was virgin, he said. Chivers claimed to have lost his old one and obtained a replacement. 'Maybe he's got another tucked away somewhere under a false name. He could have a second home we don't know about, an accommodation address or something.'

He had obtained some of Chivers' financial statements. Since he hadn't applied for a court order, Todd judged it prudent not to ask how.

Oddly, Nixon went on, there were no items of expenditure around the time the killer had been in Cuba. 'There may be bank accounts and credit cards we don't even know about.'

He planned to trace cars Chivers had owned in the past couple of years. Now he would add hired cars to his jobs to do.

To ease his workload, Todd volunteered to tackle Harvard and son. Then he told Nixon of the problems the leaked story about his trip had caused.

Nixon worked his lips, didn't whistle this time. He was on his travels at the time, but knew there had been a flap. Debby had told him when he checked in on the phone that she'd had to work all through one night on needless details of vice crimes – 'to dig you out of some sort of shit with the police over there.'

'Until I've flushed out the new mole, I'm not giving her this Cuban stuff to feed to HOLMES,' said Todd, firmly. 'I don't want anyone calling it up on screen and leaking it to Morton.'

Nixon grinned, almost boyishly. 'I'm 'onoured you don't think it's me.'

Todd poked fun. 'You're too 'umble to be a suspect. No desire for personal publicity, no ego, see.' He shook his head rather sadly. 'Without the right image, you're never going to make it to the top.'

Nixon looked him straight in the eyes. 'Who, in his right mind, wants the soddin' top?'

Sometimes Todd asked himself that question, most recently on the ride in the police Lada from Havana airport. Eventually, the answer was always the same: Me.

The official debriefing in the Quiet Room was an anticlimax. Nixon asked a few soft questions, pre-arranged over breakfast, Carole Waites hardly any.

The farm show, she reported, where her Stan's series had started a year earlier, had passed without incident this time. 'No movement at all,' she added, lethargically. In Todd's view, she'd been off the boil since that raid on Maddox had been legally blocked.

While Nixon had worked hard to find a way round the veto, she'd lost heart. Or maybe she was just winding down for an imminent family holiday in France. She looked as though she needed it.

Debby was in high spirits. PR Pam's request to pillage by remote control files on sex crimes had caused computer chaos, she said, but they'd been deleted now and things were back on an even keel.

Police in Pattaya hadn't a clue about the nationality of the killer who slashed the throat of their prostitute and dumped her by the expressway two years ago. 'He could have come from anywhere.'

Their pathologist said pre-mortem and fatal wounds had been inflicted with scissors, but that was the only connection with Ed's crimes here. There'd been no postcard to any police officer disclosing the whereabouts of her handbag which had never been found.

'I'd still like the names of British visitors in Thailand at the time,' Todd said.

Debby nodded.

'Then what?' asked Carole in a tired tone.

'Give them and the Cuban list to HOLMES and see if we get a match.'

Beth, Harvard's housekeeper, served Cuban coffee in the sitting-room; too good an opening to miss, so Todd abandoned the introduction he had rehearsed on the way here in the misty rain.

'Tasty, this.' He sipped and studied his china cup. 'I've just brought some back with me from Havana.'

'Oh,' Lord Harvard's eyebrows rose with interest. Toby showed none at all.

'A forensics conference.' Todd looked up. 'Ever been there yourselves?'

Harvard shook his head briskly. 'Too much red tape, I understand.'

'Ever been to Jamaica?'

'Not in years, I'm afraid. We usually stick close to our place in Barbados, don't we?'

He glanced rather anxiously at Toby who said 'Yer' offhandedly.

'You didn't see much cricket then?' asks Todd.

'One Test and a one-day international.' Harvard launched into a critique of both games and, from England's point of view, the whole unsuccessful series.

It gave Todd time to think. He could ask to see their passports and the log of their cruiser, he supposed, but why show his hand? He'd wait till the visa lists came in.

He fell back on his original plan, apologising for the inconvenience caused by his officers going back through the travel records of his employees.

'It's bound to have caused your staff unease. It might help if we let it be known that we had gone right to the top excluding no one.' He gave the dates of the murders in March and December last year and asked, 'Would you mind telling me where you were?'

'Certainly, if it assists,' said Harvard pleasantly, rising from a deep armchair with a pattern, sage leaves on a cream covering, that matched the roomy couch where Todd sat.

'Why?' asked Toby bluntly, sitting at a polished table in front of a long narrow window with a view of the recently mowed park.

Todd shrugged. 'Good public and industrial relations.'

'Yes...' Toby motioned towards his father who had reached the door. He laughed harshly. '... but he doesn't drive a lorry.'

So taken aback was Todd that all he could say was, 'Sorry?'

Toby began to mumble. 'Thought it was only lorry...'

'That...' His father stood at the door, hand on the brass knob, and spoke sharply. '... was changed to all drivers.'

Toby shook his head slowly, confused.

Todd leaned forward. 'What made you think we were only looking at lorry drivers?'

Toby looked away, dumbly defiant.

Todd shot a long look across the room at Harvard. 'You're aware, are you, that we are checking all company drivers, not merely – '

'Yes, yes, yes.' Harvard broke in again, irritated. 'My transport director told me.' He pulled back the door and disappeared.

Nothing was said for several minutes, Todd's mind racing, until Harvard reappeared, head down, thumbing a small black diary as he walked back across the thick, tan-coloured carpet. He sat down again and reeled off where he'd been on both dates and who'd seen him at the crucial times.

'Thank you.' Todd turned to Toby. 'Would you mind telling me where you were – ?'

'Don't work at the plant.'

Todd explained he was now talking about the nights of the non-fatal attacks.

'Why?' A belligerent tone. 'It's nothing to do with me.'

'We're asking everyone between fifteen and fifty. People who were out and about on those nights might have seen something helpful to us. Now, let's start with the first Saturday in May last year.'

The reply came immediately. 'Don't know.'

Harvard looked ill at ease. 'Wasn't that the day you damaged your hand?'

Again his son answered without a pause for thought. 'I don't know.'

'Yes, it was,' said his father, positively.

Toby thought at last. 'Yes, it was. At the hospital, I was then.'
A petulant expression. 'Satisfied?'

'How did that happen?' Todd asked casually.

'A barney at the farm show.' Toby brightened a bit at the memory. 'Some stallholder was offensive to Beth's daughter.'

'I remember seeing that in the file, now you mention it,' Todd chattered on. 'Maddox, wasn't it? What did he say to upset her?'

'Reckoned she wasn't wearing underwear. Very rude, he was. Can't have that. She's only fourteen or fifteen.'

'Do you know Maddox?'

'No,' huffed Toby.

'Have you seen him before or since?'

'No.'

'It was all settled,' said Lord Harvard with a soothing smile.

Toby glared at Todd. 'Are you satisfied now?'

'Thank you, yes.' Todd went on through the dates on which Stan had struck.

The initial response was always an irked 'Don't know' or 'Can't remember.' Harvard helped out on a couple of occasions by referring to his own diary and recalling they were in together.

He summoned back Beth and asked her to fetch a kitchen calendar. She was able to alibi Toby on another occasion. On the rest Toby claimed to have been in alone. Mostly inconclusive, Todd decided.

'He's not usually out much,' Harvard said with an expression that was becoming increasingly concerned.

Todd reached the night of the last attack. Toby didn't even remember it was Haxey Hood day and that he'd shown Todd around the stable block until reminded.

When the vital time was reached, Beth claimed to have been cooking in the kitchen and to have seen Toby. Everybody but Todd seemed to have forgotten that Harvard had told him he had given her the day off.

Toby didn't bid goodnight when Todd rose, just turned his head away and sat staring out of the window.

'Sorry about that,' Lord Harvard apologised at the black door. 'He's not in the best of moods today.'

Neither was Todd. Someone had told Toby that the hunt for the killer was focused solely on lorry drivers employed by the company. Harvard had heard from his transport director that the inquiry had been widened to include all drivers, but clearly had not informed his son.

So who, he was asking himself, walking back to the stable block, told Toby about lorry drivers in the first place?

'Good journey?' asked Dr Peck, strolling into the Quiet Room.

Did he read Morton's piece or has someone told him about my trip? thought Todd bitterly. Normally he used the word 'fascinating' that came to him when he first walked the streets of the old city. Today he said, 'Interesting.'

'Any joy?' asked Peck.

Sitting at his desk, Todd gave his standard reply. 'We'll know when we've got and gone through all their immigration records.' He gestured to a chair by the wall. Peck sat down.

'I've asked you in, because I'm rather disturbed,' Todd began.

Again Peck treated him like a patient. 'What's the problem this time?'

Todd told him of his call on the Harvards. 'Toby thought we were looking at only lorry drivers employed by his father's company.'

A puzzled frown.

'On my instructions the search through records was extended to all drivers.'

From his surprised look, it was clearly news to Peck.

Todd continued, 'Why did Toby think that, do you suppose?'

Peck bristled a bit. 'How do you expect me to know?'

Todd stiffened his tone. 'Have you discussed your profiles with the Harvards?'

No reply.

'Yes or no?' Stiffer still.

'I'm trying to think back.'

The answer came slowly. He'd dined at Temple Hall on more than one occasion, having become quite friendly with Lord Harvard since the extortion case. Obviously the attacks on the Isle had been a topic of conversation. 'Everyone's talking about them.'

Todd didn't respond, forcing him into repeating that Lord Harvard had been interested in psychology since his days in the Army Medical Corps and had used Peck's services in-company.

He seemed to make up his mind and straightened himself to take the consequences. 'I'm sure we did. Yes. Why?'

'Because the agreement between us is that I and I alone should make public your findings.'

A little wave of a hand, dismissive. 'It was a private dinner party. That's hardly making matters public.'

'They are members of the public. I take it Toby was present when you discussed your interest in lorry drivers.'

Peck sighed. 'You've always displayed more than a passing interest in him, haven't you?' He smiled thinly. 'I do assure you, you are looking in the wrong direction.'

'How can you be so certain? He's being treated in Harley Street. He's not a patient of yours.'

'Do you seriously think that Lord Harvard would fund a reward to capture his own son?'

'So,' said Todd, slowly, 'he told you that, did he?'

'Well, yes, it was mentioned.' Peck realised another confidence had been broken and tried to pass it off. 'Come on now. I don't intend to broadcast it, I do promise you.'

Compromised, Todd chided himself, alone with his scrambled thoughts in the Quiet Room. I've compromised the whole sodding inquiry.

I've accepted thirty grand and free accommodation from Harvard whose son is a suspect. I've hired a specialist who's close to him, both professionally and socially: too close.

Peck came cheap for all the time he's put in; too cheap. Could he be getting supplementary pay from Harvard, some sort of retainer, a guarantee of future consultancy work? A bribe to point me away from Toby?

'You're wrong about this,' said Sergeant Reith, sitting in the passenger seat of the Volvo.

So everyone keeps telling me, Todd brooded. 'Just tell me about her.'

'She's an ex-stripper, worked the clubs around Sheffield.' Reith began to rattle through Beth's background from memory faster than Debby could pull out and screen a record. 'She split up with her husband, so she's had to fend for herself and daughter. Old man Harvard gave her a job. The bungalow comes with it. A good mother and worker. She's as honest as the day is long.'

Beth opened the back door of a bungalow with a long garden dotted with trees, apples among them, their white blossom gone. 'Tom,' she said, smiling warmly. She addressed Todd more formally. 'Hello, sir.'

Reith cocked his thumb at his boss. 'He wants to ask you a rather personal question.'

Todd came straight out with it. 'Have you ever had underwear stolen from your clothes-line?'

Her face went from bright to thoughtful. 'Missing. I couldn't say stolen.'

'What went missing?

'A couple of pairs of pants.'

'Whose?'

'Mine and my daughter's.'

'When?'

'Ages ago.' She seemed to think for ages. 'About a year back.'

'About the time of the farm show?' Reith ventured.

'About, mmm.' She gave it deeper thought. 'Yes. That week, I think.'

'You didn't report them missing,' he complained, looking a little let down.

'They could have blown away in the wind. I never gave it much thought. They weren't exactly G-string stage custom.' She smiled mischievously and Reith shuffled unhappily from one foot to the other.

'Tell me,' Todd resumed, 'does Toby Harvard ever pop round here – socially, I mean?'

'Once a week.' She gestured to the garden. 'He cuts the orchard. He brings his own machine. It's too much for us.'

Reith leant forward slightly. 'And, tell me, does Maddox, the woodman, ever call?'

'We get our logs off him.'

*

'It's Maddox,' said Tom on the way back.

'You want it to be Maddox,' Todd replied, not at all testily, rather admiring Reith's faith in his conviction. 'I'm going to see the legal director and tell him, bugger the consequences. I'm taking out search warrants on 'em both.'

'When?'

'Next week.'

'Not Monday, I hope. It's Whit bank holiday, the Wesleyan Street Market.' He looked up into a blue, cloudless sky, the year's first really warm spell, praying, Todd guessed, that the weather would hold.

Carole Waites will be on holiday next week, Todd reminded himself. It had been his idea to flood the Isle on special events days when Stan had struck in the past. He'd have to personally ensure the patch was well covered. He glanced away from the windscreen towards Tom. 'I doubt that Maddox will be out and about.'

'He seems to be making a good recovery, from what I've seen of him.' Reith revealed he hadn't relied entirely on the surveillance camera half-way up a tree near Maddox's workshop and caravan. In person, in his own time and in civvies, he'd been making spot checks on him. 'When there's no one around he moves quite freely.'

Evidence that might be useful when Maddox's damages claim comes to court, thought Todd, impressed. 'Is that camera on Temple Hall in good working order, too?'

'Perfect.'

He drove some way in thoughtful silence. 'I don't think we should rely solely on them. Let's set up evening observations on both. Who do you want?'

'Need you ask?'

'A bottle of rum on it?'

'Rather not, sir.'

That's both drinking and gambling, really walking sideways, for a devout Methodist like Tom, Todd acknowledged, a touch guiltily.

19

All quiet in the Quiet Room.

The pubs in flag-bedecked Epworth had still been busy when Todd pulled out, but the stallholders at the Wesleyan Street Market, some dressed in eighteenth-century costume, had packed up and crowds had gone after an open air service round the grave of John's old dad up in the churchyard.

Tom Reith's prayer had been answered with a dry day, lots of sunny spells among the clouds. He'd clocked on by radio at eight. Todd playfully expressed the hope that he was dressed in camouflage more suitable for a stake-out in a forest than the black tricorn hat, white stockings and fancy shoes he'd worn for his spell behind the New Mechanics library stall of used books.

The camera at Temple Hall had monitored the return of Lord Harvard and son. The look-out assigned by Todd had reported nothing since. No movement had been recorded at Maddox's workshop. Reith's radio was silent.

Gone ten now, dark outside, and Todd was bored. Can't complain really, he told himself. This is the first bank holiday you've worked since New Year's Day and that wasn't on this job. If you can call it work, sitting here, with your legs on the desk, reading about Grimsby Town's promotion in the *Evening Telegraph*.

He'd give it till midnight, then home.

The peace was broken by a ringing phone. 'Chief Inspector Waites, please,' said an urgent female voice.

'She's on holiday, I'm afraid.' Todd introduced himself. 'Can I help?'

The caller was a staff nurse at the Cottage Hospital. 'Can you come up straight away? There's been another attack.'

Todd pulled his legs off the desk, picked up a two-way radio in a black case out of a drawer and trotted, gut rumbling, to his car in the courtyard.

It was a very short drive. As he approached the main entrance up the narrow driveway from the stable block, an oldish rust-coloured Rover came the other way, so fast that he had to use the grass verge to avoid it.

Two men were in the front. Todd couldn't be sure, but he thought he glimpsed the weedy figure of Adams behind the wheel.

The staff nurse was waiting at the entrance to Admissions. Her blue uniform was crisp. Her delivery matched it. 'Name: Beverley Pacy. Aged eighteen. Doctor's with her now. Not life-threatening.'

Todd asked what had happened. Her reply lost all crispness. She'd been brought in by private car, not in an ambulance, she explained, so there was no briefing from the paramedics.

As she understood it, she had been attacked by a man in a mask while she was walking down a lane to meet her boyfriend. She managed to struggle free and ran into a pub where she knew he'd be waiting. He had brought her in by car.

'Where's he now?' asked Todd, glancing around the room seeing no one waiting in a row of chairs.

An uncertain expression. 'Gone to fetch her mother, perhaps?' She paused. 'I'll find the duty doctor for you.'

It was a long wait, as usual in hospitals, before the doctor Todd had first met on Haxey Hood night appeared down a corridor. 'We're going to have to give her something to calm her down, so . . .' He shrugged, short of saying, 'You can't see her yet.'

'That's OK,' said Todd. He wasn't going to do the interview anyway.

'She's hysterical,' the doctor went on, 'and she's taken a fair amount of drink.'

Todd asked if she had said anything, but learned no more than the nurse had told him. The doctor lowered his head and his voice. 'It's not the same as the rest. There are superficial marks on the body, certainly, but scratches rather than cuts, and her briefs are in place.'

'Maybe she fought him off,' Todd ventured.

'Maybe.' The doctor's expression was neutral. 'You'll know better when you've talked to her tomorrow. Station an officer here overnight, if you wish.'

Todd thumbed on the transmit button of his radio and lifted it to his mouth. 'Detail a woman officer – '

Control broke in. 'You ought to know, sir, that Sergeant Reith has asked for back-up with silent approach.'

Todd crossed the Trent at Gainsborough, then headed north, more than twenty miles in fifteen minutes, the last few on bad roads that led to the edge of the forest.

He glided to a halt when a peak-capped patrolman stepped out from a bank of fern and flagged him down. He wound down the window. 'Is he OK?'

'Fine, sir, and in communication.' The patrolman pointed down a dirt track. The moon and stars were behind still purple clouds, but a wooden shack was clearly visible in an oasis of light among dark pine trees. 'The workshop. He's close to, keeping silent obs.'

So silent that all Todd could hear was a constant low humming. Not wildlife, he decided. Must be a generator providing power to the workshop. Within a triangle of pale yellow from the opened double doors was a dirty white caravan, interior lights on, and a car, all lights off.

He had no time to make out the model or colour as an engine came frighteningly alive and two beams shot out from thick bushes to his right.

'It's on,' said the patrolman, very loudly. He turned and ran towards a patrol car Todd hadn't even noticed behind a line of tall rhododendrons with drooping purple flowers.

He slammed down his feet, raced through the gears, had only reached third when he skidded to a halt, bonnet almost up to the open door of the clapboard workshop.

Two figures were running out towards him, heads down. One was big, one was small and that's all he made out.

He flung open his door. The smaller figure ran into it. He yelled obscenities, fell backwards, rolled, scrambled on all fours among the forest litter.

Todd was out and astride him before the patrol car stopped behind him. He pulled his captive's unresisting arms behind him and shouted over his shoulder, 'Cuff this one.' Two patrolmen appeared at each shoulder. One took out handcuffs as he knelt among the crackling twigs.

To the other, Todd called, 'Go after that big bugger.' He stood up gingerly. Pain stabbed his right knee.

The first patrolman bent, yanked the captive to his feet and turned him round.

Adams, face bloodied, blinked mournfully at him.

Todd limped into the brightly lit workshop, lined with planks and poles. Sitting on a stool was Maddox, head hanging. He was in his underpants. He was shaking uncontrollably, and not from cold.

Round his neck was a noose. Rope dangled down his white bare chest that glistened with sweat. More rope was tied to a beam above him. The ends had been neatly cut.

Stooping, with an arm around Maddox, was Reith in dark civvies. In his other hand was a Stanley knife.

Scattered about a chipped bench was a pile of clothes, different colours, all vaguely H-shaped.

What the fu – , he began to ask himself, and then he could see that they were women's briefs which had been cut on both sides.

Beams from flashlights danced among the trees. The barking of dogs and the shouts of men echoed through the forest, putting wildlife into scampering flight.

Maddox and Adams had gone now in separate cars to different police stations.

Reith had slumped down on the stool. Beside him Todd placed a hessian sack on a heap of fresh sweet-smelling sawdust; pine from its scent.

He lent right back and stretched out his legs so his head dropped lower than Reith's to give the appearance of sitting at his feet. He looked up to him and said, 'What happened?'

From his hide in a patch of broom, Reith had seen the Rover arrive, recognised it as belonging to Adams's father. His son was at the wheel. He also identified Ivers as the passenger.

They drove up to the caravan and went in without calling or knocking. He heard muffled voices for some ten minutes or so, then shouting. He couldn't make out the words.

The caravan began to rock on its wheels. Dressed only in his underpants, Maddox was dragged out and frogmarched into the workshop by Ivers and Adams.

Reith crawled closer through the undergrowth, had to lie doggo when Adams made a quick return trip to the caravan.

Eventually, he got close enough to the workshop to hear Ivers shouting: 'You've had a go at my bird, you bastard.'

Maddox, crying: 'Not me. No. I've not been out all night.'

Ivers: 'Don't give me that shit. You've had a go at her, like the rest.'

Maddox: 'Not Bev. Never would. No. Never. She's yours.'

Adams, sounding breathless: 'Look what I've found under his mattress.'

Ivers, screaming: 'Pervert. You dirty pervo. On here. Stand on here. On here.'

Reith could hear sobs and pleading and scuffling.

Ivers again: 'Where's the fucking knife?'

Reith couldn't hear the reply, only what sounded like a stiff drawer being pulled.

Adams, excited: 'This one.'

Maddox, miserably: 'Yes.'

Ivers, again: 'You're going to tell us all, the lot, and then we're going to turn you in.'

Maddox, begging: 'Please. No. Please. Please.'

Ivers, at the top of his voice: 'The lot.'

'OK. OK. OK. The rest, yes, but not Bev. And not those dead pros. Honest.'

Ivers: 'We want everything, I said.'

Maddox: 'Honest. I'm telling you . . .'

Ivers: 'Bev, too. Why Bev, you bastard?'

Maddox: 'If that's what you want me to say. OK, but please, please . . .'

Solemnly, as if giving evidence, Reith looked directly at Todd and said, 'I judged it no longer safe to delay taking action.'

He burst in. Maddox was standing on the stool, the rope round his neck. At the sight of him, Ivers and Adams fled, one dropping the Stanley knife.

'I didn't give chase,' he monotoned on, 'as I thought cutting free Maddox was the first priority. He was shaking violently and on the point of collapse.'

Todd could barely hold off trembling himself. Jesus, this had been a skin of the teeth job.

Tom looked away, picking his words carefully. 'We'll never know if they would have gone through with it, staged it as suicide or something, but I reckon Maddox was telling the truth. It was as close to a condemned cell confession as I'm likely to hear.'

We've got Stan, no doubt about it with all his trophies scattered around, Todd agreed privately, but there was no joy in that realisation. A second or two later and we could have had a lynching on our hands, all because you didn't have the guts to take a legal gamble and sanction a raid on this place and find the evidence that's been here all the time. Phew, this was a close call.

He patted Reith's knee. 'Thanks, Tom.'

A smiling inspector tapped on the car window as Todd was about to start up. 'Got the other one in a hedge-bottom a mile down the road.'

'Good,' said Todd. Then: 'Shine your light on this door, will you?' The inspector switched on his flashlight. 'Is it marked?'

'Rather badly, sir.'

Shit, thought Todd. 'Ah well.' Suddenly, and unusually, feeling very humble, he flashed back a smile. 'Well done and thank all the boys, girls and dogs for me, will you?'

All night, with just a two-hour break for refreshment and rest rather than a nap at Reith's bungalow, and all next day, Todd and the sergeant shuttled between police stations.

The solicitor who had issued the writ against Todd turned up at all three interviews, but, after a brief talk with Maddox, announced he was withdrawing from representing him.

'Conflicting interests,' he explained. You mean, two bites at the legal aid cherry with Ivers and Adams are better than one, Todd thought bitterly.

In the Padded Cell, sitting alongside a new lawyer, Maddox looked almost relieved. 'It's all over, you know. Behaved myself, I have, for five months now, stayed right outta trouble.'

'Sure it wasn't your broken knee keeping you in at nights?' asked Todd acidly.

Maddox firmed his tone. 'I'm over it, all finished, I'm telling you.'

It had started years ago, he said, with stealing panties from clothes-lines. 'I don't really know why.' His expression was puzzled. 'I just like the feel of 'em, I suppose.'

Twelve months ago, he had taken the briefs from Beth, the housekeeper's washing. Boozed up at the farm show, feeling daring, he'd poked fun at her daughter. 'It was just a bit of harmless chat.'

And it would have gone no further, he insisted, had Toby Harvard not punched him on the nose. 'He made me look such a wimp in front of her.'

He got a lift home from hospital where he had to leave his truck on medical orders. He brooded on it and decided to vent his frustration on Beth's daughter. He'd built his own boat which he moored by the river. He took his bike across on it.

Once he'd landed on the Isle, he felt woozy and decided it was too far to cycle to Beth's bungalow. Instead he pounced on the first girl he saw walking on her own.

'All I wanted were her briefs. I didn't mean to be that rough. Sorry.'

He was taken through all the attacks, identifying his victims by the colour of the panties which an unhappy-looking Reith held up one by one, pinched between two fingers and at arm's length.

After the first attack, Maddox planned more carefully, sometimes crossing the river by boat with his bike, sometimes camping overnight in his truck.

On those occasions, Adams also slept in the back. 'He was always so spaced out he never knew if I were there or not.'

Mrs Adams, he confirmed, had washed the clothes he wore on Haxey Hood night. 'They were landed up with mud in all that rain.'

It had been Ivers' idea to go on vigilante patrol after the Hood night attack, he went on. 'He wanted the reward and his face on

TV and things. I couldn't very well refuse or they'd have smelt a rat, wouldn't they? I had to go along with it.'

Quite apart from his busted knee, he had lost both his boat and his bike, swept away in the big tide which came with the floodwaters in January.

He hadn't been to the street market, stayed in all day, working on the stool Ivers and Adams made him stand on. 'Told 'em that, I did. They wouldn't believe me. I never did that to Bev. Asking for trouble, that would be. He'd kill anyone who did. He damn well nearly killed me. He wouldn't believe me. But I didn't. I've stopped. It's over.'

At Scunthorpe police station, Adams, a pink plaster on his cut forehead, told how Ivers had dropped Maddox once he was off the road with his busted knee. 'All he ever wanted were free lifts, his wheels, like.'

Adams had gone off him, too. 'He's a total prick.' Whenever they were out together in the truck delivering logs, he was always pipping at young girls. 'Going on about 'em and knickers and giggling.'

Adams began running things back through his mind after Chief Inspector Waites gave him such a grilling following the road block. On second thoughts, there were a couple of occasions when he half remembered Maddox moving about in the back of the truck on nights of attacks.

He'd been to his caravan and workshop and seen all the tools, including a Stanley knife. Maddox had shown him hard porn magazines which featured slashings and lots of blood.

He told all to Ivers. 'I reckon it could be him.' Ivers was against shopping him, decided they should bide their time to get more evidence so there'd be no argument about who qualified for the reward.

Last night, he and Ivers had been with Bev in a pub. They were playing darts. She said she was off to see an old friend, up on holiday, and would be back in an hour.

Ivers grew worried when she was half an hour late and walked out to look for her. 'He suspected she was up to something.'

'Who with?' asked Todd.

Adams named a local youth. He went on to describe how Ivers

had found Bev running down the lane, screaming and saying a masked man had held her up with a knife and had tried to rape her.

Adams had the use of his father's car while his parents were away for the long weekend. Ivers fetched him out of the pub to drive her to hospital. On the way, she described her attacker as short and stocky and said he smelt of pine.

'That's him,' Ivers declared after leaving her in Admissions. 'Let's go and get that evidence before someone else does, give him a pasting and turn him in.'

Maddox confessed in the workshop and told them where he kept the knickers and his Stanley knife. 'We weren't going to kill him, just want to get the truth out of him, that's all.'

At Gainsborough, Ivers cockily corroborated all that Adams had said. 'Done folk around here a good turn, us. You'd never have caught him. You should be giving us that reward, not locking us up like this.'

Encouraged by his solicitor, he went on, 'He done all of 'em, you know. My Bev too. Nobody does that to my bird. Got that?' He slapped the table hard. 'Nobody. I could have killed him, but I didn't want to. I want that reward, want to see justice.'

'From what I overheard,' Reith pointed out, 'Maddox didn't admit the assault on Beverley.'

'He denied the lot at first, only natural. But he admitted it all in the end.'

'So would you, standing on a stool with a rope round your neck,' said Reith, drily.

In the Quiet Room, Todd told Beverley Pacey, 'We are not satisfied with the account you gave to this officer . . .' He flicked his head to a tired-looking WPC sitting at his side. '. . . in hospital earlier today.'

He looked down on a medical report. 'The doctors say you had intercourse last night, but no bruising occurred, suggesting, in their opinion, the possibility of consent. In their view, the marks on your person were made by fingernails, not a knife.'

Then he waved a statement Reith had taken. 'Furthermore, we have interviewed a young man.' He named him and looked up. 'As a result, I am arresting you for wasting police time.' He told her of her rights.

Even if he'd stood her on a stool with a rope round her neck, the confession couldn't have come any faster.

She'd wanted rid of Ivers for months. 'He's a psycho and a bully. He knocks me around when he drinks which is most of the time.'

When he went to jail for driving while banned, she started seeing and sleeping with a younger chap. She had to go back to Ivers on his release. 'Or he'd have done us both.'

She was still seeing her new love on the side. On the night of the market she told Ivers she was going for a quick drink with an old schoolmate in another pub in Westport. Instead she met her lover. They had sex in a barn.

She was a bit drunk and scratched his back. He scratched her back, harder.

She knew Ivers would demand sex that night and was terrified he'd question her about the marks. When she saw him walking towards her in the lane, she panicked and pretended she had been attacked.

She remembered the description of the masked man from the papers and just trotted it out.

'Why did you say that he smelt of pine?' asked Todd. 'That wasn't in the papers.'

'Jennie told me.'

The WPC looked sideways, frowning quizzically.

Todd double-checked. 'The girl who was attacked on Haxey Hood night?'

Bev nodded. 'We work together at the timber firm.'

Well, thought Todd when he was alone again, he wasn't going to break the news to Ivers that his girl had made it all up because she'd been screwing someone else. He phoned his lawyer and told him. 'Rather you than me,' he added, gleefully.

*

From Sheffield, where he was tracking his prime suspect Raymond Chivers, Ben Nixon phoned in. He whooped with joy, though it wasn't his case.

Todd phoned Carole Waites at her holiday villa. 'Sorry I couldn't be there,' she said, understandably disappointed.

'So am I,' Todd replied sympathetically. He sketched in the background.

'Oh, that bloody writ,' she sighed.

Todd sensed she was still blaming him and said nothing.

She recovered. 'Merv Peck was on the ball again, then, by the looks of it. Phone him and say thanks, will you?'

Dr Peck was unassuming about the accuracy of his profile. 'Pity we didn't get him earlier,' he said glumly.

'No harm done,' said Todd cheerily.

Debby Thompson was even more subdued, paled when she heard how Reith had stopped a possible lynching. 'Are you OK?' asked Todd. 'Exhausted,' she said. She looked it. Todd told her she was well overdue for a few days off and to take them.

With no one to drink with, just a celebratory half-pint would have done, Todd drove home, eighteen hours behind schedule.

Next morning Maddox appeared in court, accused of nine attacks. Ivers and Adams followed him into the dock, charged with conspiracy to murder. To make sure they didn't meet up again in prison, the magistrate remanded Maddox to Lincoln jail and the other two to Nottingham.

Soon after the story broke on local radio, the Quiet Room phone rang. 'Harry Morton here.' Post Mortem sounded very cross. 'I thought we had a deal.'

'Sorry?' Todd felt more jet-lagged than on his return from abroad.

'For getting you off the hook in Cuba. So why wasn't I told about this yesterday? It's a pearler of a yarn.'

'But we'd charged them by mid-afternoon. Once they're charged it's contempt of court to go into detail.'

Morton snorted derisively. 'I could have worked round it.'

'I'm not running the risk of having a case thrown out because of prejudicial publicity.' Todd decided to enjoy himself. 'Anyway, having built them up as heroes, did you really want to turn their up story into a down.'

Morton was not amused. 'We had a deal.' He slammed down the phone.

Todd held on to his, studying it. That's right, he acknowledged. If Morton had got the tip early enough, before it became *sub judice*, lynch mob caught in the act would have been a big earner for him.

A smile spread over his face. Morton's mole had missed out.

20

SUMMER

In his blue Cuban short-sleeved shirt, Todd sat at his desk in the Quiet Room, anticipating, if not trouble exactly, then certainly inconvenience.

Lord Harvard had phoned, requesting a quick chat. Since he owned the place, Todd had said, 'Any time.' He fretted that he was about to get notice to quit, and, while hoping not, had to accept that the main cause of local concern was behind bars now and the stable block was underused.

Carole Waites and her team had returned to base. Most of the files on Maddox and his assailants had been completed while she was on holiday. The Crown prosecutors didn't think conspiracy to murder would stick against Ivers and Adams and were preparing to scale down to grievous bodily harm, still worth four or five years apiece; about right, Todd judged.

No such luck for Maddox. His new lawyer was probing his background in the hope of running a medical defence. He was facing unlimited time in the State Special.

Debby Thompson's week off had turned into a month, with a doctor's certificate diagnosing severe stress. Todd had phoned her seaside flat a couple of times. 'I'll drop in to see you when I feel a bit better,' she said, somewhat sadly, making it sound like she planned to hand in her notice.

He didn't tell her this, but she wasn't being missed that much in the Hayloft. The workload had been cut by half and a woman sergeant she'd trained up on HOLMES was proving an efficient deputy.

Nixon's squad continued to operate from the incident room, tracking down and grilling weirdos. He still fancied Chivers as Ed, and had come up with the fact that he was a regular customer at a porno shop. Neither he nor Todd wanted the hassle of relocating.

Dead on time, Harvard tapped on the door and politely waited for a 'Come in.' Just as politely, he took off a straw hat matching a lightweight oatmeal-coloured suit that must have been useful in the Caribbean. 'I owe you an apology,' he said, even before he sat down.

Here it comes, Todd groaned inwardly – eviction. He motioned to a chair.

As he sat, Harvard nodded beyond him to the window through which the sun shone. 'The grass. It's very unsightly.' Todd hadn't even noticed how long it was till he half turned. 'I'm afraid Toby did his hand in again yesterday, same hand.'

He'd broken a couple of fingers, driving in a fence post with a lump hammer, and couldn't handle the mower's controls. If he wasn't fit soon, an outside contractor would be hired.

Todd told him not to worry on his account, but Harvard explained that cutting the hospital grounds was their responsibility, too.

He's got to have more on his mind than uncut grass, Todd knew. He wondered if he was expecting an apology in return for quizzing Toby. He wasn't going to get one, not until he'd seen those lists of tourists to Cuba and Pattaya.

'You did well on the masked attacks,' said Harvard, still not getting to the point. 'Everyone on the Isle is greatly relieved, a load off every family's mind. Congratulations.'

'Tom Reith did most of it,' said Todd, giving credit where it was due.

'Will he qualify for the reward?'

Todd shook his head. 'Part of the job.'

'So who should we pay?'

Todd explained that the reward stipulated information leading to the arrest and conviction of the attacker and the case was unlikely to be heard for months yet. 'Nobody, the way things stand. Certainly not Ivers and Adams.' He smiled thinly.

'How about Dr Peck?' asked Harvard.

Todd worked his head into a No.

'But he was accurate, wasn't he?'

So, Todd realised, the old boy has seen the whole report, not just heard a bit of dinner party chit-chat concerning his company's drivers. He didn't respond.

Harvard had to go on. 'He's had two remarkable successes – here and with our extortionist.'

And one failure on the fire raiser, Todd reminded himself, but he said, 'It was sound stuff, but, as an insider on the inquiry, he doesn't qualify for the reward.'

'Oh.' A mixture of surprise and disappointment flitted across Harvard's face.

'Why?' asked Todd, bluntly.

'I thought his research ought to be financially encouraged, that's all.' Harvard seemed to dismiss it. 'Never mind.'

They talked about Toby's injury for a while, then, obliquely, Toby. 'Have you children?' asked Harvard.

'A small daughter.'

'You worry about them all the time, don't you?' he sighed, heartfelt. 'It gets no easier as they get older.'

They drifted on to cricket and it was another ten minutes before Harvard rose, almost reluctantly. 'I'll let you get on.'

Todd swivelled in his chair, looking out of the window, still not noticing the long grass or pondering the problems of parenthood.

What was all that about? he wondered. A plea for understanding Toby? Or seeking the all-clear to bung more money at Dr Peck?

Ah, well, at least he's not evicting us. And he let it drop.

Dr Peck arrived, unannounced, a couple of days later. Todd interrupted a call home to say 'Come in' and carried on talking to Em as Peck did so.

Putting down the receiver, Todd nodded to a chair, but Peck remained standing in front of the desk, looking beyond him through the window. 'What a mess.'

Look in the mirror, mate, thought Todd. His face was drained and his brown sports jacket and cords dowdy on another lovely day. Without turning his head, Todd explained the grass was long because Toby was out of action with smashed fingers.

'Yes, I know,' said Peck, finally sitting. He'd heard about it over dinner last night. 'John . . .'

Who the devil's John? Todd queried himself.

'. . . had me round for dinner at Temple Hall last night, a sort of thank-you.'

Todd had been acquainted with Harvard on and off for more than six months and never knew his first name was John. 'I was thinking of something on those lines myself.' Todd smiled. 'The budget's holding up, despite Cuba.'

'Oh, please.' A flustered headshake to say: You misunderstand me. I'm not bumming a free meal.

Peck forced a smile back. 'That's what I came to talk to you about. Cuba. Now that Stan is out of the way, I've been addressing my mind to Ed.'

He paused. 'These sex tourist murders.' Another pause. 'You've never briefed me on them, shown me photos or statements.' A hurt expression. 'I thought you might have done.'

'To be honest,' said Todd, truthfully, 'you can forget all but two of them.' He explained how the story that had made the paper had been concocted to placate the Cuban police. 'The Pattaya one we still know little about. A prostitute with a slashed throat by a roadside and that's all.'

He shrugged. 'Cuba? A teenager with a slashed throat by the roadside, but not a prostitute.'

'Not a prostitute?' Peck echoed. 'That could change things.'

'Yes, but he could have thought she was.' Todd enlarged on his own encounters with *jineteras* on the streets of Havana.

'Was there a postcard?' asked Peck.

'To the police via Canada.' Todd explained how returning tourists posted letters for locals.

Peck looked away in thought and then back again. 'Is there any chance of my seeing a file?'

'You can have what we've translated. It's not much. We're still hoping for more.'

Peck cocked his head, slightly. 'You must see that this could materially affect my original conclusions.'

Todd nodded, acknowledging that the more cases any forensic scientist studied the more he or she learned. After all, he had been forced personally and dramatically into a change of mind about the identity of Stan.

Both rose and walked out of the Quiet Room. Climbing the stairs to the Hayloft, Peck said, 'Would you mind if once again I didn't pick your brains until I've seen what you've got and compared it with the other two cases?'

'Fine,' said Todd, easily.

In the HOLMES room, the acting team leader began to pull together copies of the Cuban case.

'Have you heard from Debby?' Peck asked her.

'Making slow progress, I'm afraid,' the sergeant replied.

He turned to Todd. 'Have you?'

'Spoke to her last week. She was pretty low, but said she'd pop in to see us soon.'

'Only ...' Peck hesitated. 'She was supposed to join us for dinner last night, John's specific invitation. She didn't turn up.'

Odd, that, thought Todd idly. A night out might have done her good.

'We called, but only got her answering machine,' Peck went on. 'I called again today. She's still out.'

He looked round the room addressing everyone in it. 'Does anyone know if she's gone away?'

No one did.

Oh, dear God, no.

Todd sat at his desk at HQ, feeling hot and cold flushes chasing each other around his bloodstream.

Chin on clenched fist, he was staring down on a seaside postcard addressed to Superintendent Trench.

Every communication arriving at HQ for Trench over the last seven months had been bagged in a see-through holder, touched by no one other than the mail room supervisor and brought to Todd's office immediately.

Predictably, publishing the Chesterfield and Hull postcards in the New Year had resulted in half a dozen or so hoaxes with +'s and i's dotted with o's, but that nuisance mail, all of it written in pen and with first class stamps, had dried up long ago; so long ago that he'd almost forgotten them until now.

But this was new; the same, yet different.

He looked at the picture again – a statue of a small boy wearing a cap and standing on a plinth in a lily pond. He wore one boot and held up the other in his right hand. He couldn't decide what was odd about it.

He turned the plastic holder and saw again the green second class stamp, franked three days earlier. His eyes went to a printed caption at the bottom. 'Cleethorpes, Boy with Leaking Boot.'

He looked at the message again. The smudged pencilled writing reminded him of the letter he'd mailed for that Cuban hitch-hiker, the envelope so soiled by humidity that he wondered sometimes if it ever found its destination.

Either this postcard had been carried in a pocket in the summer heat or a very sweaty hand had written it. Or maybe looking at it through its cellophane wrapping was playing tricks on his eyes.

For the umpteenth time, he read the message, 'T+h+e+ . . . w+a+g+e+s . . . o+f . . . h+e+r . . .'

Already he'd studied it for so long that he had no need to read further. Think, he urged himself. What's the same? The style of writing? Let experts decide on that. OK, then. The address box, use of pencil, the second class stamp.

So what's different? The choice of picture, he finally decided.

OK, Peck didn't pick up on the possible phallic symbolism of the crooked spire and Wilberforce monument, but Nixon had, albeit jokingly. And the Cuban postcard showed a missile. Yet this one has a small boy with a leaking boot.

Something's wrong and I don't know what, a feeble voice within said. Then bloody well find out, urged a firmer voice that sounded like his grandfather's.

He sat there, losing all track of time, his mind going back to the New Year and beyond, recalling who said what, where, when, picturing the face, time and place.

Oh, Jesus, no. His brain went numb. Then, thawing slowly: I can't believe this.

That lecturing voice again: Police work isn't about belief. It's about finding proof.

Now, you have had a thought, a dreadful thought, but that's all it is. The trick with a thought is to research it and turn it into an idea and then a plan.

He thought of the scene in Maddox's workshop. Is that the way? he asked himself urgently. Dangle some rope and invite the killer's head into it?

Maybe. Think about it, research it, talk about it with people you trust, plan. Don't snatch up that phone, barking orders. From now on in, act cool or you'll never get the proof.

He picked up the phone. Calmly he told his secretary, 'Chief Inspector Nixon, please.'

Hanging on to the receiver, his eyes went to the ceiling. Oh, God, let me be wrong about this.

'Trouble, Ben,' he said when Nixon came on. 'The worst sort.'

Nixon heard him out, then confirmed his darkest fears, with, 'Oh, fuck me, no.'

'Urine,' said the Forensics man over the phone.

'What?' Todd was standing, receiver to his ear, at his desk in the Quiet Room, about to leave with Carole Waites and Dr Peck for a hastily arranged thank-you dinner for catching Stan.

'Urine,' Forensics repeated. 'A drink-drive sample burst in a mail bag and contaminated several documents.'

'Just as well I didn't handle it then.' Todd smiled grimly to himself. 'How long will it take to decipher?'

'If we can.' A gloomy tone.

'What do you mean, "if"?'

'It's soft lead, not ballpoint. There'll be no indentations.'

Todd groaned.

'We'll do our best.'

'As soon as poss, please.' Todd put down the phone and walked to the door where Peck and Carole waited.

Outside, Nixon was heading along the walkway from his office. Bedding plants in the stone troughs had started to wilt without Toby's daily watering.

Todd told Nixon about the call he'd just taken. 'The lab's not all that confident they'll get a result.'

'Does it matter?' asked Nixon as they crossed the courtyard towards Todd's car.

'Does what matter?' Carole demanded, walking between them and irked about the conversation going on over her head.

Todd didn't reply until everyone had got in. Another wages of sin postcard had arrived at HQ addressed to Trench, he told them. The message looked as though it had been written in pencil in pouring rain. 'Now we know why.'

'You might. I don't,' said Carole huffily.

Running through the gears, Todd explained the tests that Forensics had done for him and the conclusion reached. 'If the address block had been as badly pee-stained, it would never have arrived.'

'Wish it hadn't,' Nixon grumbled in the front passenger seat.

'Come on, Ben,' said Todd, gruffly. 'It can't be ignored.'

Nixon told one of his tales about a hoax 'wages of sin' card that took two weeks to track down to a husband fed up with his wife spending housekeeping on scratch cards. 'I'd have charged him with wasting our time, only I didn't want more publicity and more fucking phoney cards.'

'What's on the front?' asked Carole from the back.

'The Cleethorpes boy with a leaking boot,' said Todd. 'It's a sort of landmark there, apparently, a gift from an immigrant boy who made it big in shipping or something.'

'Debby lives there,' said Peck sitting next to Carole.

'You're not suggesting there's a connection, surely?' said Nixon.

'Oh, no,' said Peck softly. 'Is she coming tonight?'

Carole nodded towards Todd. 'Neither of us could raise her.'

Todd parked on the brick frontage to the Red Lion. Tom Reith was waiting in the comfortable bar, drinking tonic water. Todd ordered scotch and waters for Peck and Carole, a pint of Guinness for Nixon and a half of lager for himself.

They carried their glasses to a corner by the laid, unlit, fire. They sat in low leather couches. Todd looked around at the plaster and beam ceiling and the panelled walls. 'Nice place, Tom.'

'Hmm,' said Tom, non-committal.

Peck took a longish drink. 'I'm concerned about that postcard. Can I see it?'

'There's a copy back at the incident room.' Dully, Todd added, 'For what it's worth.'

Nixon took a much longer swallow. 'It's another phoney. We've had scores of 'em.'

'No more than half a dozen,' Todd corrected him.

'You see . . .' Peck lowered his voice and looked around the bar, not quite asking: Is it all right to talk in here? 'I've been studying the Cuba file.' He looked at Nixon, almost apologetically. 'I'm beginning to modify my view.'

Nixon smirked into his pint glass.

'It seems I may have underestimated your Ed. He's clearly got available money to go to places like the Caribbean and Thailand . . .'

'Pattaya is not firmed up,' said Todd, very firmly.

'No.' Peck shook his head in acceptance. 'But rather than a lorry driver, I'm moving towards a motorist in a higher socio-economic group. He appears to have more intelligence than I credited him with.'

'Exactly,' exclaimed Nixon. 'He got a tourist to post his card from Canada back to Havana to confuse the police there. He's changed tactics. He's not going to revert to sending cards to Trench direct.

'If Ed reads the papers, as you say, he'll know he . . .' He nodded towards Todd. '. . . is running the show. Trench hasn't had a mention in the media all year. If and when we ever hear from him again, it will probably come via Greenland addressed to him.' Picking up his glass, Nixon worked his head in Todd's direction again.

'Don't you see . . .' Peck's response was just as emphatic. 'In February, he was a stranger in a foreign land, a totalitarian state. He wanted his fun, yes, taking the rise out of the police, but he didn't want to run the risk of being trapped on a small island.'

Nixon interrupted. 'You're second-guessing.'

Peck ignored him. 'That's why he smuggled the card out to Canada. Here he knows the lie of the land, is free to come and go as he pleases. He's reverted to type.'

Everyone sipped, no one commented.

'All I'm recommending is that this new postcard shouldn't be ignored,' Peck concluded.

'I'm not ignoring it,' objected Todd. 'I've got the lab boys trying to clean it up so we can read it fully.'

'I mean . . .' Peck's face had become mournful. '. . . in connection with Debby.'

Nixon shook his head as Peck repeated what he'd told Todd about her not turning up for dinner with Lord Harvard. He turned to Carole. 'Have you spoken to her recently?'

'Last weekend. She seemed on the mend.'

'But no one's been able to reach her this week. I've tried.' Peck circled his head to take in both Carole and Todd. 'You've tried.'

Nixon shrugged, unconcerned.

'I'm very, very worried,' Peck went on. 'She told me once that she thought she had been followed home.'

'She never told me,' said Carole, alarmed.

'I told her to.'

Todd groaned.

'Come on, boss,' Nixon pleaded. 'Why should anyone want to follow her, do her any harm?'

No one had an answer, so Peck asked a question. 'Have you interviewed any suspects at the incident room?'

'Several,' Nixon snapped.

'Did she come into your office . . .'

Nixon came in too quickly. 'Never.'

'. . . with info you requested, walk past the cell?'

'Never,' Nixon repeated. 'She knows no suspect personally.'

'She'd know their secrets from records though,' Carole pointed out, deep in thought.

'Aren't you both forgetting something?' Peck raised his voice slightly. Then, quieter: 'Ed's not out to silence anyone. He wants to make fun of you. What greater taunt . . .' He left it there, his face funereal now.

'Er.' All eyes went to Tom, whose own were on Nixon. 'That suspect you're very keen on.' He was too well trained to mention Chivers' name in company that wasn't all police. '. . . I drove him away when you'd finished with him. You'd impounded his car for tests. Remember?'

Nixon nodded.

'She was looking out of the HOLMES room when we drove away.'

'Yes,' said Nixon, edgily, 'but did he look up?'

'I can't honestly say.'

Everyone fell into a silence. 'If Ben and his boys are overstretched, I don't mind putting out feelers,' Carole eventually volunteered.

Nixon relented. 'And I'll circulate Vice Squads to see if any girl is missing, unaccounted for, off the streets.' He pulled a pained face. 'Again.' He straightened it. 'Tomorrow.'

'Can't we start right away?' asked Peck anxiously.

'Let's eat first,' Nixon begged.

'Gone off the idea,' said Peck. 'Sorry.'

'Me, too,' said Carole.

Todd sighed.

Dinner for five became dinner for two.

Back in the stable block, Peck turned a photocopy of the postcard over and over. He peered to inspect the postmark. 'Did it rain the day this was posted?'

'It's leaked urine,' repeated Todd patiently.

Carole came off the phone. 'Still on answering machine. I'll get on to her family first thing in the morning.'

'Not now?' asked Peck anxiously.

'I'll have to get into her flat to get her mother's number.'

'Can't we do it tonight?'

'Go home, Merv,' said Carole sharply. Then, soothingly, 'I'll let you know the minute I've located her.' She touched his arm. 'Don't worry yourself.'

He looked worried to death.

21

A cadet in shirt-sleeves burst into the Quiet Room and blurted 'Quick' without adding 'sir'.

Panic on, Todd deduced, gut tightening. He got up, walked round his desk and followed him down the covered walkway. The sweet smell of mown grass hung on the warm air.

Slumped in a chair in front of the U-shaped reception counter was Toby Harvard. The top buttons of a dark blue boilersuit were undone. His face was glistening and ashen, his eyes shut.

The WPC on desk duty came in from the direction of the kitchen, carrying a glass of water. 'He just ran in, out of breath, looking like that. He tried to say something and almost passed out.'

She offered the glass to Toby who opened his eyes to take it in both hands. He put it to his mouth. His hands shook so badly that he spilt more down his square chin than he drank. By way of an excuse, he freed a hand and held it up to display two fingers covered in stained gauze.

Todd knelt on his good knee on the grey-blue carpet. 'I'll run you to the hospital.'

Toby's head shook now, very determinedly. His free hand pointed in no particular direction. 'In the grounds.'

Todd was about to take his hand, decided it would bring more pain than comfort. 'Let the doctor give you a quick check-up.'

'N-n-no.' Toby pulled himself not quite upright. 'In the grounds. By the gang-mower.'

'Have you had another accident?'

'N-n-' He was stuttering in shock. 'No. Not me. Someone has. Dead.' He tried and failed to get the glass back to his mouth. 'You go. I'll be all right. You go. Please.'

Todd drove out of the open gates of the stable block, stopped, engine idling.

He looked ahead of him up the narrow driveway to the Cottage Hospital. A few patients sat in the July sun at tables on the terrace.

He looked to his right and saw that the grass had been cut all the way to an ancient wall that marked the southern boundary of the grounds.

Left now and his eyes found a grey tractor several hundred yards away, close to the motorway.

He pulled his left hand down and moved in low gear towards it. There was no track but the earth had been baked hard and the grass cut so short that it was more straw-coloured than green. The going was reasonably smooth.

He could see two sets of mowers behind the tractor. Just beyond that was a three-bar fence that divided the grounds from the motorway.

The double mowers had cut a wide short swathe close to the fence from the west. The far set looked out of alignment with its twin machine. A strip of longer, greener grass remained ahead of the tractor.

He pulled up, switched off and got out. The engine of the tractor throbbed constantly above the more distant whine of motorway traffic. The cab door was open.

He took a step up and heaved himself inside the cab to turn the key in the ignition. He looked over the steering wheel and out of the other side and he saw what had knocked the far mower off line.

A body lay on chewed-up grass. One arm had snagged in the blades and been partially torn away. Exposed skin was mottled, so discoloured that it was difficult to tell if it was black or white, let alone a man or woman. The task, he recognised, would be made all the harder by the damage the cutters had caused.

The ground around looked spongy, mossy green compared to the paleness of the shortened grass. The scent of new mowings was being overpowered by the rank, unmistakable smell of a death that had occurred some days ago.

He'd been expecting, fearing this, but he was still unprepared. His eyes could take no more. He closed them and looked heavenwards. God, he cursed, you've let me down.

The stable block had never been so well staffed, the Quiet Room so noisy.

An even bigger team of officers was at the north end of the grounds where Todd had left them erecting a high tarpaulin square around the corpse to prevent passing motorists from seeing the dreadful job they were about to undertake.

A body bag, black plastic with a zip, was on the cut grass but would not be filled for hours yet, until the scenes of crime specialists and photographers had finished.

Their leader walked up to Todd's desk. He wore white overalls, white cap, green boots. A face mask hung from his chin. 'A woman, sir, white, naked apart from pants, a sort of pinkish hue, at first sight, but we can't be sure 'cos they're faded, you see.'

Todd had seen and nodded.

'Throat injury. Impossible yet with these temperatures to estimate how long she's been there.'

Todd looked at Carole Waites. 'Have you got her dental charts?'

'Yes.' In the week since their cancelled dinner, Carole had got just about all there was to know about Debby Thompson. 'I'll go and sit with her mum until we find out for sure.'

'Take her to a safe house, if she'll go,' said Todd, already worried about the media fall-out.

He transferred his gaze to Sergeant Reith. 'Break the news gently to Dr Peck, will you?'

PR Pam had arrived with two assistants. Her clipboard was clutched to her ample bosom. 'No media inquiries yet,' she reported.

'Can you hold them off for an hour till Carole and Tom have made their calls?'

'I'll try.'

'OK then.' Todd leant back to think. 'Body believed to be that of a woman found in hospital grounds.'

'You'll not get away with it.' A bleak expression. 'They came here for the reward announcement, remember, so they'll know you're based here.'

Todd shrugged; nothing he could do about that. 'No hint of a name, age, cause of death, nothing like that. We need time.'

'Say that because of the weather conditions and elapse of time identification might be difficult.'

'OK.' He wasn't interested in any of this.

'A statement in an hour and you'll be available for newsbites and footage here, say, two hours after that?'

'OK.'

The courtyard was crammed. There was none of the orderliness of the news conference that had launched the inquiry.

Even in the stable block's halcyon days of hunting, there couldn't have been more baying, more jostling for position.

Scores of journalists surrounded him, but, oddly, no Morton. They were shouting, elbowing each other with cameras and tape machines, to get closer, record every word, film every expression.

He felt like a hunted-down fox encircled by hounds about to make their kill.

He read from a statement Pam had prepared, had no need to invite questions.

'Is this the work of Scissorhands?' demanded a northern voice belonging to a reporter he'd not seen before.

'We'll be able to answer that when the post-mortem examination is complete.'

'But you are treating it as his work?' he insisted.

'Our initial inquiries are proceeding on the lines that it may be linked with our other two cases, yes.'

'Only two?' growled a veteran.

'We've said that all along.' Pam glowered at him.

He smirked knowingly. 'Officially, anyway.'

'Has he dumped it on you as an act of defiance, do you think?' asked a woman with a tape recorder.

'We'll know that when we catch him,' Todd replied.

'You've had fifteen months since the first murder,' the veteran needled, 'and the second was just down the road ...' He thumbed westward in the direction of the Chase. '... so when will you catch him?'

Hang on, Todd wanted to say, we have collared a nine-times sex offender while we've been here, got him bang to rights, but he knew that would be contempt of court. Instead, he trotted out the last tot-up Debby gave him, more than a month out of date now, on the number of actions the squad had taken.

To queries on wounds and what the victim was wearing, he had a stock reply, 'Early days. We'll know when the PM's complete.'

'Are you linking it with any missing prostitute?' asked another questioner.

'When we've an age and description for the victim, we'll be looking at the files of all missing females,' Todd answered.

'Is it connected with all those sex tourist killings abroad?' asked the veteran with a cynical smile.

He must be a rival of Morton's, getting his own back, because he missed the Cuba story, Todd speculated. Tomorrow he'll hang me out to dry. He waffled about Interpol co-operation and computer analysis of several unsolved murders overseas.

The questions kept on raining down but were becoming repetitive and Pam broke it up, breasting her way through the throng, Todd in tow.

In the haven of the Quiet Room, he lowered himself into his chair, drained. 'I didn't notice Morton there, did you?'

'No,' said Pam. 'He's not been on the blower either.'

Reith had returned from his assignment. 'Dr Peck took it very badly. He's convinced it's her, blames himself for not collecting her for that dinner date with Lord Harvard.'

Nixon, summoned back from surveillance on his prime suspect, smiled grimly at Todd. 'Keep your nerve, boss.'

'M-Way Madman Dumps Victim On Police Doorstep' was the headline that just about summed up the rest.

Todd had stayed overnight at Reith's bungalow and, surprising himself, had managed four hours of sound sleep. He looked better than most who crowded into the Quiet Room.

'Definitely her, sorry to say,' said the Forensic chief. 'Her teeth are a perfect match with the dental chart. Cut throat, but such is the deterioration and the mower damage that we're not sure about the other knife wounds that are his usual trademark.'

Oh, God, Todd groaned to himself. A workmate.

'How long she been there?' asked Nixon, matter-of-factly.

'A guesstimate, at this stage.' The specialist shrugged. 'A couple of days either side of a week.'

'Will you be able to narrow it down?'

Another nod, less certain. 'From the incubation period of insects' eggs, maybe, but, to follow the time-scale and get conditions right, those experiments will take time to set up. Don't expect any answer for two to three weeks, and even then . . .' He shrugged again, promising nothing.

Todd looked at Pam. 'Once they've got her ID, the media will call her a police girl, won't they, whether she's a civvy or not?'

It was Carole who responded first. 'A WPC is with her mum at a holiday cottage in the Wolds, well out of it. It's a small family, widely scattered.'

'Any close friends?' Todd asked.

'It was the devil's own job to trace anyone who said anything other than "A nice, quiet girl who kept herself to herself."'

Pam finally came in. 'If we issue a couple of photos of her, make their job easier, they won't be so keen to go knocking on doors, asking questions that could lead to her job here coming out.' She turned to Carole. 'Have you got one?'

'Several.' Carole thought. 'So her employers are the weak link.'

After the meeting ended, Todd called the computer company who had hired out Debby's services to the police force to operate and train staff on HOLMES.

He broke the news to the personnel director who said the usual shocked, 'Hard to believe ... How dreadful.' Then she said, 'We haven't seen her here for some time, of course, so we know nothing of her social life.'

'That's understandable,' Todd agreed, 'since she's been working with us.'

'But not for several weeks, as I understand it,' the director said tentatively.

'She's been on sick leave,' Todd confirmed.

'So she told us in her resignation letter.'

Todd was jolted. 'She'd quit then? She hinted at it but never actually told us.'

'She was going to, once we had accepted it. She said so in her letter.'

'When did you get her resignation?'

'A week ago.'

'What reason did she give?'

'She said she'd explain personally to you. We knew she'd been suffering from exhaustion, thought she might get better and rethink it. We haven't formally accepted it yet.'

Todd came to the point of his call. 'If the media get in touch, just say she was an ex-employee who had left on health grounds, will you? We'd appreciate it if you didn't mention she was contracted out to us.'

'It's always our policy to safeguard customer confidentiality,' she said, rather tartly.

'The Cuban embassy,' said Todd's secretary from HQ. 'I'm rerouting him.'

Soon a new voice, male. 'Mr Phillip Todd?'

'*Hola*,' said Todd, cheering up.

'A package for you. Air courier from Havana. From Captain Nadel. You are expecting, yes?'

The short tongued accent was music to his ear, sadly only distant music with the passing of time. 'Is it very big?'

'The size of a small telephone book only.'

He said he'd get a dispatch rider to pick it up.

The HOLMES sergeant looked harassed when she heard what was on the way from London. Thai police had faxed their list. The sheet ran from the machine across two or three yards of floor in the Hayloft.

Next day, the story naming Debby was front-page again, but there was no reference to 'police girl'.

Morton's mole still hadn't resurfaced and Todd knew why.

The sergeant sat at the HOLMES keyboard in the Hayloft and looked over her shoulder at Todd, as if expecting him to raise a conductor's baton. Not knowing the score, he merely held out a limp hand and half twisted it. After you, he was trying to say.

'Let's see if we can get a match on the Pattaya and UK lists first, shall we?' she suggested.

Totally in her hands, he nodded.

She straightened her back, shuffled her bottom on her swivel chair.

This is it, Todd knew. His heart screwed itself tight.

She tapped figures and letters, answered screened questions with ticks. Up came a block, white letters on black: 'Find match'. Beneath it were half a dozen lines that stayed empty for several seconds, an agonisingly long time.

In the blinking of an eye, a name and address filled the top line.

Standing at the sergeant's other shoulder, Nixon gulped noisily enough to have swallowed his Adam's apple.

Todd pressed his lips together, biting on his apprehension. OK, they had established he was in Thailand when their vice girl was killed and dumped, but there was nothing at all in the Pattaya file to prove he was the murderer.

The other spaces stayed unfilled and 'Command completed' appeared on the bottom line.

The sergeant swivelled round. 'Shall we match Cuba with UK?' This time she didn't wait for an answer. She turned back. Her fingers played. More letters, figures and ticks and the same black and white block appeared.

A much longer wait, half a minute that seemed like half an hour. Simultaneously top and bottom lines were filled with 'Nil' and 'Command completed'.

Nixon shook his head heavily and gritted his teeth.

Beginning to get the hang of it, Todd said, 'Try his name and home address against the Cuba file.'

She poked figures with one finger and then touch-typed in the details her first search had thrown up. She selected and pressed the button to tick 'Find'.

All too soon 'Nil' and 'Command completed' came back.

Shit, Todd screamed inwardly. We've blown it. Depression rushed through him like an aegir tide from the Humber down the Trent.

'Er ...' Nixon blew out air over his lips, making a sound like a horse whinnying. '... can you compare addresses?'

'What files?' asked the sergeant.

'All UK addresses with Cuba visas.'

The keys clacked under her feather-light touch. Seconds dragged by. An address which meant nothing to Todd skittered across the top line.

Nixon gripped the sergeant's shoulder as if making an arrest. 'Got him.' He beamed at Todd who frowned back. Nixon's hand was resting on her shoulder now. 'Can you ... er ...'

The sergeant helped him out. 'Source them?' She tapped out fresh instructions, ticked, and there they were in black and white.

An address which Nixon had dug up on his travels and the address of the holder of a visa who had gone through Passport Control at Havana airport ten days before and four days after Rosa Melena was murdered.

The same.

'Is it enough?' asked Nixon, looking at the screen as if he couldn't believe it.

Not to convict him, Todd realised. 'It's enough to get a search warrant on that address.' Pointlessly, he pointed to the screen.

Nixon looked from it to him. 'To pull him in, I mean?'

Up to now he hadn't cracked and Todd doubted if his solicitor would let them have a real go at him.

'Couldn't we stick him up on an ID parade and fly that Cuban cop over?' Nixon persisted. 'Jesus, that should be enough for the magistrates to grant an application for us to hold on to him.'

Yes, but for four days maximum, Todd knew.

Only four days and so much to do.

There was Nadel to brief. He'd bump another poor old Saga traveller out of his seat – at the point of his oft-used gun, if necessary – to get Rosa's cousin on board, so no problem there.

There was Lord Harvard to see and two prisoners at Lincoln jail, a trip to the State Special, computer experts to consult, and Post Mortem Morton to bribe, so much to do and all in four days. Could it all be done? Todd asked himself.

'Yeah.' He smiled confidently, his mind made up. 'Pull him in.'

22

Dr Peck walked slowly into the Quiet Room, slow enough to be in a funeral march. Ten in the morning and he looked like Todd felt after three consecutive sixteen-hour days – exhausted.

'Thanks for coming in.' Todd gestured to the easy chair. 'I'd like to pick your brains, if I may.'

Peck sat heavily.

'We've made an arrest,' said Todd.

'Who?' The news hadn't cheered Peck up.

'Raymond Chivers.'

Peck's face registered blank.

'The suspect Ben Nixon's been chasing for months. The pro golfer his deputy mentioned in here back in – when was it? – spring. You were here.'

It was hard to tell if Peck remembered or not.

'His solicitor went ape and sued. We needed some fancy footwork to dance round a damages claim.'

'You've found more evidence?' Some interest finally passed over Peck's face.

Todd told him HOLMES had established Chivers had been in both Thailand and Cuba on the dates of their murders. 'We're pretty pleased with progress, but we're getting confused and only partial off-the-record admissions. We're wondering if you could put us right.'

No offer came.

Todd tried again. 'If you feel it's too close to home . . .'

Peck frowned. 'What do you mean?'

'Well . . .' Todd shrugged, on the defensive. 'Debby, you, me and the rest. We were all working colleagues together . . .'

'That doesn't seem to have stopped you getting on with the job.'

'Someone has to.'

'I suppose so,' Peck conceded.

Todd again: 'If you feel too closely connected, I can always consult someone else.'

Silence.

'It's just that you know the background.'

No response still.

'Saves time and we're up against it.'

Guardedly, Peck asked. 'How can I help?'

'With interview technique, lines of questioning.'

'All right,' said Peck, all attention now.

Todd placed his feet on the carpet, both hands on the arms of his chair, lifted himself an inch or two, then eased back and stretched out. He knew he would be talking for a long time.

Chivers had been arrested three days ago, he began. In the back of the police car, he had said, 'You've taken your time.'

'Not an untypical reaction,' Peck came in, much sooner than Todd expected. 'Several serial killers have been recorded as saying something like "What took you so long?" The end, in a strange sense, comes as a relief to them too.'

On the way to the station, Todd resumed, Chivers became chatty, despite being repeatedly told, 'Save it till we get there.'

Unprompted, he said, 'I suppose you want me for that blackmailing bitch in the hotel.' Quite freely, he admitted he regularly used prostitutes.

He claimed he couldn't remember picking up Patsy Evans at the motorway service station, but did recall on one occasion well over a year ago having a row with a prostitute on the M18 about the price and ordering her out of his car.

He admitted giving a lift from Hull to a woman who, he claimed, threatened him with a knife and eventually managing to bundle her out.

'Same story with Cuba – yes, there was a pick-up, a row over money and he booted her out the car. At the station – '

Peck broke in again. 'What about Debby?'

'I'm coming to her,' Todd said, a touch testily.

At the station, he went on, Nixon handed Chivers over to the custody sergeant and found a desk to write down the conversation in the car.

The solicitor arrived and the formal taped interview began. 'It was a rerun of our previous interrogation, with the solicitor answering everything with, "No comment . . . He declines to answer that . . . He has nothing to say on this."'

Nixon informed the solicitor, 'He's already had plenty to say' and read out into the tape the notes he had just made in his pocketbook.

The solicitor asked for a private consultation with his client. An hour later, he came back and said he was unable to represent him any longer.

Todd interrupted his own story. 'You know what that means, don't you?'

Peck shook his head.

Solicitors, Todd explained, could not go along with a denial after a client had admitted guilt to them in private.

'If the defendant says to them, "Well, of course, I did it, but I want you to say I didn't," they can't. They can try to mitigate the offence, get the charge reduced, but, once they've been told "I'm guilty," they can't run with a blanket "Not guilty" to everything.'

'I didn't know that,' muttered Peck, mildly surprised.

Todd expanded. 'When you read that a man in the dock has dismissed his solicitor, it can mean they have fallen out over tactics. But it can also mean the client has confessed his guilt in private but still insists on pleading his innocence in court. Ethically, the lawyer has no choice but to withdraw.'

He sighed. 'But, of course, we can't question the solicitor; privileged info and all that.'

Peck nodded approval, not saying: It's the same with doctors.

'Next day,' Todd continued, 'Nixon and his team searched his home and golf club and came up with leads, all of which will take time to check out.'

'Such as?'

'Wait one,' replied Todd, meaning: Give me a minute to get to it, and he recounted how Nixon applied to the magistrates in private for permission to keep Chivers in custody.

Peck didn't wait a minute. 'Couldn't he have charged him with wounding that call girl and got him held on remand?'

Todd was forced to answer. 'That would have meant a public hearing and the media know Nixon's on the case. They might put two and two together and conclude we've got Ed. They'd start asking awkward questions like "Is the hunt for Scissorhands over?" Don't want that, do we, until we're absolutely sure we've got the right man and not some nutter.'

Peck grimaced, didn't answer, so Todd went on, 'Besides, the call girl's taken off on holiday and we don't yet know if she's prepared to come on side again.'

Chivers, Todd continued, declined further legal representation but the magistrates, while granting Nixon's request for an extension, assigned an appropriate adult to him.

Peck looked puzzled and Todd launched into another legal lecture. They are appointed to see fair play in the way police handle prisoners, he said. They make sure there are breaks in interviews for sleep and refreshment and can call a halt to interrogations.

'They're sort of minders. Usually they sit in at interviews with juveniles, but they can be used where there's some doubt about mental disturbance and the magistrates are obviously worried about Chivers.' He paused. 'So are we.'

Peck tried to say something, but Todd pressed on, recounting how the taped interviews recommenced in the presence of the appropriate adult.

Nixon went back to the beginning. Yes, Chivers admitted, he'd been as a sex tourist to Thailand and he may have beaten up a girl there, but not knifed her. 'Ditto Patsy Evans, Lynn Dawes, Rosa and Debby.'

Peck cleared his throat. 'What did he say about her?'

'Yes, he was in Cleethorpes for a golf tournament. It was a rainy day. He hadn't won anything, had a migraine and didn't hang around for the presentation. Yes, he stopped for a newspaper on the prom and he did get chatting to a young lady sheltering at a bus stop.

'According to him, she was waiting for a bus to a place he'd never heard of off the M180 which, he said, was on his way home. He dropped her off. She was alive when she left him. She waved her thanks. He knows nothing about any handbag or postcard to anyone called Trench.'

'Nothing at all?' asked Peck, frowning.

'So he says.'

'What's happening over that contaminated card?' Peck asked, almost by-the-way.

'Forensics have sent it to Aldermaston to fire atoms at. They think they'll get there, but perhaps not in time.'

'It's all very unsatisfactory,' grumbled Peck.

'Yesterday,' Todd continued, 'Nixon took Chivers on the same journey we made in the winter.'

Chivers identified the service station as a regular stop, said he'd picked up a girl there and drove on to the M18. When they came off at a roundabout, they rowed about the price. 'He likes to haggle and beat them down. She wouldn't come down, so he opened the passenger door, pushed her out and drove off leaving her stranded.

'A few miles down the road he noticed she had left her handbag in the foot well, so he opened the window and lobbed it out. He took Ben to within a hundred yards of the spot where our dogs sniffed it out.'

'He's covering himself in case you found any fingerprints on the bag,' Peck ventured.

Todd nodded. 'Nixon took him on to Hull. Yes, he picked up a woman near the docks, drove her to a golf course he knew from playing there to have sex with her.'

'But her pants were in place,' Peck pointed out.

'She complained he'd been rough with her. She didn't like him using a knife and . . .'

Peck's eyes widened. 'So he admits to possession of a knife?'

'A knife, not scissors, for scraping mud off his golf shoes.' Todd went back. 'She hiked her price up. He bundled her out. She was alive and fully dressed, he says. He knows nothing about her handbag or any postcard.'

Peck pondered for a few moments. 'He's sexually dysfunctional, most probably impotent, and uses a weapon as a penis replacement.'

'In all cases,' Todd summed up, 'he's in effect saying, Someone must have killed them after I left them.'

'Is that his stance on Debby?'

'The appropriate adult demanded a break, so we're doing that run today.'

Peck smiled sympathetically. 'I can see you have problems.'

Todd nodded gravely. 'These days juries give no great credence to partial confessions to the police that aren't recorded. They think we make them up. What's on tape so far falls short of admissions anyway.'

He sighed. 'And the call girl may not reinstitute her complaint, even when we trace her, so we may not be able to use that as a holding charge.'

'Mmm,' said Peck, unhelpfully.

'We've got some decent stuff from his locker at his club which he uses as a care-of address – scissors that could fit the wounds, passport in a phoney name, stamped for Cuba, lots of soft-leaded pencils for marking scorecards.'

'But it isn't enough,' Peck agreed.

A tired nod. 'We're tearing apart his car and tracing others he's owned or hired. The lab's trying to match the scissors with the wounds, but it all takes time.'

An anxious expression. 'We've got to charge him with something by tomorrow or let him go. So, really, I'm seeking your thoughts on how to tackle him today.'

Peck moved his head in the direction of the Padded Cell. 'Is he here?'

'Christ, no.' An alarmed look. 'Not secure enough. He's on his way, though, in a custody van with an armed response patrol in tow.'

Peck leaned back, seemingly relaxed for the first time. 'Can you tell me a bit about him?'

Todd had no need to look up the details and briefed him in a military style. 'Aged thirty-seven, but looks older. Only child. Rich dad, a property dealer, who had money in the club. Stayed at school until he was eighteen, but didn't add to his modest academic qualifications. Spent too much time playing in good grade amateur championships, youth stuff.

'Became an assistant, but didn't sweep the shop floor and clean members' shoes like other trainee pros. Just practised and played. Never made the big circuit. He's not raking it in, living on his inheritance, in the main.'

'Is his father a keen golfer?' asked Peck.

'Was. Collapsed and died two years ago.'

'He was living out his sporting fantasies through his son, an old story.'

Todd ploughed on. 'Married at thirty-three, separated within a year, but his ex-wife won't say a bad word against him. Nixon thinks her alimony is hush-money.'

'Nothing in his medical history that flagged a mental problem?' asked Peck, aping Todd's clipped delivery.

'Well.' Todd slowed. 'Both his ex-wife and his mum speak of migraines. He pulled out of one competition complaining of a headache. He's very grey for his age.'

Peck smiled, a rather embarrassed smile. 'I was way off with my analysis on Ed, wasn't I?'

Todd shrugged, unconcerned. 'You were dead right with Stan. Along with Fish Finger Fred, that makes two out of three. I wish all my detectives had a sixty-six per cent record.' He decided not to mention the failure on the triple arsonist. 'It's how we proceed from here that counts. What do you recommend?'

Peck replied in a confident tone, without further thought. 'He's ring-fenced his memories of events. Don't storm his barricades.' He paused. 'Is Mr Nixon an interviewing officer?'

'He's the case officer.'

'But he is . . . er . . . rather confrontational.'

'He knows every detail.'

'He didn't get to the bottom of it in the spring. And, having escaped detection then, Chivers won't tell him all immediately.' Now he did think. 'Are you going with them to Cleethorpes?'

'Yes.' Todd tilted his head, appealingly. 'Want to come?'

'It would have to be low-key.'

Todd got the idea. 'Informal, friendly, first names, you mean?'

'Get him talking about his family first, his sport, build a rapport, inch him towards the truth very gently, get through those defences without him realising we're there.'

A relieved expression flickered across Todd's tired face. 'So you'll come?'

'On those conditions.'

The dark blue custody van pulled up in the courtyard. With black grilles on all windows, apart from the windscreen, it gave the impression of a dog-catcher's truck.

A white patrol car drew up behind it. The observer got out. He wore a dark blue baseball hat, sweater and sharply pressed trousers with elastic bottoms over black ankle boots. On his belt was a holstered revolver.

Nixon got out of the back of the van, leaving the double doors ajar. Two faces, both men, looked out. They were sitting next to each other in seats with steel poles each side that ran from floor to roof.

In one seat was a silver-haired man, dressed in white overalls. He was cuffed by wrist and ankle to one of the rails.

The man next to him was older, heavier, balding, and wore a dark jacket and grey flannels. He was free to stand with a stoop and stretch, but did not get out.

Behind them was a long grille which separated passengers from the cab. The driver remained at the wheel.

Todd led Peck up to Nixon. 'Merv's agreed to accompany us.'

Todd walked on to the back of the van, pulled the doors open wider and addressed both men. 'Dr Peck . . .' He thumbed over his shoulder. '. . . has volunteered to join us today, unless you have any objection.'

The balding man looked at the manacled man who worked one shoulder into a lazy shrug. 'That's OK by us,' he said.

Todd climbed into the back. Peck joined him on a red plastic-covered bench facing the two men. Perched on the seat between them was a tape recorder.

Nixon shut and locked the doors behind them and reappeared at the passenger door. As he was getting in and belting up, the driver turned away from the wheel, unfastened the grille and half rose, very awkwardly, to push it up into clips on the interior roof.

Only when he'd resettled did Todd make the introductions. He threw out a hand towards Peck and said, 'This is Merv.' He nodded to the balding man. 'This is Bill, whose duties I've explained.' Bill nodded back.

Todd's hand went towards the manacled man. 'And this is Ray.'

23

'Not quite the Malecon, eh, Ray?' grinned Todd as they drove down the seafront.

'Some sand, at least,' said Ray, looking out on a sunlit beach so big that holiday-makers were being ferried in ex-army amphibious trucks to the distant water's edge.

'That's an odd thing for a golfer to say,' said Merv, just making small talk.

'Not if you know how to get out of it,' replied Ray in an aggressive tone he'd not displayed before.

On the way, Merv, as everyone but Ben Nixon was calling Peck, had tried to coax family details out of Ray, as everyone but Ben Nixon was calling him.

Sure, he thought a lot about his late dad, Ray'd agreed, but he loved his mum too. An expression of such sorrow flooded his face that Merv changed the subject.

'Take your time,' Peck had advised. The driver seemed to act on that as an order and a journey of forty miles had taken more than an hour.

Ray had been more forthcoming about his profession, a game about which Merv clearly knew little. He blamed his slump in form on the yips on the putting green. To keep a limping conversation going, Todd suggested extending his index finger down the grip to steady the club.

'And what do you play off?' he'd asked, unimpressed, all the more so when he heard Todd's handicap.

Throughout it all, Nixon had stayed silent, thumbing through a file on his knees, refreshing his memory. Now he turned in his front seat, pulled a Romeo y Julieta out of his top pocket and waved it alongside Ray's ear. 'Have a few of these in Cuba, did you, Raymondo?'

'I don't smoke,' said Ray disdainfully.

In silence, they travelled a further mile or two past amusement parks and packed car-parks until a golf course came up on the right behind a tree-dotted bank.

The van pulled up in front of a clubhouse, half brick, half stucco, with red roofs. On a white pole, green and yellow flags flapped in a brisk breeze.

'Right,' said Todd, businesslike. 'Exit from here at what time?'

'I can't remember.' Ray hunched his shoulders and sat back, body language for going back into his shell.

'Take your time,' Merv repeated.

'Let's see if we can help.' Nixon rustled through some papers on his knee. 'Your starting times were 9.25 and 2.34. So you'd be finished playing at what?'

Todd suggested four hours and Nixon added half an hour to shower and change and departure around seven was agreed by Ray with a nod.

Nixon moved him on. 'A drive down to the seafront, then, eh?'

Another nod and they drove back the way they came, so slowly in heavy traffic that a kiddies' train chugging beneath a string of fairy lights outpaced them.

'And you stopped where?' Nixon was asking all the questions.

'I forget.' Ray looked out aimlessly through the grille. 'They all look the same.'

True, Todd conceded. Opposite a short pier were several rows of similar shops, all with iron balconies.

'For a paper?' Nixon prompted.

'Aspirin.'

'At the station, you said a newspaper.'

'And aspirin.' Ray smiled slyly.

Nixon smiled slyly back. 'And to buy that postcard of the boy with the boot full of water you sent Mr Trench?'

'I didn't.' Ray stiffened his tone. 'Why should I? It was a day trip, business, not pleasure, not a holiday.'

Nixon let it drop. 'So where did you see her?'

'Sheltering somewhere around here.' Ray waved a hand.
'Who spoke first?'
'She did.'
'Saying what?'
'What a bad evening it was. We just got chatting, that's all.'
'About what?'

The weather, he said. The rest came out in a rush – about how she'd missed a bus to Scunthorpe, how she planned to complete her journey from there by taxi down the M180 to a place he'd never heard of and still couldn't recall, and how late she was running for an appointment.

He slowed down. 'Since I could go home that way, I offered her a lift.'

He went back to 'Can't remember' and 'Forget' when asked what she was wearing, her accent, any sort of personal detail about her.

'Are you sure you weren't looking for a prostitute?' asked Nixon in a starchy voice.

'No.'

'Is that a negative or not sure?'

'Trick question,' protested Bill, his minder.

No, Ray replied angrily to the next question, he wasn't looking for a prostitute, and no, his plan wasn't to scout the streets around the docks in Grimsby for one, and no, the girl he picked up didn't just happen to be in the wrong place at the wrong time.

'You thought she was on the game,' said Nixon bluntly.

'No.' To emphasise his denial, Ray clenched his fist and rattled the rail. 'No. No. No.'

Nixon gave him no respite. 'You don't remember what she looked like because you've used so many that they merge into one in your mind, don't they? Just sex objects.'

Suddenly calm, Ray replied, 'I treat 'em well and pay 'em well.'

'Really.' A mocking exclamation. 'Tell that to the call girl you carved up in that hotel.'

'I never did.'

'You said so, admitted it, in the car after we collared you.'

A pained expression crossed Ray's face. 'I don't recall saying that.'

'For christsake.' Nixon appeared to be close to losing his temper. 'I told your lawyer on tape and you didn't dispute it.'

'Former lawyer,' Bill corrected him.

Nixon talked closer to Ray's ear. 'Are you accusing me of making it up, like you invent everything?' Then he turned to Bill. 'I'll play it over when we get back to base, if you like.'

Going through Grimsby, Ben waved airily towards a water tower, over three hundred feet high, that dominated a skyline of cranes, chimneys, yacht masts and floodlight pylons. 'Since you're into phallic symbols, why didn't you send a postcard of that?'

Ray's only response was a short hollow laugh.

Heading inland Nixon nagged on about what had been discussed between the two of them in the car. The weather, Ray insisted. Even Bill, his minder, who was beginning to look very bored, wouldn't accept that. 'Surely there must have been another topic over this distance? Your job? Her job?'

Ray fell into a sulky silence. Merv tried to encourage him out of it. 'Let's think quietly about the place where your passenger said she was going.'

So quietly was Ray thinking that he was silent for half a mile.

'The colours of the rainbow,' Merv suggested. 'Let's picture them.'

If Ray pictured grey or green, he wasn't putting them into words.

'That appointment,' Merv pressed on, patiently. 'Was it a job interview, a date, a meal?'

Ray just wasn't biting.

Rejoining the motorway, Nixon took over again. He thumbed north towards the Humber Bridge and the golf course beyond where Lynn's bag was found. 'Let's run through that little trip again.'

Merv looked anxiously at Bill who did not intervene. 'Can we not stick to this case today?' he asked rather nervously.

'Why?' Nixon snapped. 'He committed a murder up there and another back on the coast and used this route both times.' He eased himself up to speak right into Ray's ear. 'You go out with murder in mind, don't you?'

Ray pulled his head away.

'You actually buy those postcards before you kill them, don't you?'

Ray's head was on his chin now.

Just short of the turn-off for Grey Green, Nixon ordered the driver to stop on the hard shoulder. He got out of the nearside, left the door open and swept an arm over the grounds where Debby had been found. 'And this is where you dumped the lady from Cleethorpes, isn't it?'

'I don't remember,' Ray mumbled at his chest.

'Don't remember?' An incredulous expression, Nixon giving the impression of a man on the verge of a breakdown. 'You know . . .' He steadied himself. '. . . I just might buy you not remembering what happened in Thailand. Personally, I'd like to think that if I cut a woman's throat I'd remember but it was two or three years ago after all; benefit of the doubt and all that.'

He pointed west. 'Patsy.' He stopped suddenly, then with deep sarcasm, 'Forgive me, but you never ask their names, do you? The girl you picked up at the service station. That was fifteen months back, too long for your memory, so let's give you the benefit of the doubt again.'

A menacing pause. 'But the lady from Hull you dumped there . . .' He gestured towards the Chase. '. . . was killed just before Christmas and this poor girl here was only two weeks ago.' A furious face, a raised voice. 'What do you mean, "Can't remember"?'

'I can't.' Ray almost sobbed it.

'Right.' Nixon got back in his seat and slammed the door. 'Drive on towards the Chase and stop there. We'll go through it all again.'

'I need a pee,' said Bill miserably. 'Let's take a break.'

Back in the courtyard, Nixon unlocked Ray from his poles, cuffed him to a wrist and went with him to the toilet. The armed guard followed. So did Bill.

Todd led Peck into the Quiet Room. From behind his desk, he looked at Peck in the easy chair. 'It's not working, is it?' Finding first names difficult to drop, he added, 'Merv.'

Peck had no such problem. 'Nixon's not helping.'

'He's had this runaround for three days now. He's bound to be pissed off.'

'It's not the way to the truth.'

'What is?'

Peck told him.

Ray was fastened to his seat in the back of the van. Nixon, Bill and the driver stood close to the open rear doors, Ben smoking a cigarette. The armed guard hovered.

'Change of plan,' Todd announced. He threw an arm round Nixon and shepherded him away from the other two, not quite out of earshot because they looked around, startled, when Nixon asked a stunned, 'You what?'

Todd ushered him further away, talking all the time. Peck joined the other two. Todd turned Nixon back and beckoned the trio away from the van. The armed guard replaced them at the doors.

'Dr Peck suggests a different approach.' He looked at Bill, the minder. 'Only him and Ray in the van on this trip. Any objections?'

Bill hesitated.

Peck pushed gently. 'It's just that towards the end you seemed to display a slightly questioning attitude.'

'Well, yes.' Bill leaned forward, confidentially. 'This lost memory stuff is eyewash. I'm getting fed up with it. Three days I've had it now.'

'Exactly,' said Peck. 'And that lack of faith may well have transmitted itself. He's got to have confidence in people around him, feel someone cares, understands.'

Bill looked uncertainly at Todd who said, 'It's your decision.'

'If you think it will help.' Bill still seemed very unsure.

'I've no view one way or the other,' said Todd cautiously.

'I'm certain it will help,' said Peck, positively.

'What about the tape machine?' asked Bill.

'I'd prefer it off,' said Peck. 'Once or twice he's looked at it. I think he finds it inhibiting and that's what we must break down.'

'But you use them in consultations, surely?' Todd said, an eyebrow raised.

'Not in circumstances where it would be counter-productive.'

'If he's not on bloody tape,' Nixon seethed, 'how the hell are we going to prove anything?'

Peck nodded at Todd. 'He knows.'

Todd knew, but didn't reply.

'I must protest this, boss,' Nixon dissented.

Todd tried conciliation. 'We've nothing to lose.'

'We could lose him.'

'Oh, come on.' Todd jerked his head at the armed response patrol. 'These boys will be on his back fender and we'll be with them. Just double-check his cuffs, that's all.'

'I want my objection noted,' Nixon insisted.

'Noted,' Todd snapped. 'Now let's get on with it. Time's running out.'

Nixon relaxed in the back of the patrol car, but only as far as the motorway. 'He's going the wrong way.'

'Only to turn and double back.' Todd laughed thinly, worried himself.

The van ahead was going slowly, no more than thirty, and Todd wondered if Peck was having difficulties with the controls after the shortest of briefings from the now redundant driver.

Soon, it signalled left and pulled over on to the hard shoulder. 'Oh, Christ, he's having trouble,' Todd sighed.

The patrol car pulled in behind it. 'Trouble, my arse,' grumbled Nixon.

Todd recognised the spot on the Chase where Lynn Dawes had been dumped, a scene he and Peck had surveyed back in winter.

No one got out of either vehicle but Todd could see Peck's head turned into the back. 'He's taking him through the Dawes job, too,' said Nixon unhappily.

The van moved off again, didn't double back but went north up the M18.

'What the fuck's going on?' Nixon bent forward as if suffering from gut ache. 'Cheeky bastard. He's going to do the round trip. He's cross-checking every cough and fart.'

*

Todd sat back, closed his eyes and began to cross-check with himself.

Jesus, this is a dicey operation. It could all go so badly wrong.

But he needed, desperately needed, the truth about Debby Thompson's death. She was a good workmate. He owed it to her.

The case against Chivers on Debby was non-existent and on Patsy very thin. On Lynn, he comforted himself, it was building nicely and they were a hundred per cent sure on Rosa Melena.

He hadn't confided this to Peck, but they found a Labatt's cap among a collection of porn in Chivers' locker at the golf club, the care-of address he used for correspondence in his false name. Better still, Rosa's cousin had picked him out in a line-up only yesterday.

With Chivers' impounded credit card records to work from, Nadel had already traced the red car he'd hired on the island. A waiter at the Servico remembered it and its driver, because he didn't get all that many foreign motorists calling on that crumbling, deserted, wonderful road from Havana.

He smiled to himself at the memory and mused on.

In Chivers' car, the lab boys had already found spots of blood, Lynn's type, in the bottom of the driver's door tidy that never gets cleaned out because the Hoover nozzle won't go in. The DNA test, he prayed, would clinch it.

Best of all, they'd traced an old school sweetheart who'd been taking an A level in computer studies and was working abroad now. As a joke, Chivers used to write her love notes with + between letters and o's dotting the i's. 'He was a lovely lad, kind and gentle,' she'd said.

Neither Todd nor Nixon could make head nor tail of him – partial confessions one session, flat denials the next.

One interview had to be abandoned, Chivers claiming a headache so severe that he couldn't see.

Rather than a psycho playboy with a vacuum where a conscience should be, Chivers might have a physical problem, Todd conjectured, a tumour or something that caused brainstorms or spasms which explained his homicidal behaviour.

At his trial, he was convinced, they'd run a medical defence when they'd seen all the evidence to pack him off to hospital rather than risk extradition to Cuba.

That, unhappily, would not give up the secret of Debby's death. This, dicey though it was, was the only way.

Nixon's words in the Quiet Room came back to him. 'Keep your nerve, boss.'

He actually felt himself nodding to himself.

Peck had driven Ray to the power station, stopped, chatted, then headed towards Hull, the patrol car in the van's slipstream. At the golf course where Lynn's bag was found, he stopped for some time, gesturing with a hand.

He'd finally doubled back and taken the toll bridge south to pick up the start of the M180.

Todd looked at his watch. The stop and start round trip of more than sixty miles had taken almost two hours.

The van pulled in again at the scene were Debby was found. This time Peck got out and walked to the nearside, looking down on the hospital grounds.

Getting somewhere, thought Todd, feeling some faint relief.

He watched Peck return to the driver's side, get in, start up and drive on just a mile to the turn-off for Grey Green.

The van came to a halt at the foot of the slip road. Is he about to abort and return to base? Todd asked himself, gut grinding.

The van went under the motorway and headed north for a mile or so.

As bad as aborting, Todd wanted to wail.

The van signalled left and entered a driveway leading to a golf club. 'Not this old location again,' groaned Nixon.

Todd was too tense to speak.

The van didn't go in far before halting and didn't stop long, just long enough for Peck to look to his right to a raised tee with a white marker.

He drove on very slowly, turned in the car-park and took the road back the way he came, under the motorway, towards Grey Green.

Shit, panicked Todd, he is calling it a day.

Not yet, his heart sang, as the van ignored the sign for the Cottage Hospital and drove towards Epworth.

At the approach to a rise with a white tower on top, the van indicated right and waited for an oncoming tractor before turning on to a pot-holed drive to a picnic area.

Ash surfaces for parking had been cut out of grassland. On the lawns were wooden tables with bench seats. To the left were bog-standard toilets, square, brick, flat roof; to the right, children's slides and swings. Before the playground was a small, stone column for a commemorative plaque or a sundial, Todd guessed.

The van scrunched to a halt on the ash and the patrol car drew up alongside. Everybody but Ray got out of the vehicles.

'Come with me,' a beaming Peck ordered.

Trying not to smile, Todd and Nixon followed over a patch of grass towards the square column.

Peck gestured to a long, thick tangle of brambles spilling over a boundary fence. 'I think you'll find what you're looking for in there.'

24

'Mervyn Peck.' Nixon placed a hand firmly on his shoulder. 'I am arresting you for the murder of Deborah Thompson.'

'But you . . .' The smile flowed from Peck's face as if gurgling down a plughole and seemed to block his voice box.

'Are you . . .' He couldn't get out more than two words together. The shock was taking away his balance.

Nixon hooked a hand under his armpit to hold him steady. Todd gripped his other arm.

As they walked him like a drunk back over the grass, Todd could feel some strength returning. At the opened doors of the van, Peck wriggled in a feeble attempt to work himself free. 'There's no need . . .' He could manage no more.

Standing on the ash covering, facing the now-unmanacled Ray, Nixon told Peck of his rights to a solicitor and to a copy of a tape recording.

'Scandalous.' Voice and balance restored, Peck glared at Todd. 'This is scandalous, shameful.'

I'll second that, thought Todd, angrily.

*

It had begun, like so many crimes, with a bit on the side.

The hotel and restaurant records Carole Waites had unearthed and the statements from receptionists would prove that Peck and Debby started their affair while working on Fish Finger Freddy at Lord Harvard's company.

The offender profile Peck produced was not the result of professional expertise. In Lincoln jail, Freddy confirmed he'd been interviewed by Peck during assessments he'd carried out as a company consultant. As Peck had not been called at his trial, the connection wasn't made.

Via Debby, Peck campaigned to get himself engaged on the investigations into Stan and Ed. They wanted to continue their affair under the cover of working together. She'd fed info to him about disagreements within the police service on the use of such profiles. Dr Peck, not Trench, tipped off Post Mortem Morton.

Morton's statement disclosed his publishing contract was for Peck's casebook in which the M-Way Madman would have made a chapter. They were on a fifty-fifty split, including payment for the story, leaked by Debby, about the hunt going global which caused such aggro in Cuba.

Questioned in Lincoln prison, Maddox had told how, as a schoolboy, his father had taken him as a private patient to a doctor because of his passion for ladies' garments on washing lines. He described the house where the Pecks lived. Another younger doctor took part in that consultation in the den, but he couldn't remember much about him.

Todd had pointed out that Peck was present in the Quiet Room when Maddox was on the carpet over the vigilante road block. Disappointingly, Maddox couldn't remember him from that occasion either. He'd been flustered, he explained, because Carole entered the Quiet Room. Women always flustered him when he was sober, Todd guessed.

But Peck, Todd was certain, recognised Maddox and immediately earmarked him as Stan, a suspicion confirmed in his interviews with the victims, especially their descriptions of the smell of pine.

Acting on inside info, as with Freddy, he was able to draw up a stunningly accurate profile compared with his woefully inaccurate work on Chivers.

Peck thought tracing Chivers would be so difficult as to be a near-impossibility, but he was unaware of the progress Nixon was making and that ignorance led to his believing he could get away with murder.

Far from being a sleeping partner in Three Counties Clinic, its collapse left Peck with heavy debts, according to the former director interviewed at the State Special.

Lord Harvard had revealed he had given Peck a grant in recognition of his work on Fish Finger Freddy and Maddox.

Peck, Todd suspected, intended to settle his debts with it. Instead of employing researchers to extend his database, he'd used Debby to pillage police records to get case files for nothing. They'd find the evidence, he hoped, when a computer expert on standby examined Peck's disks in his den.

No wonder he'd got Peck's services so cheaply, Todd finally realised. He'd have worked for nothing for the long-term benefits of free material and eventual media fame.

Debby, Todd was sure, had been happy to go along with her lover until Maddox's capture. She'd have been appalled by his near lynching, he theorised, and she'd realise that Maddox could and should have been safely behind bars instead of at liberty to assault other girls and at risk himself.

Instead of coming clean, Peck had held back, seeking more glory, another thrilling chapter for his ghosted book, celebrity status. And so she came to her senses, accepting for the first time just what a dangerous game they had been playing.

Pure conjecture, that, Todd had to accept, but it was a proven fact that her health had then gone into swift and steep decline. Her doctor had confirmed she was suffering from deep anxiety resulting from stress; a stress so great, in Todd's view, that she was quitting her job and had promised to give him her reasons.

And, for that reason, Peck killed her – to keep her silent about the truth of his phoney profiles, his stolen research. Not only killed her, but, using his insider knowledge, did it in such a way as to pass it off as yet another motorway murder.

He wasn't to know that Nixon's team had been tracking Chivers even before HOLMES had thrown up his care-of address in the lists of Cuban visas.

So, if not Chivers, who? Todd had pondered.

Peck made himself a suspect. Debby was just a colleague on sick leave, as far as anyone in the incident room knew at the time. Yet, more than once, he'd asked around if anyone had seen her, spoken to her. He'd pointed out she came from the resort on the postcard. He'd whittled about her. He'd chuntered about the long grass in the hospital grounds which Toby Harvard couldn't cut because of his smashed fingers. Peck wanted her body found, the sooner, the better.

In a missing person case, Todd had learned to look closely at the relative, friend or neighbour who bleats the loudest, makes all the running, when everyone else thinks, He or she will be back soon. Sometimes killers can't wait for the next chapter to unfold naturally. They can't stand the suspense. They have to know if they are going to get away with it, if their plot will work.

Peck doubled Todd's suspicions when Tom Reith gave him the news of the discovery of the body. He blamed himself for not picking her up to go to dinner with Lord Harvard.

Why, when even the experts couldn't be precise about the date of death, should Peck link it with that particular night?

Because he'd killed her and dumped her on the way to Temple Hall and he planned to use a life peer and his benefactor as his alibi.

Much of this, Todd acknowledged, was circumstantial and he'd always known that the case would stand or fall by what happened here, now, today.

The armed escort climbed out of the back of the van where he'd unlocked Ray. 'Can I stand down surveillance?'

'Sure, and thanks, inspector,' said Todd.

The guard strolled towards the toilet block where a watcher lay on the flat roof observing the bramble thicket. A relay of them had been there since Todd had looked down on the picture postcard of the boy with the leaking boot.

It had been perfectly readable, but seeing it through crinkly clear film inspired a suspicious thought that became a researched idea and then a plan.

The Forensics chief suggested urine contamination as an excuse for not being able to decipher the message and recover the handbag immediately. His call had been timed to coincide with Peck dropping into the incident room *en route* to that dinner at the Red Lion. The row with Nixon in the stable block had been well rehearsed, too.

Looking as though he couldn't believe his ears and eyes, Peck watched the guard walk away, then turned back to Todd. 'This is outrageous, disgraceful.'

Todd shrugged, easily.

Peck flicked his head towards Ray, still sitting in the back of the van. 'Is this some sick charade to get him to say more?'

'There's nothing he can tell us about Debby's death,' said Todd, quietly. 'Outside of me, Ben, the HQ mailman and Forensics, nobody knew where her handbag was.' He paused. 'Other than her killer. You were the only one in the van on that round trip who knew where you'd dumped it.'

Peck looked frantically over his shoulder. 'He directed me.'

Todd smiled. 'The tapes will tell us who said what to whom.' There'd be lots of examples, he was sure, of Peck putting words into Ray's mouth like, 'Shall we try that golf course? No, well, this picnic area then. Over there. Is that where you threw it?'

Peck looked down at the switched-off tape machine on the seat, and missed the mikes concealed in the black steel grille fastened to the inside roof. 'He wrote that card to Trench,' he almost shouted.

'Hardly,' Todd shook his head. 'I don't think you've been formally introduced.' He nodded at Ray. 'This is Superintendent Trench.'

Peck started to struggle, more than a token this time, and Nixon firmed his grip. Todd leant sideways slightly to talk in Peck's ear. 'You wanted him back on the inquiry. You've got him. And we've got you.'

Trench climbed rather shakily out of his seat. Head bent to avoid the roof, he took a few tinny steps, rubbing a wrist with the other hand. He reached out and took Peck's arm from Todd and began to pull him in.